author

DAYDANCE

Joanna Brady Mysteries

"In the elite company of Sue Grafton and Patricia Cornwell. . . . J.A. Jance has really hit her stride with her Joanna Brady series."
Flint Journal

"Jance is one of those authors who makes readers feel as if they had lived all their lives in the setting of which she writes. . . . Joanna Brady is a real person."
Cleveland Plain Dealer

"The Arizona desert comes to life in the mysteries of J.A. Jance."
Arizona Republic

"She can move from an exciting, dangerous scene on one page to a sensitive, personal, touching moment on the next."
Chicago Tribune

"Jance beautifully evokes the desert and towns of her beloved southwest as well as the strong individuals who live there."
Publishers Weekly

"Brady is a multidimensional character dealing with harsh reality in a harsh, if dramatically beautiful landscape. . . . Jance creates such a strong sense of place, you can feel the desert heat."
Colorado Springs Gazette

"Any story by Jance is a joy."
Chattanooga Times

Books by J. A. Jance

Joanna Brady Mysteries

J.P. Beaumont Mysteries

and

DESERT HEAT

J. A. JANCE

HARPER

An Imprint of HarperCollins Publishers

HARPER

An Imprint of HarperCollinsPublishers

This is a work of fiction. Names, characters, places, and incidents are drawn from the author's imagination or are used fictitiously and are not to be construed as real. Any resemblance to actual events, locales, organizations, or persons, living or dead, is entirely coincidental.

HARPER

An Imprint of HarperCollins*Publishers*
10 East 53rd Street
New York, New York 10022-5299

Copyright © 1993 by J. A. Jance
Excerpt from *Fire and Ice* copyright © 2009 by J. A. Jance
ISBN 978-0-06-177459-1

First Harper Premium paperback printing: July 2009
First Avon Books paperback printing: February 1993

Printed in the United States of America

Visit Harper paperbacks on the World Wide Web at www.harpercollins.com

10 9

To the real Jeff and MaryAnn,
who, in a time of need, were friends indeed

DESERT HEAT

PROLOGUE

"WRITE IT," Antonio Vargas ordered, without raising his voice. "Write it now."

Wayne M. "Lefty" O'Toole looked down at the piece of gold-embossed, creamy-white stationery from the Ritz Carlton in Phoenix. He had taken it from his room the morning after he stayed there, as proof to himself that he had been there once, that a kid who had grown up on the wrong side of the tracks in Bisbee, Arizona, had made it big time enough that the Ritz had once rolled out the red carpet for him. But now that time seemed eons ago—another lifetime, maybe even another body.

The aging RV, a converted school bus, was stiflingly hot. Rivulets of sweat dribbled down his face as Lefty picked up the pen, a fiber-tipped Cross—another relic from his salad days—and studied the scrap of paper Vargas had placed on the table in front of him. Typed on it were the words he was expected to copy. He glanced back at

Vargas who was lighting yet another cigarette although the cramped room was already thick with a haze of smoke.

"Couldn't we talk about this, make an arrangement of some kind?" Lefty asked tentatively.

He had hoped they wouldn't find him in this godforsaken corner of Mexico, but now that they had, he knew he was a dead man. Still, it didn't hurt to try. Never give up, right? Never say die. It was funny that he could make jokes with himself about it even then, but Tony Vargas wasn't laughing.

Studying Lefty impassively and without blinking, the way a cat might watch a doomed and cornered mouse, Vargas drummed his fingers on the table. Lefty hadn't noticed it before, but Tony was wearing a pair of thin, flesh-colored rubber gloves—surgical gloves. That was a bad sign, a very bad sign.

"The time for talking ended some time ago," Vargas said with an indifferent shrug. "There will be no arrangements. Our side doesn't make arrangements. I think you have us mixed up with those other guys, your good friends at the DEA. They're the ones who do all that plea bargain shit. We're more straightforward."

Lefty let his breath out in a tired sigh. How did they know about those negotiations? The fact that he was asking to get into the Federal Witness Protection Program was supposed to be top-secret. His life had depended on those negotiations being kept secret, but someone had betrayed him. That's why Vargas was here, wasn't it?

With hands that shook despite his best efforts to control them, Lefty put pen to paper, copying the text verbatim from the typewritten crib sheet:

A. B.,

By now you should have received the money. Thanks for all your help. My associates are pleased, and we will be back in touch when we need assistance with another shipment. In the meantime, my best to your wife. She shows a good deal of talent for this kind of work.

                Regards,
                Lefty

After scribbling his name, Lefty shoved the completed piece of paper across the table. While Vargas examined it, Lefty was aware of more trickles of acrid sweat. These coursed down his rib cage from under his arms. He had done his stints in Nam flying numerous combat missions. He recognized the rank stink of his own fear, but he tried to ignore it.

"Who's A. B.?" He asked the question casually, as though it were only a matter of idle curiosity, although, with sinking heart, Lefty suspected he already knew the answer.

In reply Vargas sailed the piece of paper back across the chipped formica table top. "Not good enough," he said. "It looks like my grandfather wrote it. Do it again."

Lefty swallowed hard and picked up the paper. Vargas was right. The handwriting was so frail and spidery that it might have come from the hand of an elderly person suffering from an advanced case of Parkinson's disease. In this case it was impossible to tell the difference between the ravages of old age and the tremulousness of sheer terror.

Lefty reached for yet another piece of Ritz Carlton stationery—sorry now that he had taken so many—and began again, concentrating on the shapes of each individual letter in exactly the same way he had once struggled with the exercises in penmanship class. The sharp-tongued nuns had insisted that he make endless rows of a's or o's. They required that all the letters slant at exactly the proper angle and point in the same direction. He had always been lousy in penmanship, but his second attempt at copying the note passed inspection.

"Fold it," Vargas directed, "and put it in this envelope. Here's the address. Copy it, too."

Taking both the envelope and the scrap of paper, Lefty studied the words that were written there—"Andrew Brady, Box 14, Double Adobe Star Route, Bisbee, Arizona, 85603."

As soon as he saw the familiar name and address, Lefty knew the name and face of his betrayer. He had bet everything on the wrong horse. It all made terrible sense. They had used Andy—who would ever have suspected Andy?—as bait to flush him into the open. It had worked like a charm. Nothing like sending one of your old students on a killer, end run play.

For the first time he fully understood the depth of his betrayal, and the realization robbed Lefty

O'Toole of his last possible hope. Sitting there across the table from his executioner, it was all Lefty could do to keep from wetting himself. At last, ducking his head, he laboriously bent to copying the address onto the envelope. It wasn't just Andy's address he was writing. Lefty O'Toole knew he was signing his own death warrant.

When the envelope was finished, Lefty handed it across the table. This time Vargas smiled as he took it, revealing a mouthful of expensive gold dental work. "Good," he said, sealing the envelope and placing it in the pocket of his sweat-dampened sports jacket. "Let's go."

"Where?" Lefty asked.

"For a ride," Vargas replied.

Lefty knew that if there was any chance of escape, it had to be soon. He had to make the attempt before they left the mobile home park where, if he called for help, there might be a chance of someone hearing him and coming to his aid. But Vargas lifted the hand in his coat pocket, the one that held the huge .357 Magnum, and motioned toward the door. "Move it," he said. "Now."

It occurred to Lefty then that perhaps he should leap up and lunge across the table, grabbing Antonio Vargas by the throat and throttling him, but there wasn't much hope in that, either. He might be lucky enough to escape Vargas this time, but other enforcers would be sent for him later. It was clear to him now that even the damn Witness Protection Program was full of holes. Sooner or later they'd get him.

Resigned to his fate and without another word,

Lefty rose and moved toward the door with Vargas only half a step behind.

When he opened the door, the desert's overpowering September heat hit him full in the face, instantly drying his sweat-slick skin. As he stood on the shaky wooden step and looked around, he found, much to his surprise, that his limbs were no longer quaking. Knowing he had passed through the worst of the fear gave him renewed courage, restored his determination not to whimper or beg. No matter what, he still owned that much self-respect.

"What now?" he asked.

"Like I said," Vargas replied, mopping his brow, "we go for a ride in your car. If anyone sees us, I'm an old friend from the States, and we're going into town for a beer."

"Where are we going really?"

"Out into the desert. Something may go wrong with your car. In this heat, who knows what will happen? Maybe you'll be lucky enough to find your way back to the road. Let's go."

In the searing noontime heat, they took Lefty's Samurai and drove slowly through the little *gringo* retirement enclave outside Guaymas. It was high noon, *siesta* time, and none of Lefty's friends or neighbors were anywhere in evidence. The Samurai traveled north through the barren Mexican desert. Thirty miles from town, where the narrow ribbon of cracked blacktop seemed to melt into the mist of a road-eating mirage, they turned off the pavement into trackless, powdery sand. They drove for several more treacherous miles before, on a small rocky knoll, Vargas told Lefty to stop.

"This will be fine," he said.

"What now?"

Lefty had been paying close attention to the way they had come, remembering landmarks. Several months out of rehab, he was in good physical shape, better than he had been in years. Even in the afternoon heat he could probably make it back to the road.

"Get out," Vargas said. "Now you walk."

Lefty O'Toole's mouth was too dry to speak. "From here?" he croaked.

"It's not as far as you think," Vargas returned.

Slowly Lefty started to get out of the Samurai. Then, in one final act of defiance, he grabbed the keys from the ignition and flung them as far away as he could throw them. He had been a hell of a passer for the University of Arizona in his day, and the keys sailed far into the air, with the sun glinting off them as they sped away. The sudden, unexpected movement caught Vargas unawares and for a moment he was too stunned to react.

"You crazy bastard!"

Before the keys came to rest thirty or forty yards away, Lefty O'Toole spun around and bolted across the desert. A strangled noise that was half-sob/half-cackle rose in his throat and escaped his parched lips. He felt good, weightless almost, gliding effortlessly over the powdery sand. It was like one of those good old LSD trips, the early ones, that had been more like flying than flying.

Lefty had tricked Antonio Vargas by God! He

had caught him flat-footed. The very idea filled him with unreasoning delight.

In fact, he was just starting to laugh when the first powerful bullet caught him directly between the shoulder blades, propelling him forward faster than his legs could move, smashing him face forward into the yielding, smothering sand.

Not even Lefty O'Toole ever knew that he died laughing.

Cursing the dead man under his breath, Tony Vargas didn't bother to go searching the trackless sand for those missing keys. His early training had taught him how to hot-wire cars, and he did it now with only a minimal amount of difficulty. Driving carefully, he made his way back to the deserted airstrip where his plane and pilot were waiting.

"You took care of him?" the other man asked anxiously.

"I'm here, aren't I?" Tony returned. "Let's go."

"Is it going to work?"

"Don't worry. I told you I'd handle it."

Once the plane was airborne and heading north, Tony leaned back in his seat, closed his eyes, and thought longingly about Angie Kellogg's lush, lithe body. He could hardly wait to get home and take her to bed. Killing people always made him horny as hell, and Angie always did what he wanted.

ONE

JOANNA BRADY stepped to the doorway of the screened back porch and stared out into the night. The moonlit sky was a pale gray above the jagged black contours of the Mule Mountains ten miles away. September's daytime heat had peeled away from the high Sonoran Desert of southeastern Arizona, and Joanna shivered as she stood still, listening to yipping coyotes and watching for traffic on the highway a mile and a half away. Beside her, Sadie, Joanna's gangly blue-tick hound, listened as well, her tail thumping happily on the worn, wooden floor of the porch.

"Where is he, girl?" Joanna asked. "Where's Andy?" Happy to have someone speaking to her, the dog once more thumped her long tail.

Up on the highway, a pair of headlights rounded the long curve and emerged from the mountain pass. Speeding tires keened down the blacktop, passing the Double Adobe turn-off without even slowing down. That one wasn't him, either. Disappointed, Joanna sighed and went back inside, taking the dog with her.

In the living room she could hear the drone of her mother's favorite television game show while Jennifer, her daughter, was eating dinner in the kitchen.

"Is Daddy coming now?" Jennifer asked.

Joanna shook her head. "Not yet," she answered, trying to conceal the hurt and anger in her voice. She kicked off her heels, poured herself another cup of coffee, and settled into the breakfast nook opposite her blonde, blue-eyed daughter. At nine, Jenny was a female mirror image of her father.

Despite Joanna's soothing words to the contrary, Jennifer assessed her mother's mood with uncanny accuracy. "Are you mad at him?" she asked.

"A little," Joanna admitted reluctantly. A lot was more like it, she thought. It was a hell of a thing to be stood up like this on your own damn wedding anniversary, especially when Andy himself had insisted on the date and had made all the arrangements. He was the one who had first suggested, and then insisted, that they get a room at the hotel and spend the night, reliving their comic opera wedding night from ten years before.

At the time Andy had suggested it, Joanna had asked him if he was sure. For one thing, staying in the hotel would cost a chunk of money, an added expense they could ill afford. For another, there was time. Not only was Andy a full-time deputy for the Cochise County Sheriff's department, he was also running for sheriff against his longtime boss, Walter McFadden.

The election was now less than six weeks away. Joanna had been through enough campaigns with her father to know that conserving both energy and focus was vital that close to election day. In the meantime, Joanna had her own job to worry about. Milo Davis, the owner of the insurance agency where she worked as office manager, had offered her a partnership. To that end he had started sending her out on more and more sales calls, letting her earn commission over and above her office-duty pay. But it meant that she, too, was essentially holding down two full-time jobs.

Joanna was the first to admit that between the two of them, she and Andy had precious little time to spend together, but staying in the hotel overnight seemed to be overdoing it. Andy, however, had laughed aside all Joanna's objections and told her to be ready at six when he'd come by to pick her up.

Well, six had long since come and gone and he still wasn't home. Eleanor Lathrop, Joanna's mother, had been at the house watching television since five-thirty. Since six sharp, Joanna's small packed suitcase had sat forlornly by the back door, joined now by her discarded shoes, but at seven forty-five, Andrew Roy Brady was still nowhere to be found.

"Maybe he had car trouble," Jennifer suggested, snagging a piece of green chili from her plate and stuffing it back inside her grilled cheese sandwich from which she had carefully removed all the crusts. Joanna bit back the urge to tell Jenny to stop being silly, to shape up and eat her discarded bread crusts, and to stop casting herself in the role of family peacemaker, but Joanna Brady had embarked on a conscious struggle to be less like her own mother. She let it pass. After all, there was no sense in turning Jennifer into any more of a family Ping-Pong ball than she already was.

"You're right," Joanna agreed finally. "That's probably what happened. He'll be here any minute."

"Are you going to tell Grandma to go on home?" Jenny asked.

Joanna shook her head. "Not yet. We'll wait a little longer."

Jenny finished her sandwich, pushed her plate aside, and started in on the dish of sliced peaches. Eva Lou Brady, Joanna's mother-in-law, had canned them herself with fruit from the carefully nurtured freestone peach trees planted just outside the kitchen door. Joanna got up and dished out a helping of peaches of her own. Two hours past their usual dinner hour, it was a long time since lunch, and she was starving.

"Was I premature?" Jennifer asked suddenly.

The jolting question came from clear out in left field. A slice of peach slid down sideways and caught momentarily in Joanna's throat. She coughed desperately to dislodge it.

"Premature?" Joanna choked weakly when she was finally able to speak.

Joanna Brady had always known that eventually she'd have to face up to the discrepancy between the timing of her wedding anniversary and Jenny's birthday six short months later. But she had expected the question to come much later, when Jennifer was thirteen or fourteen. Not now when she was nine, not when Joanna hadn't had time to prepare a suitable answer.

"What makes you ask that?" she asked, stalling for time.

"Well," Jennifer said thoughtfully. "Me and Monica were talking about babies. . . ."

"Monica and I," Joanna corrected, pulling herself together.

Jennifer scowled. "Monica and I," she repeated. "You know, because of Monica's new baby sister. She says babies always take nine months to get born unless they're born early because they're premature. Today's your tenth anniversary, right? And I turned nine in April, so I was just wondering if I was premature."

"Not exactly," Joanna hedged, feeling her cheeks redden.

"What does that mean?"

"You were right on schedule. The wedding was late."

"How come?"

"Because."

There was no way Joanna could explain to her daughter right then how a dashingly handsome Andrew Roy Brady, five years older and considerably wiser, had returned from his two-year stint in the army on that fateful Fourth of July weekend ten years earlier. Parked down by the rifle range and with the help of a cheap bottle of Annie's Green Spring wine they had seduced each other in the back seat of her father's old Ford Fairlane while Bisbee's annual fireworks display lit up the sky overhead. Joanna Lathrop had simultaneously stopped being a virgin and started being pregnant.

Now, faced with her daughter's uncomfortable question, a convenient television commercial rescued her. Eleanor Lathrop limped into the kitchen and helped herself to a dish of peaches. "Isn't that man here yet?"

"Not so far," Joanna answered.

The older woman leveled a meaningful stare at her granddaughter. "Shouldn't you finish up and go to bed pretty soon?" she asked. "Don't you have school in the morning?"

The child returned the look with a level stare of her own. "It's too early," Jenny returned. "I'm in the third grade now, Grandma. I don't have to go to bed until nine o'clock. Besides, I want to stay up and kiss Daddy goodnight."

Eleanor Lathrop shook her head disparagingly. "That's silly," she sniffed. "It could be all hours before he gets here. Besides, he's probably off politicking somewhere and has forgotten completely what night this is."

"He didn't forget," Joanna asserted firmly. "Something must have come up at the department, some emergency. He just hasn't had a chance to call."

"Men never do. He's already almost two hours late, you'd think he'd have the common decency. . . ."

Not waiting for her mother to finish the sentence, Joanna hurried to the kitchen wall phone and dialed the Cochise County Sheriff's department. The local telephone exchange was small enough that it was only necessary to dial the last five digits of the telephone number. The clerk who answered said that Andy was out. Unable to provide any further information about how long ago he had left or where he might be, the clerk offered to put Joanna through to Chief Deputy Richard Voland who, despite the lateness of the hour, was still in his office.

"Hi, Dick. It's Joanna Brady. What's going on that everybody's still at work?"

"I don't know about anybody else," Dick Voland replied, "but I'm catching up on a mountain of paper. Ruth and the kids are bowling tonight, so I'm in no hurry to get home."

"Have you seen Andy?"

"Andy? Not for a couple of hours. He lit out of here right around five o'clock. I thought from what he said that he was pretty much going straight home. Isn't he there?"

Joanna felt a tight clutch of fear in her stomach, a cop's wife's fear. "No. Did he say he was going somewhere else before he came home?"

Dick Voland didn't answer immediately, and

Joanna heard the momentary hesitation in his voice. "One or two of the day shift guys are still out in the other room. Let me check with them. Hang on. Someone will be right back to you."

Half a minute later, someone else came on the line. "Joanna, what's up?"

She was relieved to recognize the voice of Ken Galloway, one of Andy's best friends in the department.

"Andy's late getting home, and we were supposed to go out tonight. Do you have any idea where he might have gone?"

"Christ!" Ken exclaimed. "It's almost eight o'clock and he's not there yet? I thought he was on his way home hours ago. He mentioned a couple of errands, but nothing that should have taken this long. Maybe he had car trouble."

The knot in Joanna's stomach tightened into a fist. Jennifer's suggestion of car trouble had been annoying. Coming from Ken Galloway, the supposedly comforting words sounded patronizing. She bridled. "If it were car trouble, don't you think we'd have heard from him on the radio by now?"

"Seems like it. Where are you?"

"At home."

"I'll do some checking from this end and give you a call back."

Joanna put down the phone. For a moment she stood there indecisively, then she spun around and marched to the back door where she pulled a worn pair of suede work boots on over her pantyhose, then she took Andy's old Levi's jacket down from its peg beside the back door. Sensing an outing, Sadie eagerly nosed her way to the door and waited for Joanna to open it.

"Where are you going?" Eleanor demanded.

"To look for him," Joanna answered simply. "Something's wrong. I know it. He may be hurt."

"But why should you go looking? The department will handle that. That's what we pay them for," Eleanor Lathrop pointed out. "That's what your father always said."

Invoking the name and memory of Sheriff D. H. Lathrop, Joanna's father who had been dead now for some fifteen years, had been Eleanor's foolproof way of winning almost every intervening argument with her daughter. This time it didn't work. Joanna didn't knuckle under.

"Mother," Joanna answered curtly. "Andy's my husband, and I'll go looking for him if I want to."

Jenny slipped out of the breakfast nook and hurried to the door. "I'll come too."

"No. You stay here with Grandma."

With that, Joanna turned on her heel and sprinted out the door, taking the dog with her. She had gone only a few steps when the single floodlight in the yard came on. Joanna looked back and waved to Jenny who was standing beside the yard light switch with her face pressed longingly against the fine screen mesh.

"I'll be right back," Joanna called. "You wait here."

Sadie raced ahead toward the detached garage, knowing from the noisy jangle of the key ring in

Joanna's hand that she would be taking the car. While the dog danced in happy circles, Joanna backed her worn Eagle station wagon out of the garage. Moments later, with the dog once more in the lead, they started down the rutted dirt road that was little more than a pale yellow ribbon winding through a forest of mesquite.

In the still but chilly desert night, moonlit leaves cast delicate lacy shadows on the ground. Sadie gamboled along ahead of the car for only a few yards before she raced off into the underbrush, nose to ground. Within moments the dog set up a noisy racket—the characteristic booming—that meant she had scared up some desert quarry. It was probably the same old wiry, neighboring jack rabbit the dog always chased. In stylized ritual, the dog pursued the rabbit hour after hour, day after day, without either one of them ever fully putting their hearts into the contest.

Joanna, smiling to herself, was comforted by the familiar baying of the hound and by the jack-in-the-box antics of kangaroo rats who leaped fender high in their scramble to get out of the approaching car's path. Their comical frolics made her feel somewhat better, but still she worried.

She made her way out to the cattle guard that marked the boundary of their property, the High Lonesome Ranch, and swung onto the wider dirt road of the same name. During the early twenties, when water was plentiful, the High Lonesome Ranch with its mail-order Sears Craftsman house, had been one of the larger and more prosperous spreads in the Lower Sulphur Springs Valley. During harder times, one chunk of land after another had been sold off until all that remained of the original ranch was the scraggly forty acres that still held the house and outbuildings.

Just across the cattle guard, Joanna stopped the car, switched off the engine, and got out to listen. Here in a natural depression that was also the roadway, she was unable to see headlights, but she could hear the steady whine of rubber tires on blacktop. While she listened, three separate vehicles went past without any of them turning east on the Double Adobe Cutoff.

Panting, Sadie trotted up to her side. "He's not here, girl," Joanna said, stroking the dog's smooth forehead. "Let's go on down to the corner and see if he's there."

They started south on High Lonesome Road. This time, Sadie was content to follow along behind the car, sticking to the left-hand shoulder of the road. Between the ranch and Double Adobe Road, High Lonesome crossed a series of four steep washes on the rickety spines of four narrow, one-lane-wide bridges. The bridges were old and no longer strong enough to handle heavy loads. Each year, after the rainy season, the county sent a bulldozer out to grade a track through the sand for over-sized loads.

Joanna was speeding across the third bridge when the moonlight glinted off something in the wash below. Jamming on the brakes, Joanna stood the Eagle on its nose, almost fishtailing off the road in her haste to stop the car. With dust still billowing up around her, she leaped out of the Eagle and ran back to the bridge while her headlight-handicapped vision adjusted to the sparse moonlight.

"Andy," she called. "Andy is that you?"

Without remembering how she got there, she found herself standing in the middle of the narrow bridge looking down on what she instantly recognized as her husband's Bronco. It seemed to be mired down in the sand. Near the pickup's front bumper she could barely make out a dark smudge on the lighter sand. Her first fleeting thought was that Andy had accidently hit a stray head of livestock, but that was only a trick her mind played on her to shield her from the terrible truth.

"Andy," she called again. "Are you down there?"

There was no answer, but now she caught sight of a ghostly figure darting past the truck and realized that Sadie must have detoured down from the upper level. The dog stopped short near the smudge in the sand, although Joanna's eyes still hadn't adjusted sufficiently for her to see clearly.

"Andy!" Joanna shouted, more frantically this time. "If you can hear me, for God's sake say something."

For an answer she heard a terrible, low moan, one that struck terror in her heart. He was down there, out of sight and hurt, too. Petrified now, Joanna darted back to the end of the bridge and started scrabbling, hand over hand, down the steep embankment.

"Hang on," she heard herself shouting. "Hang on, Andy. I'm coming."

She found him sprawled face down in the roadway while Sadie, tail wagging, eagerly licked the back of his neck. Roughly Joanna pushed Sadie aside and fell to her knees beside the still, prone figure of her husband.

"Andy," she cried desperately, while her heart hammered wildly in her chest. "What's the matter? What's wrong?"

"JoJo," he groaned. "Help me."

Andy tried to raise his head, but the effort was too much for him. He fell back helplessly into the dirt.

"Andy, you're hurt. Where? Tell me what happened."

She was almost shouting in his ear, but there was no answering response from him. The only sounds in the desert came from Sadie's heavy panting and the faraway, high-pitched yip of a distant coyote. Searching for answers, Joanna's eyes scanned his back, but she saw nothing. With one hand on his shoulder, she waited for him to take another breath, but he didn't, not for a long time. The realization that her husband was dying hit her full force.

Grunting with effort and blessed with a strength beyond her capability, she managed to turn him over onto his back. Only then could she see the ink-black stain that spread from just above his belt buckle to his crotch. Fearing the worst, she touched the dark spot with the tips of her fingers. They came away wet and sticky and covered with sand.

"Oh, God!" she whispered. "Help me." It was both an exclamation and a prayer.

Andy's eyes fluttered open momentarily. He coughed and a shower of wet sand spattered Joanna's face, but at least he was still breathing. Fighting back the urge to scream, she leaned close to his ear. "It's bad, Andy, real bad. Wait here. Don't move. I've got to get help."

Leaping to her feet, she scrambled over to Andy's Bronco and tried the door. It was locked. She ran around to the other side and tried that one as well. It too was locked. For a moment she panicked, then she remembered the extra key to the truck on her own key ring in the Eagle. At once, she climbed back up to the roadway, raced to the idling car, shut off the engine, and grabbed the keys. Afraid she might drop them scrabbling back down, she shoved the keys deep in her hip pocket before starting the steep descent.

Once back in the sandy wash, she hurried to the door of the Bronco, pulling the keys out as she ran. Her hands shook uncontrollably as she tried to shove the key into the lock. It took three attempts before the key clicked home and turned. Sick with relief, she wrenched the door open, lunged across the seat, and grabbed the radio microphone down from its clip on the dashboard.

She pressed the button. "Officer down," Joanna shouted into the microphone. "Officer down and needs assistance."

"Who is this?" the dispatcher demanded in return. "State your location."

Joanna Brady took a deep breath and tried to calm herself. "Joanna Brady," she answered. "I've just found my husband. I think he's been shot."

"Where are you?"

She forced herself to answer clearly, rationally. Otherwise, help would never be able to find them. "Half a mile off Double Adobe Road on High Lonesome. We're down in the wash beneath the second bridge."

"Hang on," the dispatcher told her. "Help's on the way."

Joanna flung the microphone back into its clip and ran back around the truck where she once more knelt beside Andy's still, silent form. He lay just as she'd left him. This time when she knelt beside him and lay one hand lightly on his chest, he didn't respond at all. "Andy," she said, but still there was no answer.

In an agony of fear, she groped at his wrist. There was a faint, weak pulse, but his skin was icy cold to the touch. Rising panic threatened to engulf her, but she fought it off, rejected it. From some dim corner of memory, her Girl Scout first aid training reasserted itself and clicked into action.

Shock. Andy must be going into shock. Once more she scrambled away from him, this time returning from the Bronco with the clean but worn blanket he always kept in the back seat with his first aid kit and tool chest. Hastily she spread the blanket over his motionless body. She knelt beside him, holding his hands, willing her own warmth into him.

Neighboring coyotes heard the sound long before she did. Only when that first eerie chorus died back could Joanna hear the faint wail of an approaching siren that had set them off.

"Do you hear that, Andy?" she asked. "Hang on. For God's sake, please hang on."

But if Andy heard her, it didn't show. Sadie whined and crawled closer on her belly until her nose touched Joanna's leg. It was though the dog, too, was in need of comfort. She waited an eternity for Andy to take another shallow breath. But he didn't. Three miles away, she again caught the faintly pulsing wail of the siren. Followed by another echoing chorus of coyotes. And still Andy didn't breathe again.

A shiver of despair shot through Joanna's body, leaving her totally devoid of hope. She rocked back on her heels and screamed her outrage to the universe. "No," she wailed, flinging her desolation upward toward a moonlit but uncaring sky. "Noooo."

All up and down the lonely stretches of the Sulphur Springs Valley, howling coyotes took up this new refrain. Somehow the sound of it snapped Joanna out of her unreasoning panic, reminded her of another part of her first-aid training.

Heedless of the blood, she bent over her husband's inert form. Afraid of hurting him but knowing being too tentative could prove fatal, she placed both hands on his lower rib cage and pressed down sharply. Then, molding her lips to his, she tried to force the life-giving air back into his lungs.

"Don't leave me," she whispered between breaths. "Please don't leave me."

♣ TWO

AN AMBULANCE and two Cochise County Sheriff's vehicles arrived almost simultaneously followed by an officer from the Arizona Highway Patrol. When the arriving officers scrambled toward them down the embankment, Sadie barked frantically. Joanna didn't want to stop what she was doing, but the only way for the professionals to get close enough to do their work was for Joanna to leave Andy long enough to drag the dog out of the way.

Clutching Sadie by the collar, Joanna led the protesting dog back to the Eagle and shut her inside for safekeeping. Weak with fear and spent with effort, she leaned against the fender of the car and looked down at the group of Emergency Medical Technicians clustered around Andy's motionless body. Their hurried shouts and frenzied actions gave her some small hope that perhaps they weren't too late and Andy was still alive.

She was still standing there looking down at them when Ken Galloway found her. "How bad is it?" he asked.

Shaking her head was all the answer Joanna could manage.

Ken took her arm. "Come with me," he said. "You're better off not watching."

Holding her solicitously, Galloway guided her through the growing collection of haphazardly parked vehicles that already littered the area around the bridge. He opened the rider's side of his still-warm patrol car and eased her into the seat. She was shaking violently. Inside her head chattering teeth rattled uncontrollably.

"My God, Joanna, you must be freezing," Ken said. "Wait right here."

He disappeared, returning moments later with two blankets and a cup of coffee. He handed her the coffee then wrapped the blanket around her legs and tossed the other one over her quaking shoulders. Joanna held the coffee in her hands without taking a drink while she stared at the place where people clambered up and down the embankment. From this perspective, the people on the floor of the wash were totally out of sight.

"He stopped breathing," Joanna explained woodenly to Ken Galloway. "I tried doing CPR, but I don't know if it worked or not. Go check for me, Ken. Please."

"You'll be all right here alone?"

She nodded. Ken strode to the head of the bridge and then disappeared down the bank. He came back a few minutes later, shaking his head.

Joanna's heart sank. "Is he still alive?"

"Barely. At least they've got his heart beating again. You kept him going long enough for them to be able to do that."

Joanna didn't know she had been holding her breath until she let it out. "Thank God," she murmured.

With a grateful sigh she took a first tentative sip of coffee, letting the hot liquid warm her chilled body from inside out. She drank without ever taking her eyes off the path that emerged from the wash just at the end of the bridge abutment.

"I can't believe it," Ken Galloway was saying, although Joanna was paying little attention. "I saw him right around five when he got off shift. He was fine when he left the office. What the hell happened? Where did all the blood come from? Did he drive off the bridge and run the steering wheel through him?"

"The truck was locked and he was outside it," Joanna said numbly. "I think somebody shot him."

"No. You gotta be kidding."

"I'm not kidding."

Ken Galloway shook his head. "Jesus, Joanna. I can't tell you how sorry I am. Sorry as hell." For a moment Galloway stood there as if vacillating over whether to stay or go. "I'll go back down and check again," he said quietly. "If I stay here, I'll make a damn fool of myself."

With that, Ken Galloway hurried away. Left alone on the sidelines, Joanna saw people she knew coming and going in an eerie glow of flashing blue and red lights. Even though they saw her and knew she was there, for the most part they ignored her. One or two of them nodded in her direction, but to a man they found themselves tongue-tied and shy in the face of Joanna Brady's looming personal tragedy. Aghast at the extent of Andrew Brady's injuries, none of them wanted to be trapped into telling Joanna exactly how bad it really was. Unfortunately, their wary silence was something she recognized all too well.

Joanna had heard that same terrible silence once before in her life. She had been ignored exactly the same way the night of her father's accident. Sheriff D. H. Lathrop, Hank for short, had been bringing a group of girls back from a camping trip in the Chiricauhuas when he stopped to change a flat tire for a stranded female motorist. He had been struck from behind by a drunk driver and had died at the scene with his thirteen-year-old daughter looking on helplessly from the sidelines. Now, fifteen years later, Joanna was once again trapped in similarly ominous silence.

With eyes glued to the top of the path, Joanna was only dimly aware that another vehicle had arrived on the scene. Within minutes, Sheriff Walter V. McFadden himself, Stetson in hand, loomed up beside her out of the darkness.

"Dick Voland called me at home," he said gruffly. "I can't believe this. I came as soon as I could, Joanna. How are you?"

"All right," she whispered.

"And Andy?"

"I don't know."

"Why the hell didn't they leave the engine running in this damn thing? It's colder 'an blue blazes. Want to come sit in my truck? It's warmer there."

Joanna shook her head. "No. I can see better from here. In case . . . in case . . ." She didn't finish the sentence, but Walter McFadden understood what she meant.

"Here. Give me your cup," he said. "I'll go get you a refill on that coffee."

McFadden returned and handed her a second cup of coffee, this one far stronger than the first. Joanna accepted it gratefully. "What happened?" he asked.

Joanna shook her head. "I still don't know. I found him here. His truck was locked, but I have an extra key. I got in and radioed for help."

"Somebody told me he's been shot. How bad?"

Joanna swallowed hard. It was what she herself had suspected, but this was the first official confirmation. "Real bad, I think," she replied.

"Damn! Could he still talk when you got here? Did he say anything at all? Tell you who did it?"

"No. Nothing."

"You got in the truck?" McFadden asked. Joanna nodded. "Did you touch anything?"

"The doors, I guess. And the radio. That's all I remember touching."

"I'll be right back," McFadden said. He marched away from her and disappeared into the wash. He returned a few minutes later, puffing with exertion.

"I checked the Bronco," he said. "There's still a

set of keys in the ignition. Are they yours or Andy's?"

"They must be Andy's," Joanna replied. "Mine are right here in my pocket."

She pulled the heavy key ring from her jacket pocket. It jangled heavily with its collection that included house, work, and car keys as well. Andy had often teased her that her key ring looked like it would have been more at home on a school janitor's belt rather than in a woman's purse.

"You say the doors were locked when you got here?"

"Yes. Both of them. Who would do this, Walter?"

"I don't have any idea, Joanna, but believe me, we're going to find out."

"I want to help," Joanna whispered fiercely.

McFadden looked down at her and shook his head. "You already did enough just getting help here as soon as you did. Your job right now is to be there for Andy. Let us handle it, Joanna. Answer the questions when the detectives get around to talking to you, but other than that, leave well enough alone. He's one of our own. We'll take care of it."

Joanna gazed up at him. "You will, won't you?"

"Damned right," McFadden responded. "You'd better believe it."

Just then a small, frail voice came wafting through the cool desert air. "Mommmmy," Jennifer called from somewhere back down the road in the direction of the house. "Mommmy, where are you?"

"Dear God in heaven," Joanna exclaimed. "It's Jenny. What in the world is she doing out here?"

"Jenny?" Walter McFadden asked. "Your little girl?"

Joanna nodded. She put down the coffee cup and threw off the blanket that had been wrapped around her legs while McFadden squinted up the darkened roadway. "There she is," he said, pointing.

Joanna peered into the darkness and caught sight of a small figure running toward them. "She probably saw the lights and came to see what was happening. We'd better head her off."

With Joanna leading the way, they rushed past the parked Eagle where a confined and miserable Sadie whined and bayed, wanting to go along. When they intercepted Jennifer, she was sobbing and out of breath.

"What happened?" she demanded. "Is it Daddy? Is he all right?"

Joanna gathered the frantic child into her arms. "Hush," she said. "Stay here. It's Daddy. They're working on him right now. We mustn't disturb them."

Jennifer struggled hard and tried to get free, but Joanna held her fast. "How'd you get here? Is Grandma coming?"

The child gave up trying to escape and sobbed against her mother's breast. "No. She sent me to bed so she could watch TV, but I saw the lights and snuck out through the window. I didn't ask her if I could come. I knew she wouldn't let me. Is Daddy okay? Is he dead?"

Joanna shook her head. "I don't know."

Jennifer turned to Walter McFadden. "Do you?" she asked accusingly.

"No, ma'am," McFadden returned in his soft east Texas drawl. "I don't know either. You stay here with your mama, and I'll go back down and see what I can find out."

Walter McFadden hurried away from them. Jennifer clung more tightly to her mother, and Joanna wrapped the remaining blanket around both of them. Maybe she couldn't protect her child from anything else, but at least she could ward off the cold.

"What happened?" Jennifer asked. "What happened to Daddy?"

Joanna faltered momentarily before she could answer. "I think somebody shot him."

"Who did, a crook?"

When Andy Brady regaled his fascinated daughter with stories about his work life, the bad guys were always "crooks" or "black hats" and the police officers were always "good guys" or "white hats."

"Maybe," Joanna said. "We won't know that for a while. There'll be an investigation."

"But why would someone shoot my Daddy?" Jennifer asked. "Were they mad at him?"

Joanna groped for an answer. "I guess," she said. "I don't know why else they'd do such a terrible thing."

Walter McFadden returned from his

intelligence-gathering mission. Joanna turned to him questioningly, but he bent down so his lean, weather-beaten face was on the same level as Jennifer's.

"Is that your dog over yonder in your Mama's car?" he asked accusingly.

Jennifer wiped the tears off her face. "Yes, sir. Her name is Sadie."

"See that truck over there, the one there by the sign?" Jennifer nodded. "The man driving it is one of my deputies," McFadden continued, speaking directly to the little girl as though no one else existed. "Do you think you could help your Mama by going with him and taking that Sadie dog of yours back to the house?"

Jennifer stiffened and scrunched closer to her mother. "Why? Where's my Mom going?"

"They're about to load your daddy into the ambulance," Walter McFadden said softly. "They'll be taking him into the hospital in Bisbee for evaluation. From there he may go by helicopter to Tucson."

"I want to go, too."

Walter McFadden shook his head firmly. "No," he said. "Tonight your Mama's going to have enough to worry about without having to look after you as well. Did I hear you say your grandmother's back there at the house?"

"Yes. Grandma Lathrop."

"Good," McFadden said. "You stay with your grandmother tonight. Believe me, hospitals are no place for little kids in the middle of the night.

In the morning, I'll come get you myself and take you there."

Jennifer started to object, and so did Joanna, but she knew Walter McFadden's assessment was correct. It was going to be a long night of waiting and worrying. She'd be better off alone.

"That's right, Jennifer," she said. "You go on back to the house."

"But I want to help," Jenny insisted. "I want to be with you."

"You heard Sheriff McFadden. Taking Sadie back home will be a big help. She can't stay here in the car all night."

Meantime the emergency medical technicians had carried Andrew Brady's stretcher down the wash to a place where the bank wasn't quite as steep. The ambulance moved down the road and met them where they emerged from the brush.

Once again Jennifer tried to pull away. "I want to go see my Daddy," she insisted, but Joanna didn't let go.

"No, Jenny. You can't."

Within a matter of seconds the stretcher was loaded into the ambulance and the vehicle pulled away with its siren gearing up to full-pitched howl.

Walter McFadden took Jennifer's hand and led her toward the pickup. "You know Deputy Galloway, don't you, Jennifer? He's a good friend of your daddy's."

Jenny nodded. "Good," McFadden continued. "He's the one who'll take you and Sadie home. Will that dog of yours bite?"

"No. She's not mean."

"Well, let's go get her then."

Together the three of them hurried back to the Eagle where Joanna released the imprisoned dog. Sadie was ecstatic to see Jennifer, but she was also wary of going anywhere near Ken Galloway's pickup. Only when Jenny finally climbed into the bed of the strange vehicle and called to the dog did Sadie allow herself to be coaxed into it as well. Jennifer grabbed the dog around the neck and held her close.

"I'll ride here in back with her," the child announced. "That way she won't be scared."

Joanna bit her lip. "That's good," she managed to murmur as Ken Galloway's pickup pulled away taking both the dog and the child with it. Down the road they heard the already speeding county ambulance rumble over the last cattle guard on High Lonesome Road and turn onto the Double Adobe Cutoff. Seconds later, after crossing the last cattle guard there as well, it turned onto Highway 80. The noise of the siren faded behind the foothills.

"We'd better hurry," Walter McFadden urged. "Come on."

Together they made their way to his 4×4 which was parked just off the road with its light bar still flashing. Once they reached it, McFadden helped her inside before racing around to open his own door.

"You talked to the medics," she said quietly as the pickup lurched into reverse and circled back onto the roadway. "What did they say?"

"Lots of internal damage," McFadden replied, pressing the gas pedal all the way to the floor.

"Is he going to make it?" Joanna asked.

"They don't know. Nobody does. Like I told your daughter, they've called for a helicopter to meet them in Bisbee. They've managed to stabilize him enough to move him. That's a good sign. I told them I'd take you directly to University Medical Center."

"Shouldn't we stop in Bisbee for me to sign surgical releases."

McFadden shook his head. "Not necessary. When somebody's hurt this bad, they don't wait for releases."

"Can't I go along in the helicopter? Wouldn't that be faster?"

McFadden shook his head. "It might be faster, but with the EMTs along there's not enough room. Don't worry, Joanna. They may beat us to the hospital, but it won't be by much."

With siren blaring, they roared past the newly opened county jail, up Highway 80, around the traffic circle, and on through town. Joanna glanced at the speedometer. They were doing sixty-five when they rounded the long, flat curve by the open-pit mine, and the needle hit seventy as they headed up the long straightaway. After that, she gripped the armrest and avoided looking at the dashboard. She knew they were going fast. She didn't need to know any more than that.

Once through town the nighttime desert swept by outside the windows, washed by the alternating red and blue flashes from the light bar overhead.

Joanna ignored the intermittent crackle of voices on McFadden's two-way radio. She heard only the jumble of unanswerable questions roaring in her head. Would Andy live or not, and if he did, would he be all right? What would she do if he died? What would she do if he didn't quite die but if he couldn't ever go back to work, either?

With help from the bank they were buying the High Lonesome Ranch from Andy's parents, Jim Bob and Eva Lou Brady, who had moved into a small two-bedroom house in Bisbee proper. Joanna knew full well that it took all of Andy's and Joanna's joint efforts to keep things afloat. The monthly payments they made on the ranch constituted a major portion of the elder Bradys' retirement income. What would happen to them if Joanna and Andy could no longer keep up the payments? Joanna squeezed her eyes shut and refused to think about it anymore.

"Somebody told me that today was your anniversary," Walter McFadden was saying.

Joanna nodded. "We had a date. We were supposed to have dinner and spend the night at the Copper Queen. In fact, my suitcase is all packed. It's right by the kitchen door. Maybe you could have someone bring it to Tucson for me in the morning."

"Sure thing," McFadden answered. "Glad to do it." For a moment there was silence in the speeding truck before Walter McFadden asked, "How many years?"

Joanna's thoughts had strayed, and it took a few seconds before she answered. "Ten."

"You kids eloped, as I recall," McFadden continued. "Made Eleanor mad as all get out."

It still does, Joanna could have added, but she didn't. Her mother had never liked Andy to begin with, and when she had learned he was interested in law enforcement, Eleanor Lathrop had predicted this very kind of outcome.

"If you let him become a policeman," Eleanor had warned, "you'll end up raising Jennifer alone, the same way I had to raise you." Remembering her mother's dire prophecy, Joanna's fingers tightened around the armrest.

Again Joanna and Walter McFadden fell silent. Several miles sped beneath the vehicle's tires before the sheriff eventually asked, "Was Andy having trouble with anybody?"

"Trouble?" Joanna repeated dully. "What do you mean trouble?"

McFadden shrugged. "I don't know. At work possibly or with any of the neighbors. When you live out in the country this way, you can run into some surprising complications. Remember that case down by Bisbee Junction where two of Old Man Dollarhyde's cattle drowned in those new people's fancy swimming pool? I thought World War III was going to break out over that one for sure."

Joanna thought of her neighbors. The closest ones, Charlene and Bill Harris, lived a mile farther down High Lonesome Road on the right. They had two high school–aged girls who sometimes baby-sat for Jennifer. Then, across the road and up a shallow canyon was the Rhodes's place which belonged to a spry octogenarian named Clayton Rhodes who still rode his fence line on horseback each year rather than using his aged pickup truck. Beyond the Harris place was that of a fairly recent arrival, Adrienne West with her fledgling herd of llamas. Among the neighbors on High Lonesome Road there had never been even the smallest hint of difficulty.

"No," Joanna replied. "Nothing like that. Besides, no one out here in the valley can afford a swimming pool."

"What about work?" McFadden asked.

"None except . . ."

"Except what?"

Embarrassed, she shrugged. "You know. The election and all that."

Andrew's decision to run against Sheriff McFadden had caused a good deal of consternation in the Cochise County Sheriff's department as well as in the community at large. Walter McFadden had already announced that this was the last time he would run for sheriff. As a result, most people felt that he shouldn't have had any real opposition. Surprisingly, despite her husband's determination to run, Joanna Brady was inclined to agree with that same general opinion. After all, McFadden had been her father's undersheriff and handpicked successor. Joanna still felt a good deal of loyalty to the man, but once Andy had committed to the race, Joanna had thrown herself into the campaign with all the fervor she had once devoted to her father's re-election efforts.

Joanna realized all this now as the truck sped on through the night. Regardless of what happened at University Medical Center, this year's election campaign for Cochise County Sheriff was over for Andrew Brady.

"You're not thinking I had something to do with this, are you, Joanna?" the sheriff asked.

"Of course not," she replied honestly. "Not at all."

"Good," Walter McFadden declared quietly. "I'd hate to think you did. I'm no cheater. When I win an election, I win it straight out or not at all."

Once again neither of them spoke while the truck ate up several miles of highway. McFadden was the first to break the silence. "Tell me, Joanna. Why'd he do it?"

"Do what?"

"File against me. Andy knew this would be my last term. I'd have been more than happy to see him run next time. Why'd he have to go and jump the gun like that?"

Joanna studied the old man's angular profile. Among Arizona's collection of fifteen county sheriffs, Walter McFadden was considered something of an elder statesman. He was well liked and well respected.

"I don't know," she answered. "Andy's impatient. I guess he figured it was something he had to do. Anybody else would have fired him."

Walter McFadden shook his head. "That wouldn't have been right," he returned. "Every man's got a God-given right to make a fool of himself if he wants to, but there must have been a reason. Did I do something to piss him off? Did I make him mad?"

"If you did," Joanna answered, "Andy never told me about it."

A plane went by overhead. Joanna sat forward and scanned the nighttime sky, hoping to catch sight of the medevac helicopter's navigation lights.

"Do you see it up there?" McFadden asked.

"No. Can you? Call, I mean, and check . . ."

McFadden shook his head. "Even if they knew, Joanna, they wouldn't tell me one way or the other. Not over the air."

She nodded, knowing it was true.

The speeding truck was nearing St. David and Benson now, the halfway point of the trip to Tucson. McFadden radioed ahead to warn local officers in each little burg that a speeding vehicle was on its way through. McFadden raced through both hamlets with his truck's blue lights flashing, barely slowing for Benson's single stoplight. Once they made it up onto the I-10 freeway outside Benson, Joanna finally found the courage to ask the one question that was uppermost in her mind.

"Do they live?" she asked, her voice tight and little more than a hoarse whisper.

"Beg your pardon?"

"When people are shot that way—gutshot the way Andy is—do they live?"

In the reflected light from the dashboard she watched the grim set of Walter McFadden's lean jaw before he answered. "Not usually," he said.

"Especially when they don't get treated right away and lose a lot of blood. But then again, you can never tell."

"That's why whoever did it locked the doors, isn't it," Joanna said. "So he couldn't radio for help, so they couldn't get to him in time."

McFadden shot her an appraising look. "Could be," he agreed. Then after a pause, he added, "Miracles do happen."

"But not that often," Joanna returned. "Otherwise they wouldn't be miracles."

At that grim prospect, she hunched herself into the far corner of the seat, crying softly and trying to keep Walter McFadden from hearing. Finally, though, she straightened up and wiped her eyes. Tucson was close now. Where once there had been only a faint glow on the horizon, there were now individual pinpoints of light. "Do you know how to get to the hospital?" Joanna asked.

"Yes," Walter McFadden answered. "I've been there a time or two before."

An hour and twenty minutes after leaving High Lonesome Road Walter McFadden's Toyota 4×4 pulled into the Emergency Room portico at University Health Sciences Center more than one hundred miles away. A helicopter was parked on the landing pad nearby.

"You go on inside," Walter said. "I'll find a parking place and then come in, too."

One of the EMTs, Rudy Gonzales, met Joanna at the door. "This way," he said quietly. "The clerk you're supposed to talk to is over here. They're prepping Andy for surgery right now."

Rudy led her through a maze of cubicles to where a stern-faced older woman waited in front of a computer terminal. "Here she is," Rudy said. "This is Joanna Brady, Deputy Brady's wife."

Joanna took a seat. The last few miles of the ride between Bisbee and Tucson had given her a chance to marshal her resources. She answered the clerk's rapid-fire questions in a quick, businesslike fashion. When handed a sheaf of forms, she worked her way through them, signing each with an insurance agent's swift efficiency.

"Good," the clerk said, taking the papers and glancing through them. "You can go on up to the surgery waiting room if you like."

Walter McFadden appeared behind her. He took off his hat and nodded politely to the clerk who pointedly ignored him.

"One of the forms is missing," Joanna said.

Annoyed, the clerk peered at her over the tops of her half-rimmed reading glasses. Clearly, she didn't like having someone else finding fault with her procedures. "Really? Which one?"

"The organ donor consent form," Joanna answered firmly. "His heart's already stopped once. I want to go ahead and sign the form now, just in case."

The clerk frowned. "That's not a very positive attitude, Mrs. Brady," she sniffed disapprovingly. "Our surgeons are very skillful here, you know."

"I'm sure they are, but I still want to sign it, if you don't mind."

The clerk disappeared into a back room and returned eventually with the proper form. Joanna scrawled her signature, and Walter McFadden witnessed it.

"Will I be able to see him before the surgery?" Joanna asked.

"I doubt that," the clerk replied coldly. "I doubt that very much."

Actually, as far as the clerk was concerned, if it had been left up to her, the very fact that Joanna Brady had insisted on signing the prior-consent organ-donor form would have cinched it. No way would she have allowed that woman to see her husband now, not in a million years.

Women who were that disloyal didn't deserve to have husbands in the first place.

THREE

JOANNA WAS surprised when, without the slightest hesitation, and without having to check the building directory, Walter McFadden led the way to the elevators and unerringly pressed the button to the correct surgical floor.

"Carol had surgery here, too," he explained. "That's how come I know my way around."

"You don't have to wait with me," Joanna said. "I'll be all right."

"No," Walter McFadden returned. "These waiting rooms are tough, especially in the middle of the night. I'm not going to leave you here alone."

"Thank you," she said.

The surgical floor waiting room was bleak and impersonal with suitably uncomfortable modern furniture and a collection of outdated, dog-eared magazines. McFadden gathered up the scattered pieces of a newspaper, then he sat down with them on one of the couches, placed his Stetson on one knee, and settled in to read and wait. Joanna hurried to a telephone at the far end of the room.

Ten o'clock Arizona time was midnight in Tulsa, Oklahoma, and she woke her in-laws out of a sound sleep. "We'll be there just as soon as we can," Jim Bob Brady told her once he had assimilated the bad news. "Eva Lou is already packing our bags. We'll be on our way just as soon as she's done."

The next call was to Joanna's mother. "I finally got that child of yours in bed," Eleanor Lathrop grumbled. "She's almost as stubborn as you are. I don't know what in the world she was thinking of, sneaking out into the desert at night like that all by herself. And it seems to me that the least you could have done is to stop by here and let me know you were going before you took off for Tucson."

"There wasn't enough time, Mother," Joanna returned evenly. "I wanted to be here at the hospital before they took Andy into surgery."

"Well, it just doesn't seem fair that I'm always the last one to know what's going on."

Joanna Brady had spent a lifetime fielding her mother's chronic complaints. "At least you know now, Mother, and I need your help. Would you please call Milo and let him know I won't be into work in the morning. And let Reverend Maculyea know as well. I'm too worn out to talk to anyone else."

"All right. I can do that. I suppose I'd better pack Jennifer up and bring her to Tucson in the morning."

"No," Joanna replied. "That won't be necessary. Sheriff McFadden already offered. He'll bring my suitcase along as well. I don't have any idea how long I'll be here."

Eleanor Lathrop hadn't much wanted her husband to be sheriff, but even less had she wanted Walter McFadden to take over in the aftermath of Hank Lathrop's tragic death.

"Him?" she squawked. "Why on earth should he be the one to pick up Jennifer? Doesn't he have anything better to do? It seems to me that if people are going around shooting each other here in Cochise County, he ought to be out doing something about that. He shouldn't be traipsing around hauling little girls all over the countryside. I'm perfectly capable of bringing her up."

Grateful that her mother wasn't broadcasting on a speaker phone, Joanna put her hand over the mouth piece. "My mother says she can bring Jennifer to Tucson tomorrow if you have other things to do."

Walter peered at her over the top of the newspaper he was holding. "I promised that little girl that I'd bring her up, and I intend to do just that," he said. "Besides, I'll have to come back up anyway."

"He says he'll do it," Joanna told Eleanor Lathrop.

"I can't for the life of me see why."

Joanna was fast losing patience. "Look, Mother, I can't talk any longer. I've got to go now."

She hung up, feeling betrayed. In times of trouble, mothers were supposed to give their children comfort and consolation, not a hard time. At least that's the way it worked in books and on television. Easygoing Hank Lathrop could very well have passed for Ozzie Nelson, but Eleanor Lathrop would never be mistaken for Harriet. She had far too many sharp edges.

Joanna left the phone and paced back and forth in the small confines of the waiting room. Walter McFadden watched her over the top of the newspaper. She stopped and stood, still and unseeing, before an impossibly gaudy oil painting hanging on the far wall.

She looked like a refugee from some nearby war. The oversized denim jacket was an ill match for a torn and tattered, silk-looking blue skirt. The skirt's hem barely skimmed the top of a pair of scruffy men's work boots. There were dark stains on both the jacket and skirt, stains Walter McFadden surmised would turn out to be splotches of Andrew Brady's blood. He wondered if Joanna knew there were bloodstains on the jacket she was clutching to her body as though she were still freezing cold.

"At times like this, I miss my father," she said softly. "Even after all these years, I still miss him."

The sheriff turned the paper to a different page and then shook it sharply to smooth it out. "D. H. Lathrop was a good old boy," Walter McFadden observed solemnly. "It was crazy for him to die like that, changing a tire for a lady with a carload of kids and a spare so bad that it didn't even get her into town."

Joanna turned from the picture and walked

over to a chair, taking a seat near Walter McFadden. "Did you know he used to call me Little Hank?" she asked.

"Little Hank?" McFadden repeated.

Joanna smiled sadly. "He only used his initials in public, but Big Hank was his family nickname, and Little Hank was his way of getting back at my mother. She always insisted that if men had the babies, there'd only be one child in each family, and one was all she was having. So Daddy was stuck with me. He never got the real son he always wanted. Mother wanted me to be one of those sweet, doll-playing, mind-your-mother little girls. My dad turned me into a tomboy, mostly out of spite, I think, and not that it took much effort on his part. The natural inclination was already there. And every time he called me Little Hank it drove my mother crazy."

Walter McFadden understood that it was easier right then for Joanna to think and talk about her father than it was for her to deal with her husband's grave injuries, with the uncertainty of what was happening with Andy's surgery.

"Your dad was smart to get out of the mines when he did, Joanna," Walter said. "He saw the bottom was going to fall out of the copper business a whole lot sooner than anybody else did. He got out to run for sheriff, and once he got elected, he took me with him. Smartest thing I ever did. I owe your dad a helluva lot."

Joanna pulled the jacket more tightly around her. Looking down she seemed to become aware of the ugly stains marring the denim. She rubbed fitfully at one. When it didn't come off, she returned her gaze to Walter McFadden.

"You paid that debt in full," she said quietly. "Andy wouldn't have been hired if it hadn't been for you. I know that. His grades were okay, but they weren't that good."

"I didn't do him that big a favor," McFadden returned. "Andy was a good deputy."

Joanna Brady's eyes narrowed. "*Is!*" she said determinedly, balking at how easily the sheriff had slipped into using the past tense where Andy was concerned. "Andrew Brady *is* a good deputy," she corrected. "Don't go writing him off, Walter McFadden. It's not over 'til it's over."

The sheriff smiled. "Your daddy, Old D. H. Lathrop, was one damn stubborn hombre in his time. Is that where you get it?"

Even Joanna couldn't help but smile in return. "Actually," she said, "I think I got a double dose. Stubborn streaks are pretty strong on both sides of my family tree."

She picked up a ragged *People* magazine and made some pretense of reading it, but the words wouldn't jell in her mind. She ended up flipping randomly through the pages without even bothering to read the captions under the pictures. When she finished with that one, she didn't bother to pick up another. Instead, she stared fixedly at the clock. It seemed to take forever for the minute hand to move from one small black dot to the next.

Twenty minutes later, a swinging door burst open and the Reverend Marianne Maculyea strode into the room. Marianne was half-Mexican and half-Irish. To everyone's surprise and in spite of a strict Catholic upbringing, Marianne had turned out to be one hundred percent Methodist. She was a Bisbee girl who had gone away to college in California expecting to major in microbiology. She had returned home several years later as an ordained Methodist minister, sporting braces, Birkenstocks, and a househusband named Jeff Daniels who stayed home, baked his own bread, kept an incredibly clean parsonage, and who never hinted to Marianne that perhaps they ought to share the same last name.

This unusual arrangement inevitably caused Bisbee's old-timers to be somewhat suspicious. Scandalized was more like it. Five years after Marianne Maculyea's return, the braces were gone but the househusband remained. Even though the town as a whole languished in economic woes, the once dwindling First Methodist Church up the canyon in Old Bisbee boasted a healthy, thriving congregation. When the local Kiwanis Club began admitting women, Reverend Marianne Maculyea was one of the first women invited to join.

"I figured I'd find you here," Marianne said to Joanna, who had gotten up and hurried to meet the other woman. "Your mother called Jeff, and Jeff called me. What's the word? What's going on?"

"We still haven't heard anything," Joanna answered. "Andy isn't out of surgery yet. Mari, how on earth did you get here so fast?"

"I was already in Tucson," she said. "I came up

to meet with Deena O'Toole to help her plan the memorial service. Jeff caught me at her house out in the foothills just as I was leaving."

"Memorial service?" Joanna asked, frowning. "What memorial service? Who died?"

Marianne shook her head. "I didn't know you hadn't heard. I'm sure you remember Lefty O'Toole, don't you?"

Wayne O'Toole had graduated from Bisbee High School in the early sixties and had gone on to receive a degree from the University of Arizona before falling prey to the draft. After a stint in Vietnam he had returned to Bisbee to teach only to leave the district in disgrace three years later when he was found to be growing a healthy crop of marijuana in his mother's backyard up in Winwood Addition. It was years since Joanna had heard his name.

"I didn't know him," she said, "not personally. But Andy did. Mr. O'Toole was the line coach the whole time Andy played football, JV and Varsity both. He got fired the year I was a freshman. What happened?"

"Murder, evidently," Marianne Maculyea replied. "Someone shot him in the back. He had just gotten out of drug rehab a month or so ago. According to his mother, he was living in Mexico and supposedly getting his life back in order. Lefty's like me. He was raised a Catholic but left the church years ago. I've become friends with Mrs. O'Toole up at the Mule Mountain Rest Home. She asked me to handle the memorial service. Deena, Lefty's ex-wife, is helping with the arrangements.

Between the two of them, I've had my hands full, but enough of that. Tell me about Andy. What in the world happened? Jeff said he'd been shot, too."

Joanna nodded. "That's right. It must be an epidemic. I found Andy down under one of the bridges along High Lonesome Road. They brought him here by helicopter. He's been in surgery for over an hour so far."

"Tell me again what happened to Lefty O'Toole?" Walter McFadden interrupted.

Marianne Maculyea's total focus had been on Joanna. Now, for the first time, she seemed aware of the sheriff's presence.

"Oh, hi there, Walter. I didn't see you when I came in. The story we're getting is still pretty muddled. It happened down near Guaymas. When they found him, he was thirty miles from nowhere, out in the middle of the desert. It's a miracle anyone found him at all. His car turned up abandoned by an old airstrip, so chances are it was robbery. At least that's what the Mexican authorities are saying so far."

"And he was living down there?" McFadden asked.

"That's right. In a dilapidated old school bus someone had converted into a poor-man's RV. From what we've been able to piece together, he disappeared from the mobile home park over a week ago. The body was found this last Wednesday and the *federales* notified Mrs. O'Toole late Thursday afternoon. Since then, Deena's been trying to make arrangements to bring him home.

It's costing Lefty's mother a small fortune to get the body back across the border."

"Why haven't I heard about this before now?" McFadden demanded.

Marianne shrugged. "*Mordida* doesn't work all that well if too many people hear about it."

Joanna wasn't fluent in Spanish, but living in a border town, you didn't have to be. *Mordida*, literally translated as "the bite," refers to bribing public officials. Across the line, it was the time-honored if illegal custom by which Mexican border guards supplemented their meager incomes. If an American citizen happened to die in Old Mexico, getting him home could be a very expensive process, especially if the case received very much publicity. Then the delays could become insurmountable.

Marianne Maculyea turned back to Joanna. Taking both Joanna's cold hands in hers, she squeezed them tight. "I'm sure Andy has an army of doctors and nurses looking after him. How are you holding up?" she asked. "Can I get you anything?"

"I'm all right," Joanna answered. "So far." She extricated her hands and walked back over to the painting. In the meantime, Walter McFadden put down his newspaper, picked up his hat, and walked over to Marianne. "Reverend Maculyea, if you're going to be here with Joanna, maybe I'd better be getting on about my business."

Marianne nodded. "I plan to stay all night, if that's all right." She looked to Joanna for confirmation, but she seemed to have faded out of one conversation and into another.

"I'm sorry Lefty O'Toole's dead," she said quietly. "And Andy will be, too. No matter what happened later, Andy always liked the man. He always said Lefty would have been fine if the war hadn't messed him up. He thought Lefty deserved another chance."

Marianne shook her head. "Andy's always been a man ahead of his time," she observed. "Small towns don't necessarily make heroes out of people who turn the other cheek."

"Don't be putting down Andy," Walter McFadden grumbled. "And don't be hard on old Bisbee, either. Lefty O'Toole's been messed up on drugs for as long as I can remember. Sounds to me like he got in way over his head, and somebody took care of him."

Tipping his hat to Joanna, he stalked from the waiting room. The two women exchanged glances. "I don't think Walter liked hearing about Lefty from somebody like me," she said, "but Deena insisted on keeping it quiet."

"Don't worry," Joanna said. "He's probably just worn out. I know I am."

After McFadden left, Marianne located a vending machine and bought two cups of acrid coffee. For the next two hours Joanna Brady and Reverend Marianne Maculyea sat in the waiting room and talked. Or rather, Joanna talked and Reverend Maculyea listened. Finally, at one o'clock in the morning, the door to the waiting room swung open and a doctor dressed in surgical green stuck his head inside.

"Mrs. Brady?" he asked.

Joanna scrambled to her feet, her heart thudding heavily in her chest. "Yes."

"I'm Doctor Sanders. Your husband's come through surgery as well as can be expected under the circumstances. He's in the recovery room right now, and from there he'll be going to the Intensive Care Unit."

Feeling her knees sag, Joanna sank back down into the chair. "Is he going to be all right?"

Dr. Sanders shook his head. "That I don't know. He's been gravely injured. For the next forty-eight hours at least, it's going to be touch and go."

"How bad is it?"

"We've already been through one episode of cardiac arrest, and there may be some brain damage from that. As far as the wound itself is concerned, we're dealing with possible peritonitis as well as damage to his liver, kidney, and large intestine. Not only that, the bullet lodged against the spine, so it's possible there could be some spinal damage as well."

The hard-hitting words sent Joanna reeling: brain damage, peritonitis, paralysis. She felt as though she were flying apart, but Dr. Sanders seemed unaware of the effect his words were having. "Actually," he continued, "we should all count ourselves lucky that he's made it this far."

"Can I see him?" Joanna asked.

"No. Not at the moment, Mrs. Brady. There's not much point. He's still under anesthesia, and we're going to keep him heavily sedated for a while. With that kind of abdominal damage, we'll be leaving the incision open so we can continue monitoring exactly what's going on. Infection and all that. If I were you, I'd go somewhere and try to get some sleep. It's going to be a long haul. You'll need your rest."

"What are his chances, doctor?"

Dr. Sanders was young, not much older than Joanna. He gave her a searching look. "Do you want it straight?"

She nodded. "Please."

"He's got about one chance in ten of making it."

"Those aren't very good odds, are they, doctor?"

"No, but you said you wanted it straight."

"Then I'll stay here and stretch out on one of the couches. Ask someone to come get me when they move him from the Recovery Room to the ICU."

"All right," he said. "I can understand your not wanting to leave. I'll have someone bring in a blanket."

Reverend Marianne Maculyea kicked off her shoes. "Have them bring two," she said. "If she's staying, so am I."

"Okay," Dr. Sanders said. "Suit yourselves." He walked as far as the door and then paused as if reconsidering. "Since you'll be here," he said, "I'll set it up for you to be able to see him for five minutes once they get him to ICU."

"Thanks," Joanna murmured.

An orderly appeared a few minutes later and dropped off two blankets and two pillows. The women made makeshift beds on the couches. Reverend Maculyea padded around the room until she located the light panel. She shut off all the lights except the red *EXIT* sign directly over the door.

"Hope you don't mind the red glow," she said, making her way back to the couch, "but it looks as though that one doesn't have a switch."

Joanna settled herself on the couch and pulled the blanket up around her chin. For a moment the room was quiet, then the stillness was broken by the wail of an approaching ambulance which finally quieted once it arrived at the Emergency Room entrance.

"Mari?" Joanna asked.

"Yes."

"I'm trying to pray, but I can't remember how to do it. I've forgotten all the words."

"You don't have to remember the words," Marianne Maculyea returned. "Trying to remember the words counts. God's got a pretty good idea of what you mean, but would you like me to pray for you?"

"Please."

"Now I lay me down to sleep," Reverend Maculyea began. "I pray the Lord my soul to keep."

Joanna found the old, familiar words of the childhood prayer oddly comforting. Somehow they made her want to laugh and cry at the same time.

"If I should die before I wake," Marianne continued, "I pray the Lord my soul to take."

The prayer had barely ended when Joanna Brady fell into an exhausted and troubled sleep.

SEVEN MILES away, in his luxurious rented home in the Catalina foothills, Antonio Vargas answered his doorbell. He checked through the peephole to make certain no one was there. Sure enough, there was nothing visible on his front porch but a single briefcase.

Quickly Vargas unbolted the door and hauled the case inside. It was a good one, a Hartmann with a combination lock. He spun the locks to the correct combination and snapped open the lid. There they were, lined out in neatly wrapped bundles of twenties and hundreds—$50,000—blood money, his paycheck for taking out both Lefty O'Toole and Lefty's pal, Andrew Brady. Killing people was his job, and he was very good at it.

There had been some grumbling over the cost of this particular operation, but those damned bean-counters didn't know anything about working out in the field. It had been necessary to convince them what exactly was at stake if preventive measures weren't taken. They'd come around then, when Tony had shown them in black and white that one of the most lucrative drug routes in the country—the one through Cochise County—was at risk. After that, they'd seen things his way, and money was no object.

Closing the briefcase, Vargas stuck it up on the top shelf in the coat closet next to the door. Fortunately, Angie was either smart enough to stay out of his business or dumb enough not to know what was going on. Either way, she kept out of his way and didn't ask questions. She could cook, and she was a hell of a lay, one who seldom told him no. What else did a man want? Or need?

Tony felt his growing erection and marveled that his hard-on materialized at the very touch and smell of all that money. He wondered which for him was actually the bigger turn-on—blood or money. As he sauntered back into the bedroom, he switched on the bedside lamp. Angie Kellogg groaned, rolled over on her side, and covered her eyes with a pillow, trying to shut out the light, but Tony was not to be dissuaded. He pulled back the bedding and climbed onto the bed, turning her over onto her back and peeling back her gown.

"Wake up, Angie baby, and see what daddy has for you. He wants you to take him for a little ride."

"Please, Tony. Not now. It's the middle of the night. I'm tired. I want to sleep."

"Sleep hell! Open up!"

And she did, too, because Angie Kellogg was first and foremost a survivor, and she was far too frightened of Tony Vargas to do anything else.

✿ FOUR

JOANNA'S FIRST visit to the ICU came at three
o'clock in the morning. The daunting collection
of machines, tubes, and wires took her breath
away and left her feeling weak and angry.
The person lying there on the bed looked like
little more than a pale representation of the man
she loved. She touched Andy's thick strawberry-
blonde hair, but his eyes remained closed. There
was no response when she sat down beside him
and took his warm limp hand in hers. She huddled next to him for the strictly enforced five-
minute period while silent tears rolled down her
cheeks.

By her fourth visit, just after seven, she was
better able to handle the situation. When she
emerged that time, Dr. Sanders was waiting for
her in the hallway. "Care for a cup of coffee?" he
asked.

She glanced at Marianne who waved her away.

"Go ahead," she said. "I'll come find you if you're needed."

"Thanks," Joanna said. She followed Dr. Sanders down the hall, thinking they were on their way to the cafeteria. Instead, he led her into a tiny conference room, showed her to a chair, and then went out and brought coffee back from somewhere nearby.

"Have you seen him already this morning?" she asked. Seating himself across from her, Dr. Sanders nodded.

"What do you think? Is he going to make it?"

"He's hanging in there for the time being," Dr. Sanders replied noncommittally. "That's about as good as it gets at the moment."

He leaned closer to her across the small conference table and seemed to study her face. His searching look made Joanna feel self-conscious, and she tried to hide behind her coffee cup.

"How long have you and your husband been married, Mrs. Brady?"

"Call me Joanna. Ten years. Ten years exactly. Yesterday was our tenth anniversary."

"You love him very much, don't you."

Joanna bit her lip. "Yes."

Dr. Sanders' face was somber. His was not the look of someone about to deliver good news, and Joanna tried to prepare for it, to steel herself against whatever was coming. "What is it?" she asked. "What are you trying to tell me?"

"How has he seemed to you lately?"

"Seemed? What do you mean?"

Sanders shrugged. "Oh, you know. Has he been

despondent about anything, angry, or upset, any of those?"

"We've been busy," Joanna conceded. "We both work. We have a nine-year-old child. Andy's been running for sheriff . . ." She paused and examined the doctor's features warily. "I don't understand why you're asking about that."

"Have you ever read the story about the Little Engine that could? It's a children's book."

"Of course I've read it. Hasn't everybody? It's one of Jenny's favorites, but what does that have to do with anything?"

"You remember in the story how the Little Engine says 'I think I can?'"

"Yes."

"That Little Engine thought he could pull the train over the mountain. He wanted to do it, believed he could do it."

"Yes, but . . ."

"You asked me if I thought your husband was going to make it, Joanna, and I'm telling you. It's going to depend in large measure on his attitude, on whether or not Andrew Brady wants to recover, on whether or not he thinks he can."

"You're talking about paralysis, aren't you? You're telling me that if he's going to be crippled for the rest of his life, he may not want to live."

"No," Dr. Sanders answered slowly. "That's not what I'm saying at all. This morning I've already had two calls from one of the people down there in Bisbee, an investigator. Dick somebody."

"Dick Voland. He's the Chief Deputy, Andy's boss."

"Voland. That's right. That's the name. We talked for some time."

"What did he say?"

Dr. Sanders rubbed his forehead. "You may find this information disturbing, but I think it's only fair to warn you, Joanna. The people at the Sheriff's Department are investigating your husband's case as an attempted suicide."

The room seemed to spin around her. The last sip of coffee rose dangerously in her throat. She fought it back down. "No," she said. "You mean attempted murder."

"I said exactly what I mean," Dr. Sanders insisted. "The physical evidence there on the scene and also what we found here in the hospital—the angle of penetration, the powder burns on your husband's hands—are consistent with a self-inflicted bullet wound, what we call around here a misplaced heart shot."

He waited for Joanna to speak, but she simply shook her head. "I'm sorry to have to tell you this, Joanna. I can see it's a shock to you, but I wanted you to have a chance to compose yourself. There are several reporters down in the lobby waiting to interview you. Once you venture off this floor or try to leave the hospital, they'll be all over you. I didn't want you to encounter them without first having some warning, some time to prepare."

"Reporters," Joanna repeated stupidly, as if her stunned brain had to struggle in order to grasp hold of a single word or idea from all he had told her. "Why would they want to talk to me?"

"Cochise County may be small potatoes, but

nonetheless, your husband is a political candidate. An attempted murder of a politician always causes an uproar. As of right now, it's still being reported as an attempted homicide. That will change soon enough, but even so, when someone in the public eye attempts suicide, that's also considered newsworthy. Regardless of which way it goes, until the case is resolved, you're going to continue to find yourself shoved into the limelight."

For a long moment Joanna stared dumbly at Dr. Sanders, not just looking at him but thinking about the implication of his words. Then her mind clicked out of its temporary paralysis and into gear. "You're saying Andy tried to kill himself? That he did this?"

"Yes."

Anger rose within her, but she remained totally clearheaded. "Where's the weapon then? He didn't shoot himself with his bare hands. I was there, with him, on the ground, and I didn't see any sign of a weapon."

"Voland told me they found it under the truck this morning when they towed it away."

Suddenly she was bristling with fury. "Sure, he shot himself and threw the gun under the truck. And who the hell do you think locked the car doors?"

Sanders seemed taken aback by the sudden transformation. "I don't know anything about locked doors," he said placatingly.

"Well I do!" Joanna exclaimed. "Both doors were locked and his keys were in the ignition."

"What does that have to do with it?"

Erupting in anger, she stood up, violently crashing her chair into the wall and leaving a dent in the plaster.

"I'll tell you what it has to do with! Andrew Brady locked his keys in his car one time in his whole life. He did it once and only once, the first time he ever drove a car by himself, and it never happened again. Including yesterday! Somebody else locked those keys in his truck. When Dick Voland finds out who did that, he'll have the right killer."

Setting her shoulders defiantly, Joanna marched from the conference room and back down the hall. Marianne Maculyea saw the look on her face and immediately assumed Andy had taken a turn for the worse. "What did the doctor tell you, Joanna? How bad is it?"

Joanna fought to keep her voice under control, speaking slowly and deliberately. "He says Andy might've tried to commit suicide."

"Andy?" Marianne said dubiously. "Andrew Brady tried suicide? The doctor's got to be kidding."

"Dr. Sanders isn't kidding, and neither is the Sheriff's Department. They're investigating what happened to Andy as a possible attempted suicide."

Marianne shook her head. "Come on, now. That's ridiculous. He's a happily married man, an excellent father. Did you tell Dr. Sanders that?"

"I told him," Joanna responded. "I told him it wasn't possible, just couldn't be that it happened that way."

"Wherever did he get such a crazy idea?"

"From the Sheriff's Department. From Dick Voland. And he's wrong. I swear to you, no matter what Dick Voland says, somebody tried to kill my husband, and that's attempted murder in my book."

Marianne Maculyea looked thoughtful. "They couldn't just say that without any evidence, but . . ."

"You know what will happen, don't you?" Joanna interrupted. "They'll declare it a suicide as soon as someone can finish writing up the paper. They'll close the book on the case, and whoever really did it will get away scot-free. No one will ever go looking for him. In the meantime, while everyone's busy pretending it's suicide, all the real evidence will simply disappear."

"But when Andy comes around, surely he'll be able to tell someone what really happened."

"But what if he doesn't?" Joanna objected. "I've been going in there every hour for four hours now, Mari, and Andy hasn't moved, not once. He hasn't spoken and he hasn't responded to my touch. I think the machines are all that are keeping him alive. What if he never wakes up?"

"Then you're right. Whoever did this will literally get away with murder, won't they," Marianne Maculyea agreed.

The waiting room suddenly seemed to fill up and grow smaller as two other families arrived to keep their own separate ICU vigils. The newcomers talked in hushed, worried voices, waiting for

the time when one or two of them would be ushered into a room for a five-minute visit.

Just as the new arrivals were settling in, the
door to the waiting room slammed open again
and Jennifer Brady rushed inside. A careworn
Walter McFadden followed hot on her heels. Lack
of sleep had left dark circles under the old man's
eyes. In one hand he carried Joanna's shabby
luggage. In the other was a long white florist's
box tied with a red satin ribbon.

Breathlessly Jenny darted up to her mother,
talking full speed as she came. "Will I be able to
see him now? Sheriff McFadden doesn't think so,
but I do. They'll let me, won't they? Grandma's
mad because I rode up with Sheriff McFadden.
She thinks I should have ridden up with her. Are
you okay, Mommy? You don't look very good."

Joanna took Jennifer firmly by the shoulders.
"Jenny," she said. "I want you to go sit with Rever-
end Maculyea for a few minutes. I've got to talk to
Sheriff McFadden."

"But . . ." Jenny objected.

Marianne Maculyea headed off the objection
and led the protesting child away. Meanwhile,
Walter McFadden set the suitcase on the floor.
After placing the box on a nearby table, he gave it
a gentle tap.

"I brought this from the hotel," he explained.
"As soon as he heard what had happened, Melvin Williams from up at the Copper Queen called
and left word for me to call him. Evidently
Andy dropped this off at the hotel late yesterday

afternoon and asked Melvin to keep it in the refrigerator until you two came in for dinner. Under the circumstances, Melvin wanted you to have it right away while the flowers are still fresh."

"What flowers?" Joanna asked.

She had been staring at him, but she must not have been listening to a word he said. McFadden shook his head impatiently as though wanting her to pay closer attention.

"These flowers, Joanna. The ones here in this box. Don't you want to open them?"

"I don't give a damn about flowers," Joanna said vehemently. "I only want to know one thing. Who besides Dick Voland says Andy tried to kill himself?" Her icy tone of voice matched the pallor of her cheeks.

Walter McFadden's shoulders sagged. "You heard then?"

Joanna nodded. "I heard."

McFadden left the box on the table and moved closer to her. "I'm sorry, Joanna, sorry as hell."

"You think *you're* sorry? I want to know who came up with that crackpot idea," she insisted. "Tell me."

"Dick Voland, Ken Galloway, the detectives who worked the scene. Don't take it personally, Joanna. It was a consensus opinion."

"Consensus my ass!" she said, her eyes narrowing. "Whoever says that is dead wrong."

"You can't argue with the evidence, Joanna. It's plain as day. They found the gun, you know. Under the truck. Andy must have dropped it when he fell. It's his own gun, Andy's .38 Special. We've already checked. His are the only prints on it."

"If it's Andy's gun, of course his prints are on it. Whoever else used it probably wore gloves."

Their raised voices caused the other families in the room to turn away from their own concerns in order to watch the drama unfolding in the middle of the room—an older man using soft, placating words while he argued with a visibly angry red-haired woman who seemed ready to tear him apart.

"Look, Joanna, I know this is hard on you. Suicide's always hell for whoever's left trying to pick up the pieces."

Joanna's voice dropped a full octave. "You're not listening to me, Walter."

Of all the people in the room, only Jenny knew enough to be wary. Experience had taught her that when her mother's voice fell that low in pitch, something was bound to happen.

"Somebody tried to murder my husband," Joanna continued. "I want you and the rest of your goddamned department to find out who did it."

Oblivious to the danger signals, Walter McFadden raised both his hands. "Look, little lady, I don't know what . . ."

He never finished the sentence. With a lightning grasp, Joanna's hand lashed out, grabbed his outstretched thumb, and forced it back into his wrist. Searing pain from the nerve shot up his arm. Without knowing quite how it happened, Sheriff Walter McFadden found himself down on one knee in the middle of the room with Joanna Brady standing over him.

"Don't you ever 'little lady' me again, Sheriff McFadden," she hissed. "And don't tell me to shut up and mind my own business, either. This *is* my business. Somebody tried to kill my husband last night. According to the doctor, whoever it was did a pretty damn thorough job of it, too. Liver damage, intestinal damage. Even if Andy lives, he may be paralyzed from the waist down."

She let go of McFadden's thumb and stepped back two paces before turning her back on him and walking away. One of the men in the room made as if to come help him get back up, but McFadden motioned him aside. "I'm all right," he grunted sheepishly. "Let me be."

With both knees cracking in protest, the sheriff of Cochise County lurched to his feet. No one had ever done that to him before, and the fact that a little slip of a woman had tumbled him like a tippy-toy galled him down to the toes of his snakeskin boots. More curious than angry, he hobbled after Joanna. "How in the hell did you do that?"

She spun around and faced him again. "I'm warning you, Walter, don't close the book on this case without finding out who did it."

"Joanna, be reasonable," he countered, testing his thumb, trying to determine if it was broken. Despite the fact that it hurt like hell, it was probably only sprained.

"Reasonable!" she stormed. "My husband's in there dying, and you expect *me* to be reasonable?

I can outshoot half the men in your department. My dad and my husband both saw to that. And I can handle myself, too. It's your job to find out who attacked my husband, but if you don't solve this thing, I will."

Just then Jennifer escaped Marianne Maculyea's clutches. She rushed over to where Joanna and McFadden stood in nose-to-nose confrontation. The child's face was beaming. "Mom, that was great. It worked just like you said it would." She turned to Walter McFadden. "Mommy taught me how to do it, too. Want me to show you?"

Jennifer's unexpected interruption took the edge off the situation, although it didn't defuse it completely. In spite of himself, McFadden smiled down at the child. "No thanks," he said. "Not right now, but do me a favor, Jennifer. Go get that box off the table for me, would you?"

While she did as he asked, McFadden turned back to Joanna. "If I were in your place, I'd probably be mad as hell, too. I don't blame you, Joanna, not a bit, but in the end you're going to have to leave the investigation to the professionals."

"And take your word for it?"

"Yes," Walter McFadden said. "That, too."

Jenny walked up to them with the box in hand. "Is it a present?" she asked.

"I think so," McFadden nodded, "an anniversary present from your dad for your mother."

Jennifer held out the package, but Joanna made no move to take it. "Maybe you can get her to open it," McFadden said to Jenny. "After all, I only had to beat off half my department to bring that box up here this morning. The very idea sent Dick Voland straight through the roof. He wanted it for his investigation. They all think I need to have my head examined."

Once more Jennifer held out the package. This time, reluctantly, Joanna took the box and slid off the red ribbon. She handed the ribbon to Jenny then carefully lifted the lid and folded back a layer of delicate green tissue paper. Inside on a bed of ferns lay two dozen beautifully formed apricot-colored roses. She had always preferred apricot ones to the more traditional, dark red kind.

A huge lump formed in Joanna's throat. "Oh, Mommy," Jenny exclaimed. "They're beautiful! Can I hold them?"

Joanna nodded and started to hand the box over to her daughter. "There's a card," Jenny pointed out. "Aren't you going to read it?"

The card was nothing more than one of those tiny envelopes found on florist counters everywhere. Andy wasn't one to spend money on lavish, gold-embossed, flowery greeting cards. Joanna's name was scrawled on the outside of the envelope in Andy's careless handwriting.

With trembling fingers, Joanna tore open the envelope. Inside, on an equally tiny note card with a single red rose in the upper right hand corner were the following words:

"JoJo. Sorry it took ten years. Love, Andy."

She looked at the words, read them through twice more, but they didn't make sense, so she handed the card over to Walter McFadden. "What does it mean?" he asked.

Joanna shook her head. "I don't have any idea."

Meanwhile, Jennifer had placed the box back on the table and was slowly lifting the individual roses out of their tissue wrapping, counting aloud as she went. "Mommy," she said suddenly, "come look at this."

Joanna hurried to her daughter's side. From the bottom corner of the flower box, Jennifer extracted a tiny, velvet-covered jeweler's box which she placed in her mother's hand. Joanna flipped up the lid. Inside lay a diamond engagement ring with a single emerald-cut stone.

"Oh, Mommy," Jennifer squealed. "It's beautiful. Put it on."

The ring consisted of a single diamond on a gleaming gold band. Joanna pulled it out of its velvet-lined bed and slipped it on her finger where it fit perfectly, snuggling up against her plain gold wedding band. She held out her hand and the fluorescent overhead light fixture set the flawless stone gleaming.

Walter McFadden peered down at the ring through his bifocals. "It's pretty all right," he said. "It's just about as pretty as it can be." But then, when Marianne came to admire it, the sheriff walked away. He stopped at the door and looked back, shaking his head.

Joanna turned and caught his eye. "Be sure and tell Dick Voland about this," she said, holding up her hand and waving it defiantly so the diamond winked in the light. "Ask him if this looks like what you'd expect from a depressed, unhappy, suicidal man. Ask him, sheriff, and let me know what he says."

FIVE

THAT DAY had all the distorted and nightmarish reality of time spent at a carnival fun house. Hours dragged. The seconds and minutes stretched into eternity, except for those few precious moments each hour when Joanna was allowed to sit at Andy's bedside. Those brief interludes passed in a fast-frame blur that was never long enough.

Nature abhors a vacuum. As the hours passed, the waiting room filled and emptied of people. Neighbors from home stopped by, people Joanna knew from work or school or church. Her boss, Milo Davis, showed up with the first contingent. In a genuine show of support, all of them had willingly taken time to make the two-hour, hundred-mile, one-way drive from Bisbee to Tucson. Each time Joanna emerged from Andy's room, some of the earlier arrivals would have disappeared only to be replaced by a new crop.

The visitors eddied and flowed around her,

77

offering hugs and nervous murmurs of small talk. Someone had evidently leaked the information that the previous night's shooting incident was now being investigated as a possible suicide attempt. That was hot news in Bisbee, and most of the visitors that morning were well aware of the ugly rumor. To each other, Joanna's visitors spoke indignantly about how terrible it was that Andy Brady could do such an awful thing to his wife, child, and parents. To Joanna, they said only how very sorry they were and how she should let them know if there was anything at all they could do to help.

For Jennifer, the novelty of being at the hospital wore off within the first hour. The nurses were adamant. Children under sixteen were not allowed to visit patients in the ICU. Period. When Jennifer realized there was no way she would be allowed to visit her father, she grew more and more restless. Not long after that she began lobbying to go home. Even with Marianne Maculyea running interference between mother and child, by eleven Joanna had hit the wall and was ready to send Jennifer packing. At noon, when Marianne offered to take the child home and let her stay at the parsonage for as long as necessary, Joanna agreed instantly. They left at twelve fifteen, but Joanna's respite was brief. Her mother arrived a few short minutes later.

For years, Eleanor Lathrop had maintained a standing Wednesday morning appointment for a shampoo, set, and manicure at Helene's Salon of Hair and Beauty, in Helen Barco's converted backyard garage. The classy-sounding "e" had been added to Helen's name about the same time her husband, Slim, had installed a shampoo basin where he had once kept his table saw. Eleanor had been one of Helene's first, and was now one of her most loyal, customers. It would have been unthinkable for her to miss that appointment, especially when there was so much to talk about.

Eleanor arrived at the ICU waiting room wearing her best Sunday dress. Her hair was freshly blued and her nails freshly done. There was a striking contrast between the well-turned-out Eleanor and her scruffy-looking daughter who was still wearing that old, ratty jacket and her pair of rough boots. Her hair was a mess; her clothes were filthy.

"You look a fright," Eleanor said in her usual brusque fashion. "I sent your suitcase along with Walter. Didn't that man bother to give it to you?"

"He brought me the suitcase, Mother," Joanna replied wearily. "I just haven't had time to do anything about it."

Eleanor glanced around the room. "Where's Jennifer?"

"She was bored to tears. Marianne Maculyea took her back to Bisbee. She'll stay with Mari and Jeff until I get things under control here."

Eleanor shook her head. "I don't understand what's got into you, Joanna. First you have her ride up here with Walter McFadden, and then you send her home with someone else before I can even get here. What in the world are people going to think? That you don't believe I'm capable of taking care of her? That you don't even trust your own mother to *baby-sit?*"

Eleanor's voice had been climbing steadily, and now her eyes filled with self-pitying tears. Joanna tried her best to calm her. "It's nothing like that, Mother. Nothing at all. Jenny was bored and unhappy sitting around here. When Mari offered to take her home, it was too good to pass up."

At that moment, the room was free of other Brady family visitors, so Joanna settled her mother in front of the waiting room's only television set.

"I'll be back in a few minutes," Joanna said, switching on the set.

"Where are you going?"

"To visit Andy."

"But I just got here," Eleanor objected petulantly. "Can't you stay around long enough to tell me what's happening?"

"It's time for me to go see him," Joanna explained. "They only let me in the room once an hour for five minutes at a time. You'll barely know I'm gone."

Five minutes later when Joanna returned to the waiting room, Eleanor was engrossed in Noontime Edition, Tucson's local version of the noon news. "It's a good thing you got back in time," she said. "You'd better come watch. When this commercial is over, they're going to have something on about Andy."

Joanna hurried over to the television set. "Really? About Andy? On the Tucson news?"

"That's right."

The commercial ended and the screen switched to the newsroom set. A female anchor with a beauty-pageant smile turned her charm full on the camera.

"From Bisbee, this morning, we have learned that a Cochise County Sheriff's Deputy, who is also a candidate for the office of sheriff, has been hospitalized in critical condition with a possibly self-inflicted gunshot wound. In addition, the injured man is currently being investigated for alleged connections to Wayne M. "Lefty" O'Toole, a suspected drug-runner, found shot to death near Guaymas last week.

"Sources close to the investigation say that evidence linking Andrew Brady with the murder victim had been found by Mexican officials at the crime scene north of Guaymas. Brady is a declared candidate in a contest to oust longterm Cochise County Sheriff, Walter V. McFadden.

"For more on that, here's Noontime Edition's on-the-scene correspondent, Roger Cannon, speaking to you from the courthouse in Bisbee."

Not believing her ears, Joanna sank into a chair next to her mother.

"What in the world are they talking about?" Eleanor asked.

"Hush," Joanna hissed. "Listen."

The picture on the screen switched to a young man posing in front of Bisbee's copper-toned Iron Man, the statue of a barechested man—a well-muscled miner—wielding a sledgehammer and drill.

"Late last night and early this morning, this

small southern Arizona mining community was shocked to learn that a well-respected local police officer who is running for the position of sheriff, Deputy Andrew Brady, had been wounded in what investigators now say was an apparently unsuccessful suicide attempt. Brady was rushed to University Hospital in Tucson where he remains in guarded condition.

"Earlier this morning federal Drug Enforcement Agency officers notified the Cochise County Sheriff's department that they were beginning a wholesale investigation of Brady's possible involvement with slain convicted drug runner, Lefty O'Toole, who also hails from the Bisbee area.

"O'Toole, who once served as Andrew Brady's high school football coach, was a man who, in recent years, was suspected of utilizing his Vietnam-era piloting experience in the lucrative field of transporting illegal drugs across the Mexican border.

"People here in town have told me that O'Toole taught at Bisbee High School briefly in the late seventies, but his teaching contract was terminated over an alleged drug violation. He was living near Guaymas at the time of his death. The exact nature of the connection between Andrew Brady and Lefty O'Toole is not known at this time."

"Why, did you ever!" Eleanor Lathrop exclaimed. Joanna waved her to silence.

"I'm speaking now with Richard Voland, Chief Deputy for the Cochise County Sheriff's Department," the reporter continued. "Mr. Voland, before this morning was anyone in your department aware of the DEA's possible investigation into the activities of Deputy Brady?"

Richard Voland's face appeared on the screen looking tired and angry. "No," he said. "Absolutely not. We had no idea."

"Is it possible that Andrew Brady somehow learned of the impending investigation and that's what prompted last night's unfortunate events?"

"It's possible, of course," Richard Voland agreed, "but I don't see how Andy could have known since we didn't find out ourselves until mid-morning today."

"Cochise County Sheriff, Walter McFadden, is well known statewide for his outspoken opposition to drugs. How has he reacted to the news that one of his deputies may have some involvement with a known drug-runner?"

"I'd rather not comment on that, if you don't mind," Richard Voland said. "You'll have to ask Sheriff McFadden himself when he's available."

"Has your department taken any action against Andrew Brady at this time?"

Voland glared at the reporter. "Andrew Brady is currently on sick leave," he replied. "If and when we have access to the DEA's so-called evidence, we'll review it and then see if any further action is necessary."

"Thank you very much, Mr. Voland. Back to you, Donna."

The picture returned to the newsroom set. Once more the smiling woman's face beamed out at them, but Joanna could no longer hear what the news anchor was saying over the roar of blood pounding in her own ears.

"Why, forevermore!" exclaimed Eleanor Lathrop. "That's the wildest thing I've ever heard of. How can they get away with saying such nonsense?"

Shocked, Joanna lurched to her feet. For a moment she stood over her mother, but she didn't open her mouth for fear of what might come out. She grabbed up her purse, flung it over her arm, and headed for the door. "I can't breathe in here," she said. "I've got to get some air."

"Where are you going now?" Eleanor wailed.

"For a walk."

"Can't I come with you?"

"No. I've got to think."

"Well, you should at least change clothes before you go out. You look terrible."

"Tough," Joanna said to herself as the door swung shut behind her, stifling whatever last-minute advice or orders her mother might have been issuing.

Joanna paused in the hallway long enough to look down and examine her clothing. She could easily have passed for a bag lady. She was still clumping around in the pair of frayed, pull-on work boots. The Levi's jacket was bloodstained and torn besides. Under it, the once lovely blue dress, the one she had bought for their anniversary getaway at the Copper Queen, was also stained and tattered. Now, less than twenty-four hours later, that unkept date seemed a lifetime ago. She was embarrassed by her appearance, but she refused to go back into the waiting room and face her mother in order to retrieve the suitcase. Staying dirty was the lesser of two evils.

She fled down the hallway. When the elevator didn't come right away, she pounded down the stairway with the sound of her boot heels reverberating in the stairwell. Reaching the first floor, she galloped through the lobby, almost crashing into a delivery man carrying two huge bouquets of flowers. Once she reached the sidewalk outside, she stood for a minute in the early afternoon sun.

The air conditioner had been running full blast in the waiting room. Outdoors it was still surprisingly hot. Reflected heat from the September sun rose off the driveway's blacktop in shimmering waves, but the warmth didn't penetrate Joanna's frozen core. Instead of peeling off the jacket, she pulled it closer around her and plunged her hands deep in the pockets.

Not caring where she went, she headed across an expanse of green lawn toward Campbell Avenue. "I won't cry," she told herself determinedly. "I will not cry!"

She had already cried enough. Besides, crying would interfere with the thinking process, and that was what she had to do now. Think.

How was it that Lefty O'Toole had emerged from the dim, dark reaches of the past to some kind of suspected illegal involvement with Andy? Who the hell was Lefty O'Toole anyway? Her only real recollection of him was from a poor black-and-white photo of a necktie-clad man in the faculty section of Andy's senior-year *Cuprite*, Bisbee

High School's annual. The same grainy picture had been run in the local paper when one of Lefty's numerous subsequent scrapes with the law had brought him under public scrutiny.

Lefty O'Toole had been fired from his teaching position at Bisbee High School the year Joanna was a freshman. The place on the yearbook's faculty page where his picture should have been was blank. O'Toole had been present in Andy's book, missing in hers. Now, here he was back again. It was as though the man was some kind of terrible ghost who had returned years later to haunt her and tear Joanna's life to pieces. How was it possible? How could it be happening?

And why was Andy lying in a hospital bed—pale, stricken, barely breathing, and unable to defend himself—while the world outside the hospital room, even friends of his like Dick Voland, accused him of all kinds of unspeakable actions? Andy. He wasn't perfect by a long shot. Ten years of marriage had taught Joanna that, but he was hardworking, honest, and kind. He was the type of man who would spend a weekend helping patch a widow's leaking roof or who would agree to take a carload of noisy kids to Sierra Vista for a bowling tournament. How could a man like that, a man so very much like her own father, have anything at all to do with the likes of Lefty O'Toole?

Joanna crossed Campbell and started up Elm, striding along in her heavy, clumsy boots, not caring how she looked, letting the sunlight warm her chilled body and mind.

Had Walter McFadden known about all this

earlier when he dropped off Jennifer and the suitcase, Joanna wondered. If so, why hadn't he told her? Surely if someone in his department was being investigated by the DEA, the sheriff himself would have been properly notified. Why had the reporter interviewed Dick Voland? Why not the sheriff himself? But then, maybe with the election coming up, McFadden figured it would be better if someone else broke the news that his opponent was under investigation.

Hours earlier Joanna had thought that having Dr. Sanders accuse Andy of attempting suicide was the worst possible thing that could happen. Obviously she had been wrong. This was far, far worse. She could see how, left to their own devices, the media would convict Andrew Brady of wrongdoing without him ever having an official day in court.

A car drove by, a silver Ford Taurus with a single male occupant. She realized dimly that she had seen that car twice now in the course of her short walk. At first the idea that someone might be following her seemed too preposterous to even consider. The events of the past few days had left her edgy and skittish, she told herself. She was being silly. But when she crossed the next intersection, she caught sight of the same car again. This time it was parked half a block away with the engine still running and the driver hunched behind the wheel.

Why would someone be following her, she wondered. At home in Bisbee, she wouldn't have hesitated to walk up to the car and ask what the hell was going on, but this was Tucson, a big city by comparison, and only the night before, person or persons unknown had tried to murder her husband. Feeling isolated and vulnerable, she looked around her for someplace to turn for help. The houses nearby all seemed large and forbidding, mansions almost. The way she was dressed, in her bloodstained clothing and clumsy boots, she couldn't see herself running up to the front door of any of those houses and asking for help. They'd take one look at her, call the cops, and have her arrested.

Ahead of her she saw the pink-and-blue wall of what at first seemed to be the largest house of all, but then, upon closer inspection, she realized the building was a hotel, a public building. Small blue letters on the side of the building announced, "Arizona Inn."

She personally had never set foot inside the place, but she had heard of it. The Arizona Inn was some kind of posh resort. Maybe here she could disappear into a crowd of tourists. At the very least, she'd be able to find a telephone and summon help.

She ducked into the first available door. Looking around to get her bearings, she found herself standing in front of a small, densely stocked gift shop. Joanna had hoped for a crowd, and there was none, but perhaps the gift shop might have a pay phone she could use. Quickly, she slipped inside. The sales clerk behind the small counter was busy with someone else—a well-dressed older lady. Overhearing their conversation, Joanna learned the woman was making complicated arrangements to send gifts back home to her several grandchildren in Dubuque, Iowa.

While waiting impatiently for the clerk to finish with her customer, Joanna caught sight of a rack displaying a few end-of-summer items—bathing suits and smock-like beach jackets. Looking at them, she grew more self-conscious about the way she looked and about how out of place her bloodied, filthy clothing was in her present circumstances. She examined the clothing on the rack more closely.

At the far end of the rack was a vivid yellow smock. That particular shade had never been one of Joanna's favorites, but the size was medium, and so was she. Joanna pulled the garment off the hanger and held it up to her body, checking the price tag in the sleeve as she did so. Even at half off, the price was enough to raise her eyebrows, but at least the smock didn't have any bloodstains on it.

Joanna peeled off the denim jacket and rolled it up into a wad. On a shelf near the door sat a small collection of leather *huaraches*, Mexican-made, sandal-type shoes that visiting tourists from back East loved to take home as much for their comfort as for their value as genuine Southwestern conversation pieces. Hoping her luck would hold, Joanna edged over to the display. Sure enough, she saw a pair that was half a size too big, but half a size off was close enough for *huaraches*. She kicked off the boots and slipped on the floppy leather shoes.

By the time the saleswoman finished with her first customer and turned to Joanna, the boots and jacket were securely wrapped together in a compact bundle. Hoping to imitate the anchor lady she had seen on the news, Joanna smiled her most sincere smile.

"I think I'll wear both of these, if you don't mind," she said.

If the woman had any private thoughts about the suitability of the yellow smock with Joanna's torn dress and skin coloring, she diplomatically kept them to herself as she clipped off the sales tags and put Joanna's bundled jacket in a flimsy bag.

"Maybe I should double this," she said, hefting the weight.

"Good idea," Joanna agreed.

She held her breath while she wrote out the check, hoping against hope that it wouldn't bounce. Friday was payday for both Joanna and Andy. Maybe their paychecks would make it to the bank before this check did. Or, if they didn't, maybe Sandra Henning, the manager, would cover it for a day or so until Joanna could make it good.

"Can you tell me where to find a phone?" Joanna asked.

"Down the hallway," the woman answered. "Beyond the bellman's desk, across from the library."

Joanna scuttled across the old-fashioned lobby and found the tiny telephone alcove. Seated in front of the phone, she paused for a moment, wondering who exactly she should call and what she should tell them. Not knowing who else to ask for help, she finally dialed the Cochise County Sheriff's Department and asked to speak to Walter McFadden. When told he wasn't in, she asked for Dick Voland instead.

"Hi, Dick," she said curtly when he answered. "This is Joanna Brady. Where's Sheriff McFadden? I want to speak to him."

Voland cleared his throat uneasily. "He's not here right now."

"Where is he?"

"I can't say, Joanna. We haven't heard from him. What do you need? Can I help?"

As Joanna tried to frame an answer, a man entered the lobby from outside and walked past her. When he stopped at the bellman's desk to ask a question, she recognized the distinctive profile and realized it was the man from the Taurus, the same one who had been following her.

"Joanna?" Dick Voland said. "Are you still there? Do you want me to take a message?"

Joanna's hand shook and her heart hammered in her chest. "No," she said softly, lest the man overhear. "No message."

Carefully, she put down the phone. She had no idea who this man was or what he wanted, but it was clear that he was trailing her openly, in broad daylight as if he had a perfect right to do so.

The long lobby was nearly deserted. An old man sat on a bench next to the wall far beyond the registration desk, but except for him, the bellman, and the man who was following her, there were no other people in the lobby. The sounds of laughter and tinkling glassware came floating to her from someplace else, from a room that sounded like a dining room.

Her pursuer had stepped closer to the bellman's desk and was reading one of the newspapers lying there. The door to the dining room was just around the corner from the public telephone. Maybe if she went through the dining room, she could disappear outside through another exit.

Joanna got up and bolted around the corner, almost colliding head-on with a dining room hostess. "One for lunch?" the woman asked.

Joanna glanced back over her shoulder. Something, maybe the sudden flurry of movement, had caused the man to look up from the papers. Their eyes met, and he started toward her.

"One for lunch," Joanna said hurriedly. "No smoking."

"This way please."

The large dining room with its old-fashioned cane-backed chairs was only half-full, but the room hummed with a relaxed, convivial atmosphere. Joanna followed the hostess to a windowed table that looked out on a small patio.

"Can I get you something to drink?"

"Coffee," Joanna murmured. "Just coffee. Black."

Sitting with her hands clenched in front of her chin, Joanna watched as the hostess ushered the man into the room and seated him a few tables away. A busboy delivered the coffee and Joanna's hands were shaking badly enough that some of the coffee spilled the first time she raised the cup to her lips.

What should she do, she wondered. Make a run for it out a side door and hope to elude him long enough to get back to the hospital? She took another sip of coffee and tried to calm herself. Surely there was some way out of this if she could just force herself to think clearly.

"What can I get for you today?" a smiling waiter asked.

Joanna hadn't intended to stay, much less eat, but she felt trapped. Not eating would make her even more conspicuous. Without even bothering to check the price on the menu, she ordered a club sandwich.

She sat back and took another sip of coffee. Gradually the clanking silver and glassware combined with the enticing smells emanating from the kitchen reminded her that she had eaten almost nothing in nearly twenty-four hours.

She would eat her sandwich when it came and whoever it was who was so interested in where Joanna Brady went and what she did could sit right there and watch her eat.

It would serve him right.

SIX

ANGIE KELLOGG sat on the soft leather couch in the living room, her satin robe untied and gaping open, one naked leg tucked demurely under her. An almost empty and long-forgotten coffee mug was nestled in the soft mound of auburn pubic hair, but coffee in the cup had grown far too cold to drink. Totally alone, she sat absolutely still.

Her attention was focused on the antics of a pair of comical road runners who regarded the gravel-covered backyard as their own private preserve. Angie Kellogg was a lifetime city dweller. Initially, Tucson's strange desert creatures had been a complete mystery to her. Tony had jeered at her lack of knowledge, laughing and calling her stupid. Eventually though, he had condescended to buy her what a bookstore manager had called, "the birdwatchers' Bible," the *Field Guide to North American Birds*.

With the help of that, she had gradually learned

to identify some of her neighbors—quail, dove, road runners, hummingbirds, and even an industrious cactus wren that had taken up residence in the yard's solitary saguaro.

Drinking coffee, reading the newspaper, and watching the various birds and animals provided the sum total of Angie Kellogg's morning diversions. She was an early riser; Tony wasn't. When she was awake and he was sleeping, she wasn't allowed to turn on either the radio or the television set, not even with the volume set on low.

Instead, Angie watched for the glimpses of life her backyard afforded her. She especially enjoyed the hour just before and after sunrise because that was when the cute little cottontails sometimes ventured out to eat and play. They came scampering into the yard through a small natural depression where the wrought-iron fence didn't quite meet the ground. Sometimes she would see a horned toad or a small lizard perched in the sun on the rockery. Less often, she would spy a snake, sometimes even a rattler, sunning itself beside the graveled path. You had to look really carefully to catch sight of the snakes because they blended so well into the surrounding terrain.

The first time she had seen one, she had panicked and yelled for Tony. He had come running outside and had been only too happy to chop the poor snake in half with a shovel. It had seemed to Angie the two halves of the severed snake had wiggled forever. Months later the agonizing death of that writhing snake still haunted her. Now when she did happen to see a snake, any kind of snake, she didn't mention it to Tony at all. In fact sometimes she wished that the whole yard would fill up with slithering rattlesnakes and that Tony would go outside barefoot, but of course that didn't happen.

She envied them all—the birds, the rabbits, and yes, even the snakes—because they at least were free to come and go as they liked. Angie Kellogg wasn't.

All morning long she had itched to go check in the coat closet and see if this was the morning when the newest briefcase would appear, but she hadn't dared, not with Tony in the house and only asleep. She had learned that he was a very light sleeper, and she didn't want him to catch her prowling around where she shouldn't. Later on, if he went out, which he usually did, she'd have ample opportunity to check.

Tony knew a lot about her, but not everything. Her ability to pick the locks on briefcases, for instance, was a carefully guarded secret. Every time the doorbell rang like that in the middle of the night, she knew that in the morning a different briefcase would show up on the shelf in the entryway closet. It would stay there, for a day or two, until Tony was called out of town, then the briefcase would disappear, along with the banded packets of currency inside it.

Angie understood the connection between the intermittent arrival of money and Tony's subsequent sexual prowess. Tony regarded himself as a hell of a lay, but it was only when the money came or when he went off to do what he called a consulting job that he could come up with a decent hard-on, and those didn't last long. By the next day, he'd be after her, demanding satisfaction despite his perpetually soft dick and blaming her when it didn't work. Angie was enough of a pro to make it happen most of the time, but it was hard work, much harder than she had envisioned when Tony Vargas plucked her off the mean streets of East L.A. After the brutality of her last pimp, Tony had seemed a safe haven, at first. Now, though, she realized she had moved from frying pan to fire, and once more she was searching for a way out.

From the bedroom she heard Tony cough his first hacking cough of the day and flick open his cigarette lighter. He was awake then, finally, and had lit up the morning's first smoke. It was amazing to her that in a house that spacious—Tony said there were almost 5,000 square feet under the roof—that she could still hear the tiny click of his damned lighter so distinctly. She hated that sound. It was a signal to her, as plain as if he had punched a buzzer or rung a bell. Angie knew better than to ignore that arbitrary summons.

Pulling the robe closed around her, she went to the kitchen and switched on the Krups coffee maker that had been sitting on the counter loaded and ready since nine o'clock that morning. When Tony woke up in the mornings, he always wanted a cigarette, sex, and a cup of coffee, and he wanted them in that exact order.

"Where are you, Angie?" he bellowed from the bedroom. "What the hell are you doing out there?"

Sometimes, when she came back to the bed, he'd only want her to lie there next to him and keep quiet, but today he ran his hand over her thigh. "You on top," he told her shortly. "And take off that damned robe. I like looking at your tits."

Angie peeled off the robe and clambered on top of him. She resented it when he wanted to do it that way, lying there with one hand behind his head, smoking his cigarette and watching her while she tried to get him hard enough to fit inside her. Maybe if he'd put down the cigarette and concentrate some, it might work better.

She played with him, caressed him, knowing that if she didn't make it work, it would be her problem far more than his. By the time he finished the cigarette and stubbed it out in the overflowing ashtray on the bedside table, she thought it was hard enough, but when she settled herself on him, what little erection there had been disappeared and he flopped back out.

"Sorry, Tony," she said. "It won't go in. Maybe later."

He seized one pendulous breast in his hand and squeezed it until she yelped with pain. "It'll go in something," he said, pulling her down to him. "Use your imagination."

Seething with resentment, Angie did what he wanted, plying him with her tongue and teeth, using all the tricks nine years of working the streets had taught her. At times like this, when she knew it would take forever, she tried not to think about how long it would be, tried to ignore the scratches his jagged toenails sometimes left on her leg when he jammed his knee into her crotch.

One of the girls in L.A. had told her that the secret was to put yourself on automatic and think about something else entirely, something happy or pleasant. To do that, she had to go way back, to first or second grade, before the night when, with her mother in the hospital having another baby, her father had come to her room in the middle of the night and forced himself inside her. That night had marked the end of Annie Beason's childhood and the beginning of a nightmare that lasted for years. Two days shy of her thirteenth birthday, she had boarded a Greyhound bus and left Battle Creek bound for California.

Even there the nightmare had changed, but it hadn't ended. She had expected to make it big in California. Back home in Battle Creek, she had overheard people telling her mother how beautiful she was and how she could maybe be a model some day. Annie Beason headed for California determined to become a movie star. As the noisy bus rumbled cross-country, she had decided on her stage name—Angie Kellogg, after the company her father worked for. Once she made it big, she expected to come back home and rub his red, vein-marked nose in it. And, with a different name, if something bad happened to her along the way, her mother would never have to know.

Of course, something bad had happened, lots more bad than good as a matter of fact. In L.A.

there was a whole industry ready to snap up any and all would-be movie stars, the younger the better. On the streets she had learned that she wasn't alone, that there were lots of other girls just like her, girls from families like hers where the only sign of love or affection between fathers and daughters was a stiff poke between the legs in the middle of the night. Knowing she wasn't alone made it a little easier, but not much.

At first, as young as she was and as pretty, it was easy to make the big bucks, but Angie was bright and she noticed what went on around her. She stayed away from drugs. Girls who did drugs ended up dead more often than not, and Angie Kellogg was nothing if not a survivor. The trick was to make good money, save some of it, and stay alive long enough to get out. If you were smart and lucky, you found a rich daddy to take care of you while you still had your looks.

By twenty-two, Angie Kellogg was old for someone in her line of work. Worldly in some ways but hopelessly naive in others, she was lucky to have kept her looks. Over time, however, she had been passed down from one pimp to another until she ended up with a guy who was not only a pimp but psychotic as well. He had caught her freelancing in a neighborhood bar on her day off, and he would have killed her if Tony Vargas hadn't stepped into the middle of it and come to her rescue.

By then, it had no longer mattered to Angie who she worked for. She figured Tony was another pimp, and she expected him to put her back on the streets. Instead, he moved her to Tucson, settled her into the nicest house she had ever seen, one filled with the very best in rented furniture. He bought her food and clothing and even books on occasion. She thought at first that she had died and gone to heaven, but now that she had lived there for a while, she realized that hell was more like it.

Angie was used to having some independence, some say in spending her time and her money, but Tony didn't see it that way. He didn't let her have any money of her own, and he wouldn't allow her to leave the house without him. She wore only the best clothes, but they were clothes Tony selected and paid for. He wouldn't even let her go to the grocery store by herself. Her reading was limited to what books she managed to find at the checkout counter in the grocery or drug store.

Beneath her, Tony moaned and grasped her head, pulling her hair to make her move faster. When he came, finally, he lay gasping on the bed while she retreated to the kitchen. There she brewed fresh coffee and juiced grapefruit and wished it were poison instead of juice when she poured it into the glass.

While Tony stood under the water of a steaming shower, Angie prepared a tray with more coffee, freshly squeezed grapefruit juice and a bowl of Frosted Flakes. It was Angie's job to make sure they didn't run out of the daily staples—grapefruit, milk, and Frosted Flakes. She set the breakfast tray on the coffee table where it was waiting by the time Tony finished his shower.

He came into the living room wearing a robe and still dripping wet. He padded over to the couch and sat down, leaving a trail of wet footprints on the thick white carpeting. Angie placed the morning newspaper on the marble-topped coffee table next to the breakfast tray. Without a word she backed away to the recliner in the corner. Tony Vargas didn't like to talk to anybody until after he had eaten breakfast, read the funnies, and watched the news.

Angie sat and observed him while he ate, listening to the hollow crunch of cereal in his mouth and wondering if her father, who had once worked on the bagging line in Battle Creek, had helped make that particular batch. She didn't even know if her father was still alive, and she didn't much care one way or the other.

"What are you staring at?" Vargas demanded, glowering at her over the top of his newspaper.

"We're almost out of cereal," she said woodenly. "And toilet paper."

"I'll take you to the store this afternoon. Switch on the set would you? It's almost time."

The television had a remote control, but it was broken. Angie wondered sometimes if Tony had broken it deliberately so he'd have something else to tell her to do, another reason to order her around. She turned on the set and switched the channel selector to Channel 5's Noontime Edition. Tony Vargas had the hots for Donna Ashforth, Channel 5's blonde-bombshell noonday anchor. Hots or not, Angie suspected he probably wouldn't be able to get it up for Donna Ashforth either, if he ever lucked out and managed to corral the woman into bed.

Angie didn't watch the news itself. Like prisoners everywhere whose very existence is dictated by the moods and whims of their keepers, she watched Tony's face to see how he was reacting to whatever was showing on the screen. She had learned to recognize the danger signals, items that would throw him into towering fits of rage—elections sometimes affected him that way, and the arrests of various people on various charges. Angie had noticed that some of those arrested, especially ones connected with the drug trade, were people Tony seemed to know personally, but she discreetly kept that knowledge to herself.

Today, Tony didn't appear to be paying that much attention until, just before the commercial, they mentioned that the next item would be about an injured sheriff's deputy from somewhere down around Bisbee, wherever that was. When they made the pre-commercial lead-in announcement, he stopped chewing the food that was in his mouth. It was as though his jaw had suddenly turned to stone. Angie had seen that happen before, and she felt her own stomach become a leaden mass. She wished she had gone into the bathroom to shower or outside to swim, anywhere so she'd be out of his way. But she hadn't, and she didn't dare leave now. She sat perfectly still, hoping he wouldn't notice her.

She was holding her breath as the commercial ended, and there was Donna Ashforth's lovely face once more smiling into the camera. As soon as the woman said the fateful words "hospitalized in critical condition," Tony Vargas leaped to his feet, spilling the tray and the rest of the milk and cereal onto the carpet. He hurled the heavy crystal glass, grapefruit and all, at the television set. The sticky yellow contents sprayed all over the room as the glass smashed into the set, demolishing both it and Donna Ashforth's award-winning smile. There were a few bubblegum-like pops before the set sputtered and went out altogether.

"Tony!" Angie exclaimed.

Her remark was totally involuntary. Angie had planned to keep her mouth shut, but his sudden violence shocked her into speech. Hearing her, he swung around and shook his finger in her face, his features distorted by a spasm of undiluted fury.

"Don't you say a word to me, cunt. Not one word! Get off your dead ass and clean up the mess! Call somebody and tell them to send somebody out here tomorrow or the next day to fix the set. And if they can't do the work here, tell 'em to bring a loaner. You got that?"

Angie was left nodding while Tony stalked from the room. Numbly, she went about cleaning up the mess. Bringing a plastic garbage can from the kitchen, she picked up the shards of broken crystal and glass. Then, armed with a damp sponge, damp towels, a brush, and spray bottle of carpet cleaner, she set about cleaning up the sticky sprays of grapefruit juice that seemed to be everywhere. While she worked, she heard Tony making a series of phone calls from the bedroom. She was still working on the carpet on her hands and knees a few minutes later when he emerged from the bedroom fully dressed.

"I'm going out," he announced.

She nodded mutely, grateful that for once she hadn't been the target. He left, unlocking the deadbolt, taking the key, and locking it again from the outside.

Motionless as a light-blinded deer, Angie waited until she heard the car start up. Gravel sprayed against the outside of the house as he churned out of the driveway into the street. Only then did she get to her feet.

She stumbled into the bathroom and heaved her guts out into the toilet. When it was over, when the shivering finally stopped and her teeth no longer chattered, Angie went back to the living room and finished cleaning up the mess.

In the beginning, Tony had told her he was a business consultant. As time passed, she realized that wasn't the truth, but she didn't press him, figuring she was better off not knowing. But now she did. There could be no mistaking it. For Tony Vargas, business consulting meant killing cops.

Because she had been watching so closely, Angie knew exactly what had provoked his rage—Donna Ashforth's smiling face saying the words "critically injured." That was the problem. Whoever it was Tony was supposed to have killed—that poor deputy from Bisbee, whatever his name was—he wasn't quite dead, not yet. But Angie had seen the look on Tony's face, the cold, calculating determination, and she knew the man would be dead soon, and there wasn't a damn thing she could do about it.

Working with wet towels and the vacuum cleaner, it took Angie forty-five minutes to finish cleaning up the mess in the living room to a point where it would pass Tony's inspection. Then she hurried into the kitchen, got out the phone book, and started looking for a television repairman.

She figured it wasn't going to be easy to find a repairman who would be willing to match an appointment with Tony's schedule, so she figured she'd better get started.

SEVEN

SEVEN MILES away at the Arizona Inn, Joanna
Brady was just finishing her club sandwich. The
spacious room with its graceful tableware and bud
vases of fresh dahlias had a calming, quieting effect on her. As the food found its way into her
system, she felt her strength being renewed and
with it her ability to think.

For the first time, she remembered what
Dr. Sanders had said much earlier in the day
when he had warned her about the reporters
camped out in the lobby waiting to talk to her.
Maybe, she thought hopefully, this man was one
of those. After all, he hadn't tried very hard to
conceal the fact that he was following her.

While she was eating her sandwich, she had
caught him looking at her several times. The last
time, he stared at her openly. She couldn't escape
the feeling that she had seen him somewhere

before, that he was someone she knew but couldn't quite place.

She observed that he hadn't bothered to eat anything. He drank only a glass of iced tea while she wolfed down her sandwich and two cups of coffee. When the waiter dropped off his ticket, the man stood up immediately. Joanna breathed a sigh of relief, thinking he was going to leave. Instead, after leaving money on his table, he walked directly over to hers.

"Mrs. Brady?" he said.

She nodded. "Yes."

"I didn't want to interrupt you until after you had finished your meal, but I wondered if I could have a word with you?"

Without waiting for her to answer, he pulled out the chair opposite her and eased himself into it.

"Who are you?" Joanna asked.

He reached into the vest pocket of his well-cut suit jacket, pulled out a thin leather wallet, and handed it to her. Inside was a gold badge and an identification card showing the man's picture.

"My name's Adam York," he said, when she handed the wallet back to him. He pocketed it quickly before anyone else in the room had a chance to see it. "I'm the local agent in charge of the DEA. Glad to make your acquaintance."

He held out his hand, and she shook it. "What can I do for you, Mr. York?" she asked.

He smiled what seemed to be an ingratiating smile. She noticed that his skin was evenly tanned. His teeth were straight and very white. His expensive suit and tie to say nothing of his wrinkle-free white shirt made her acutely aware of the garish yellow smock she wore over the stained and ragged blue dress.

"Call me Adam, Joanna," he said cordially enough, leaning back in his chair, crossing his legs, and watching her expectantly. His impeccable clothing was bad enough. Combined with a haughty smile and indulgent manner, they were infinitely worse. Everything about the man set Joanna's teeth on edge.

"Haven't I seen you someplace before, Mr. York?" Joanna asked, ignoring his given name and keeping the conversation on a strictly formal basis.

"No," he said. "I don't believe so."

But just then she realized when and where she had seen him before. He had been in and out of the ICU waiting room during the morning, mingling with the people waiting there. She had assumed he was connected to one of the other families, but now it was clear that wasn't the case. She regarded him levelly across the bud vase with its single vibrantly pink dahlia. "That's not true, Mr. York. I saw you in the waiting room this morning. Why didn't you speak to me there?"

Caught in the lie, he shifted uncomfortably in his seat. "I thought you'd prefer to meet with me privately," he said. "I didn't want to cause you any embarrassment in front of your family and friends."

"Why would I be embarrassed?" she asked.

"We are meeting under very unfortunate

circumstances. I don't want to be insensitive to your needs, Joanna, but in view of your husband's activities, I need to ask you some questions."

"Like what?"

When Joanna Brady had panicked and dashed into the Arizona Inn, Adam York was sure she'd be an easy interview once he had a chance to question her. Now he wasn't so sure. Somehow she'd ditched most of her dirty, bloodied clothing. Among the brightly colored plumage of Arizona's early winter season tourists, her vivid yellow smock didn't seem all that out of place. She had sat in the dining room calmly eating a sandwich as if she hadn't a care in the world. And now she was staring back at him with a steady, unflinching gaze that successfully put him on the defensive.

He realized too late that he had lost the advantage. Somehow she had managed to take the interview initiative away from him, and he needed to get it back.

"I like your ring," Adam York said casually, without breaking eye contact. His unexpected sideways approach, geared to throw people off guard, worked as expected. Involuntarily Joanna glanced down at the unfamiliar ring on her finger as if to verify that it was still there.

"As I'm sure you know, it was a gift from my husband," she said evenly. "An anniversary present, but then you already know that, don't you? You were probably right there in the room when I opened it. What about my ring?"

"It looks expensive."

"Maybe it is. I wouldn't know about that," she returned. "As I told you, it was a gift."

"Do you know where your husband got it?"

Joanna shrugged. "From Hiram Young, I suppose. In Bisbee. That's what the box said. Young's Fine Jewelry."

Adam York smiled his white-toothed smile. Joanna remembered the lyrics from "Mack the Knife," that old song from *Threepenny Opera*, "Oh the shark has pearly teeth, dear . . ." Adam York was definitely a shark.

"Oh, come now. Aren't we being a little obtuse?"

Joanna felt the danger, as though she were about to be pulled over an abrupt edge into some terrible, unknown abyss. All around her, oblivious to what was going on, the other diners in that gracious old room continued their leisurely luncheons, punctuating their genial conversations with polite laughter.

Joanna took a deep breath and studied her adversary. One of Big Hank Lathrop's lessons came back to her from the far distant past. Eleanor had hated it, lobbied against it, even when it was happening, but her husband had stubbornly persisted in teaching the daughter he called Little Hank the finer points of playing poker. Over and over he had stressed that the secret of winning lay in never, ever showing your opponent that you were scared. Remembering her father's words, an eerie sense of tranquility seemed to settle over her.

She signaled the busboy to bring more coffee. When he did, she picked up the cup with both hands, letting her ring finger rest casually around the brim of the cup. The ring was hers. It had been given to her and she had nothing to hide. She was gratified to see that her hands didn't betray her with even the slightest tremor.

She offered Adam York a thin smile. "Obtuse?" she asked. "What's that supposed to mean?"

"Do you have any idea how much that ring of yours cost, Joanna?"

"I told you before, it was a gift. When someone gives you a present, it isn't polite to ask how much it cost, or didn't your mother ever teach you that?"

"It cost three thousand four hundred fifty three dollars and twenty two cents," he said deliberately. "One of my agents checked that with Mr. Young himself in Bisbee early this morning. He let us have a copy of the receipt. It's paid in full."

"I don't understand why the DEA should be interested in the cost of my anniversary present, Mr. York. It seems to me you'd have better things to do with your time."

He had expected her to crumple then and start spilling the information that would make it easy to nail Andrew Brady once he was fit to stand trial. Instead, Joanna stood firm and brazened it out. York had pictured her as one of two things, either the innocent and most likely wronged wife, one who had no inkling of her husband's extracurricular activities, or as a guilty co-conspirator. And despite what had been said so far, Adam York still had no idea which was which. Either way, she was very good at fighting back.

"I hope your agent showed Mr. Young the kind of respect he deserves," she continued deliberately. "Hiram Young is a sweet, frail old man. I'd hate to think one of your henchmen gave him a hard time."

"I can assure you that my agent was unfailingly polite," Adam York replied.

"I'll just bet," Joanna said with what sounded like a trace of sarcasm. She took another sip of coffee.

"Would you like to see a copy of the receipt?"

"No, thank you. That's not necessary." She, too, could be unfailingly polite. "I'm happy to take your word for it." This time there was no mistaking the sarcasm.

"So. Is giving your wife a diamond ring for an anniversary present a criminal offense these days, Mr. York? You said the DEA was investigating my husband, but all you've been interested in so far is this ring."

"And where the money came from to buy it," he said. "Have you checked your bank balance lately, Joanna?"

Adam hoped that by continuing to use her first name, he might annoy her into a telling emotional outburst, but somehow she seemed to have turned off the weakness he was sure he had detected earlier.

Her green-eyed gaze drilled into him. "Actually, Mr. York, I've been a little too busy lately with what you might call life-and-death matters to give a tinker's damn about my checking account balance, so the answer is no. I have no idea."

Adam York reached into his pocket and pulled out a piece of paper. "Allow me to enlighten you. Here's your balance as of ten o'clock this morning."

He held up the paper. She didn't even glance at it much less take it, but he could tell from the sudden jutting of her chin that he had finally landed a solid blow.

"How did you get that?" she demanded.

Again he smiled. "It's all perfectly legal. You can check with the branch manager down there in Bisbee. When federal officers show up at a bank's head office with court orders in hand, bankers usually jump to give us whatever we need."

"Then suppose you tell me what my balance is."

"Five thousand eight hundred seventy one dollars and five cents. That's after the checks for the ring and the flowers both cleared." He gave her another of his overly tolerant smiles. He thought he detected the smallest twitch in the corner of her left eye, but afterward he couldn't be sure.

"Are you in the habit of keeping that kind of money in your checking account, Joanna?" he continued smoothly. "That seems like a sizeable amount for a struggling young couple like you and your husband."

She stiffened at that remark, but she didn't say anything at first. Instead, she leaned forward in her chair and stared back at him with those disconcerting green eyes.

"Mr. York," she said at last, her voice dropping

almost to a whisper. "My father was a police officer once, and my husband still is. I am a person
who has always been in favor of law and order,
one who has utmost respect for officers of the law,
but I will tell you here and now that if you are any
indication of the kind of people currently serving
in the capacity of federal police officers, then this
country of ours is in big trouble."

With that she pulled a ten dollar bill from her
purse, slapped it on the table, and pushed back
her chair. This wasn't exactly the kind of reaction Adam York had expected, and it caught him
by surprise. He got up and trailed after her, catching her by the elbow as she stepped up into the
dining room's doorway.

"Look," he said, "if you're going back to the
hospital, I could just as well give you a ride."

She wrested her arm away from him. "I don't
ride in cars with strangers," she responded frostily. "It's a very dangerous practice."

She strode away from him, but then, sensing
that he was still staring after her, she stopped,
turned, and came back.

"By the way," she said, "if you or any more of
your so-called agents show up in the ICU waiting
room this afternoon, I promise you, I'll throw
the sons of bitches out. And if you think that's an
empty threat, you might check with Sheriff Walter McFadden."

"Oh, Miss," the busboy called to her from
across the dining room. "You forgot your bag."

He came over to her, lugging the heavy shopping bag with its bulky load of boots and jacket.

She took it, murmured a quick thank you, then turned on her heel and marched away.

"She's a cool one, all right," York muttered to himself without realizing the busboy was still listening. He, too, was watching Joanna Brady make her way through the long, narrow lobby.

"She's beautiful," the busboy breathed fervently. "Who is she? Someone on TV?"

"Not yet," Adam York replied grimly. "But keep watching the news. She may turn up there real soon."

Joanna kept her shoulders back and her head high as she walked away from him. She felt betrayed and wounded by the system. How dare they go nosing around Bisbee, asking Hiram Young questions about the ring? How dare they contact the bank about their balance? People couldn't really believe that Andrew Brady was involved in drug trafficking. That wasn't possible!

The walk back to the hospital was only a matter of blocks, but it seemed like miles. The too-large shoes slapped clumsily on the sidewalk, and it was all Joanna could do to put one foot in front of the other. Mid-afternoon sun burned down unmercifully through her double layer of clothing. The twine on the heavy shopping bag cut at her fingers, and she felt sweaty and dirty. More than that, Adam York had left her feeling helpless and violated.

Why had he treated her that way, she wondered miserably. As a police officer's wife, Joanna knew that in the aftermath of an attempted murder, family members would be expected to provide answers to painfully uncomfortable questions. She knew those questions would be coming soon enough from whatever investigators Dick Voland had assigned to Andy's case. That was no surprise. And in the light of the television news broadcast, questions from the DEA as well as the Mexican *federales* were also to be expected.

But this hadn't been the kind of kid-gloves-type interview to which she should have been entitled. Even if they suspected Andy of wrongdoing, Adam York hadn't acted at all as though Joanna were an innocent bystander. His whole demeanor and attitude told her that she, too, was under suspicion. For what, she wondered. For taking the ring? For accepting a present that might very well be the last thing her husband ever gave her?

She shifted the heavy bag from one hand to the other. As she did so, the sun caught the sparkling diamond in a flash of light. So where had the ring come from, she asked herself for the first time. Andy Brady didn't have that kind of money stowed away, certainly not money hidden from her. And as for the extra almost six thousand dollars in their checking account? That had to be a simple bookkeeping error. It might take Sandy Henning a day or two to figure out where it came from, but eventually the money would be credited to the proper account, and the Brady account balance would tumble back down to its usual level of nearly crashing and burning.

Joanna had retraced her steps back up Elm to Campbell which she crossed at the light. As she started up the sidewalk along the hospital drive-way, she thought she caught sight of her mother's purple dress in the shadow of the portico. Sure enough, as she got closer, she saw Eleanor pacing back and forth in the small patch of shade.

The moment Eleanor saw her daughter, she motioned to her frantically and then came rushing down the sidewalk to meet her. As her mother approached, Joanna was surprised to see that her mother's mascara was smudged. Obviously she had been crying.

"What's the matter, Mother," Joanna asked.

"He's gone."

"Who, Andy? Where'd he go? Did they move him somewhere else?"

Eleanor Lathrop was puffing and out of breath. "You don't understand, Joanna," she said. "Andy's dead."

Joanna stopped short, thunderstruck. "He's dead? No. When did it happen? How?"

Eleanor shook her head. "After you left, my good friend Margaret Turnbull stopped by. She and I were sitting there watching *The Young and the Restless* when some kind of alarm went off and people started running around and yelling 'code red' over the loudspeaker, whatever that means. Pretty soon some doctor comes out and says to me that it's all over, that Andy's dead."

Joanna dropped the bag, pushed past her mother, and raced into the building. She sprinted through the lobby and shoved her way inside an elevator just as the doors were closing. She stood there shaking her head, not believing it had happened. It couldn't be true. Andy couldn't be gone, not without her being there to say good-bye.

On the ICU floor she slammed open the door to the waiting room. A little knot of people stood near the painting on the far side of the room. They turned to look at her when the door opened. Ken Galloway separated himself from the group and started toward her, but she dodged around him and darted into Andy's room. The machines were eerily quiet. The bed was empty. He really was gone.

A nurse from the nurse's station looked up, saw her, and started toward her just as a pair of arms closed around her from behind. "Where is he?" Joanna demanded. "What have you done with him?"

"Hush now," Ken Galloway said, holding her, trying to calm her.

"But where is he?" she repeated, her voice rising. "I've got to see him."

The nurse was there now, too, reaching out, offering solace, but Joanna was beyond the reach of consolation.

"I want to see him," she sobbed. "Where is he? Where?"

"They took him back to the operating room."

Joanna stopped struggling in Ken Galloway's arms. "The operating room? Then he isn't dead, is he! It's all a mistake."

The nurse shook her head sadly. "I'm sorry, Mrs. Brady. We tried to find you, but he went into cardiac arrest. Afterward, we had two doctors in to check him, and they both pronounced him brain dead. The form was there in his file, and everything was in order. We contacted the medical examiner and he gave us permission to go ahead. With harvesting organs, there isn't a moment to lose. I thought you knew."

Before Ken Galloway could stop her, she lunged out of his arms and raced back out through the waiting room. Another grim-faced family was just then filing into the room to start their own vigil of waiting and worrying. Seeing them, Joanna realized that she was separated from those people by a vast, impassable gulf. The ICU and its waiting room were for those who still clung narrowly to life. The place held nothing for her anymore. Andy was dead. There was no reason for her to stay.

In the hallway, her mother was just stepping off the elevator. "Joanna, there you are."

Without glancing at her mother, Joanna rushed onto the elevator and pressed the button for the lobby. "Where are you going now?" Eleanor Lathrop asked.

"I don't know," Joanna choked as the door closed between them. "I don't know at all."

LATER SHE would have no remembrance of fighting her way through the lobby or of recrossing the busy intersection at Elm and Campbell. When she came to herself, she was sitting in a tall wooden chair in a shaded patio somewhere on the green, flowered grounds of the Arizona Inn.

She had no idea how long she'd been sitting there or how long she'd been crying, but someone was speaking to her.

"What seems to be the problem?" a woman was saying. "Are you a guest here?"

Joanna tried to stifle another sob. The woman, tall and elderly, planted her feet squarely in front the chair. She carried herself with patrician bearing—from her silver hair, cut in a short, elegant bob down to her old-fashioned saddle oxfords. One hand rested sternly on her hip while the other held an old, bentwood cane. Only when she took a step forward did Joanna notice that one leg was encased in a heavy metal brace.

"No," Joanna managed guiltily. "I'm sorry. I'm not. I'll leave right away."

"Oh, for heaven's sake," the woman said impatiently. "I didn't mean to chase you away, but you were crying as though your heart was broken, and I wondered if there was someone I should call for you or if there was anything at all I could do to help."

Joanna straightened in the chair and wiped the tears from her cheeks. The woman's small act of kindness seemed to work some kind of recuperative magic.

"Thank you," she said. "I believe you already did." She stood up.

"Where are you going?" the old woman asked.

"Back to the hospital," Joanna answered with resigned hopelessness. "I'm sure there are papers to sign, arrangements to be made."

The gaunt old woman's skin was wrinkled and

parchment thin. She must have been nearing
ninety. Age and wisdom both allowed her to see
beyond the surface of Joanna's relatively innocuous words to the real message and hurt behind
them.

She nodded slowly. "I see," she said. "So it's
like that, is it?"

Joanna nodded as well. "Yes."

The woman reached out and patted Joanna's
arm with a gnarled, arthritic hand. "It will take
time, my dear," she said kindly, "but someday
things will be better for you. Just you wait and
see."

EIGHT

LEANING ON her cane, the old woman escorted Joanna as far as the hotel lobby. There, swinging the braced leg off to one side, she sauntered off into the dining room while Joanna stopped short in front of the telephone alcove. Much as she dreaded the prospect, it was time to tell Jenny. Past time if Joanna wanted to deliver the news herself. Unless she wanted Grandma Lathrop to do it in her stead, then there wasn't a moment to lose.

Quickly she placed a long-distance call to the Methodist parsonage in Bisbee. Jeff Daniels answered.

"Hello, Jeff," Joanna began, trying to observe at least a vestige of good manners. "I need to speak to Jennifer."

"You sound upset, Joanna," Jeff returned. "Are you all right? How are things?"

She tried to answer but at first the words caught in her throat. "Andy's dead," she managed finally.

123

"It happened earlier this afternoon. Please don't tell Jenny when you call her. I want to be the one to break the news."

"She's outside with Marianne right now," Jeff said. "Hold on. I'll go get them both."

While she waited, Joanna dug her fingernails deep into the palms of her hands. It hadn't been necessary for anyone to tell her of her own father's death. She had been right there on the shoulder of the road and had seen it all for herself first-hand. Now, though, she found herself praying for strength, for the ability to find the right words to say. Moments later Jenny's cheerful, childish voice came on the phone.

"Hi, Mom. Reverend Maculyea and I have been outside playing on her swing. I think she's weird. And Jeff, too. They have a swing, but they don't have any kids."

"Jenny . . ." Joanna began and then stopped when she heard the unmistakable tremor in her voice.

And clearly her distress was obvious, even to a nine-year-old. "What's the matter, Mom?" Jenny asked. "You sound funny. Are you all right?"

Joanna took a deep breath. "I'm okay, but your dad's not," she said. "He's dead, Jenny. Daddy's gone."

Her announcement was met with shocked silence. For a moment she thought maybe she'd been disconnected. "Jenny," Joanna said. "Are you still there? Did you hear what I said?"

"Is he really?"

"Yes, really, honey. I'm sorry."

Again the phone seemed to go dead in a baffling, achingly long silence, one Joanna had no idea how to fill. Finally Jennifer said, "Why were those nurses so mean to us? Why wouldn't they let me see him? I didn't even get to say good-bye."

"I know, Jenny. Neither did I. Hospitals have rules, I guess, and everybody has to go by them, even if they don't always make sense to anybody else."

Jennifer began crying then. For almost a minute the only sound was that of Jenny sobbing brokenly into the phone. Joanna longed to be in the same room with her daughter. She wanted to hold her close and shield her from the hurt, but from one hundred miles away there was nothing she could do but listen. The sound of Jennifer's broken-hearted weeping tore Joanna apart.

At last, in the background, she heard Jeff Daniels speaking soothingly. After a shuffle, the phone was handed over to someone else while Jenny's disconsolate sobbing moved away from the receiver.

"Jeff told me," Marianne Maculyea said when she came on the line. "How did it happen? After listening to Dr. Sanders, I thought he was doing all right."

"So did I, but according to the nurse he went into another episode of cardiac arrest. This time they weren't able to bring him back. Two separate doctors came in and certified that he was brain dead. And then they took him away. I wasn't even there."

"I'm so sorry, Joanna. Do you want me to come

back up to Tucson? If you need me, I can be there in less than two hours."

"No. I'd much rather have you there with Jenny right now. I'm all right, really. I had to leave the hospital for a little while to try to get myself sorted out, but I'm on my way back there now. I'll come home as soon as I can."

"Call if you need me," Marianne told her. "I'll stay by the phone."

"Thanks, Mari. I will."

After hanging up, Joanna detoured through the hotel restroom where she used a handful of tissues to wipe her face and blow her nose. Looking at her image in the mirror, she was shocked by what she saw there—by the deep, dark circles under red, puffy eyes, by the gray pallor of her skin, by her lank, dirty hair. She still hadn't had a chance to shower or change out of the blue dress and the yellow smock, and her teeth were crying for a toothbrush. But all that would have to come later. For now she had to go back to the hospital and handle whatever needed to be handled.

Again, the walk back to the hospital seemed to take forever. As she entered the lobby, she felt shabby and dirty and ill at ease. She felt even more so when a well-dressed young woman fell into step beside her.

"Mrs. Brady. Could I please have a word with you?"

The woman was a stranger yet she seemed to know Joanna by sight. "Who are you?" Joanna asked.

"Sue Rolles. I'm a reporter with the *Arizona Daily Sun*."

"What do you want?"

"About your husband's suicide . . ."

"Murder," Joanna interrupted, correcting the reporter the same way she had corrected Dr. Sanders hours earlier.

"But I was under the impression that the case was being investigated as a suicide."

Joanna stopped in mid-stride and turned to face the reporter. Hurt and rage, the two warring emotions that had simmered hot and cold inside her all morning long, combined into a volatile mixture and came to a sudden boil. "You can talk about suicide all you want," she declared, "but not to me, and not about my husband. Do I make myself clear?" The reporter nodded.

"Andrew Brady was murdered," Joanna continued. "He was an experienced police officer. Cops know all about how guns work. When they set out to commit suicide, they know how to get the job done—they usually blow their brains out. I believe that's a statistic I read in an article in your very own newspaper.

"I'm here to tell you that Andrew Brady never shot himself in the gut. He wouldn't have done something like that in the first place, and even if he had, he never would have done it where I'd most likely be the one to find him."

Properly chastised, the reporter moved back a step just as Ken Galloway materialized out of nowhere.

"What's going on?" he asked, extricating himself from a crush of homeward-bound people exiting an elevator.

Joanna turned on him as though he were as much an enemy as the reporter. "I'll tell you what's going on," she said. "Andy's dead and I'm sick and tired of people telling me he committed suicide. I don't want to hear it anymore. I won't listen."

"Who's this?" Ken asked, nodding toward Sue Rolles.

"A reporter," Joanna answered. "With the *Sun*."

"Maybe you'd better go," Ken Galloway said hurriedly to Sue Rolles. "I think Mrs. Brady has had about all she can handle for one day." To Joanna he said, "Your mother sent me down to see if I could find you. She's waiting for you upstairs. Come on."

He started away, but Joanna didn't move. Right that moment there were few people Joanna wanted to see less than she wanted to see her own mother, but she could hardly tell Ken Galloway that. When Joanna didn't move, Galloway came back.

"I'll be up in a little while," Joanna said. "I need to stop off at the billing department and make arrangements to pay the bill." It was a lame excuse but enough to delay the inevitable confrontation with her mother for a few minutes longer.

"But what should I tell your mother? She's waiting to give you a ride home," Ken explained. "She said you rode up here with Sheriff McFadden last night and that you didn't have a way back to Bisbee."

Wearily Joanna passed her hand over her eyes. "Ken, you know my mother, don't you?"

"Some," he admitted.

"Well enough to know how much of a pain she can be at times. You may think I'm a terrible daughter, but I'm just not up to riding home with her right now. Too much has happened. I need some time to sort my way through things, some time to think without her constantly yammering at me. You're here, Ken. You have a car, don't you?"

"Yes."

"Maybe this sounds crazy, but couldn't I ride back home with you? Be a friend. Go upstairs and tell my mother that I've got things to do. Make something up if you have to. Tell her I've got to go see the Medical Examiner or talk to someone from the Tucson PD. Tell her anything, whatever you want. Just so I don't have to ride in the same car with her for the next two hours. I couldn't stand it."

Ken nodded sympathetically. "Sure," he said. "I understand. There are times when the last thing you need is a mother. You go on over to the billing department and do whatever you have to do. Then wait for me down in the cafeteria. I'll come get you as soon as she's gone. Is that all right?"

Joanna nodded. "It's what I want," she said, "but you must think I'm crazy."

"No," Ken Galloway said with a pained expression on his face. "You forget. You've been away from the hospital for the last two hours. I've spent that whole time upstairs in the waiting room with your mother and her pal Margaret Turnbull. I know exactly what you mean."

Ken hurried back to the bank of elevators and Joanna followed the signs to the billing department. She was enough of an insurance bureaucrat to understand how many things could go awry in paying a hospitalization claim. To head off as many difficulties as possible, Joanna wanted to be sure everything was in the best possible order to begin with. First she asked the clerk on duty for a computerized printout of all current hospital charges. With that in hand, she'd be able to check any subsequent bills for possible discrepancies. Her second precaution was to verify that the paperwork reflected that Andy's policy with the county would provide primary coverage, while Joanna's insurance from work would finish paying any bills that hadn't been handled in full by Andy's carrier. Finally she picked up the small plastic bag containing Andy's personal effects. She didn't even look inside it.

Having done all that, she made her way to the cafeteria. By this time it was late afternoon and the place was deserted except for a few stray hospital workers taking off-hour breaks. She bought herself a cup of coffee and took it to a table near the door.

Too tired to feel guilty about ditching her mother and too wrung out to feel apologetic about her outburst with the young reporter, Joanna stared vacantly down at the cup of coffee without even bothering to lift it to her lips. Beyond tears and almost beyond thought, she tried desperately to grapple with the reality of Andy's death, but every attempt left her with a gaping hole in her being that was beyond her ability to fathom. Maybe, if she'd been there to see him before they took him away, it wouldn't be so hard for her to believe that he was really gone.

Ken Galloway turned up, startling her out of her reverie by placing the battered suitcase on the table in front of her.

"Your mother's gone," he announced. "She and Margaret are going to caravan back to Bisbee. They told me that they'll be stopping at the Triple T for deep-dish apple pie in case we want to catch up with them on our way out of town. I said I didn't think we'd make it, that you had papers to sign, things to do."

Joanna breathed a sigh of relief. "Thank you, Ken. I'm not nearly as irrational as I sound. It's just that I couldn't face dealing with my mother right now."

"No problem. I understand completely." He settled down on the chair opposite her and earnestly studied her face. "You look like hell. How're you doing?"

"Better, I think. I'm tired though. I can barely hold my head up."

"I wonder why. Do you have any other errands to run? Do you want to stop someplace on the way and get cleaned up before we head out?"

"No. I've been a mess this long, it won't hurt me to stay that way a little while longer. I just want to go home."

"Let's do it then."

Galloway's white Bronco was parked in the hospital garage. Joanna climbed into it and settled gratefully in the rider's seat. While waiting for Ken to go around and open his own door, she realized with a pang how familiar the seat felt. This vehicle was almost the same make and model as Andy's. It hurt her to realize that she would never again have the pleasure of riding in a vehicle with Andrew Brady at the wheel. That part of her life was over forever.

Ken climbed in and started the engine. Neither of them said a word as he maneuvered out of the garage and headed south on Campbell. As she rode along, Joanna realized that it might be a long time before she had another opportunity to ask anyone else the questions that were bothering her. Ken Galloway had been one of Andy's best friends. She was sure she could count on him to give her the straight answers she needed.

"Why's Dick Voland doing this?"

Ken gave her a sidelong glance. "Dick Voland? Doing what?"

"Why's he saying Andy committed suicide? He was murdered, Ken, I know he was, but the news on TV, the woman in the lobby, they're all saying something else, that the case is being investigated as a suicide. That sounds like an official pronouncement, and it's got to be coming from either Dick Voland or from Sheriff McFadden himself."

Ken Galloway sighed. "Joanna, listen to me. Nobody's making anything up. I know you don't want to hear it, but you're going to have to listen and come to terms with it no matter how much it hurts."

"So you're saying the same thing?"

He nodded. "Look, Andy Brady was a good friend of mine, but from what I've learned the past few days, I sure as hell didn't know everything about him, and I don't think you did, either. The evidence is all there, Joanna. Believe me."

"What evidence?"

"I hate to be the one to tell you, but they found a note."

"What kind of note?"

"A suicide note, Joanna."

"No."

"Sorry, but it's true."

"Where was it? In Andy's own handwriting?"

"In one of Andy's personal files in the computer at work."

"What did it say?"

"That he was sorry to put you and Jenny through this, that he never should have taken the money in the first place. He said that even with Lefty out of the way, he was afraid the DEA was still closing in. He said he'd never let them take him alive."

Joanna shook her head stubbornly. "Somebody must have broken into his file and written it then. Andy wouldn't."

Ken sighed in exasperation. "Come on, Joanna. Get real."

For a long time Joanna didn't speak again. Despite her forcible denial, she felt as though a bucket of ice water had been thrown in her face. For the first time she felt the tiniest bit of doubt. Was there maybe some small grain of truth in what the reporter had told her?

"What about Guaymas?" she asked finally. "The reporter said something about evidence found at the scene in Mexico that linked Andy to that."

"I haven't seen it, not with my own eyes, but evidently something was found on Lefty's body, a letter of some kind from him to Andy. From the sound of it, they must have been working together for some time."

Ten minutes or so passed in silence while Joanna tried to assimilate what she had heard. If everything Ken Galloway said was true, then she had spent the last ten years of her life married to a complete stranger. None of this squared with her understanding of the man she had known and loved. And loved still.

"What if it's a setup?" she ventured.

"Look, Joanna," Ken Galloway returned gruffly. He sounded disgusted. "Andrew Brady would have been the last person in the world I would have expected to turn into a crooked cop, but the evidence is overwhelming. The letter's there, the note's there, and evidently the money's in your checking account as well."

"You've heard about that, too?"

"Bisbee's a small town. Word gets around."

"It certainly does," she said bitterly. "I can see that it does."

Not another word was exchanged for the next

ninety miles. Most of that time Joanna sat staring straight ahead of her. Resting in her lap was the small plastic bag the clerk had given her. Under the thin layer of plastic she could feel the familiar contours of Andy's worn billfold. Her fingers closed round it, and she held it tightly, as though it were some precious, life-giving talisman.

Only as they drove through the Mule Mountain Tunnel did Joanna rouse herself enough to speak. "We have to stop by Marianne Maculyea's parsonage up the canyon and pick up Jenny."

"Sure thing," Ken Galloway replied easily, swinging off the highway onto the exit. "Hang on. We'll have you both home in two shakes of a lamb's tail."

TONY VARGAS was in an expansive mood when he came home in the middle of the afternoon. He rousted Angie out of the pool for a quick fuck oh the living room floor in front of the mangled television set. This time he had no difficulty achieving an erection. As he grunted above her, Angie was grateful she'd been so meticulous about cleaning up all the shattered glass. Otherwise her bare back and buttocks would have been full of it.

Finished, he rolled off her and then lay beside her, leaning on one elbow and absently toying with her nipple. "We'll go out to dinner," he said. "I feel like celebrating."

She didn't dare ask him what they were celebrating. She was smarter than that. Eventually he headed for the bathroom to shower. She went into the kitchen, squeezed fresh grapefruit, mixed drinks, and then followed him into the bedroom. He had evidently switched on the small television set on the dresser. The local edition of the evening news was just starting. The lead story told that Andrew Brady, the wounded deputy and candidate for Cochise County sheriff, had died at University Hospital in Tucson earlier that afternoon.

Transfixed by what she was hearing, Angie stood in the middle of the room holding the two drinks. It had been bad enough, earlier that afternoon when her vague suspicions about Tony's "consultation business" had once and for all solidified into harsh reality. Then, he had broken the television in a blinding rage when he heard the news that Andrew Brady was still alive. Now, with the announcement that the very same man had died, Tony was taking her out to dinner. To celebrate.

With horror, Angie realized that somehow Tony Vargas had gone to the hospital and finished what he had set out to do, just as she had known he would. And by not doing something to prevent it, Angie realized that she, too, was somehow responsible.

And with that sickening realization came another one as well. Angie had always imagined that somehow she'd find a way to slip away from Tony and leave him, but now she understood that wouldn't be possible. He'd never let her go. And if he ever discovered how much Angie really knew about him, she, too, would be living under a death sentence.

The water shut off, and Tony stepped out of the shower.

"Hey, Angie, where the hell's my drink?" he demanded as he began toweling himself dry. "I thought you went out to the kitchen to make me a Sea Breeze."

Taking a deep breath, she stepped into the narrow bathroom beside him. He ran his hands over the bare skin of her buttocks as she set both drinks down on the bathroom counter.

"Nice ass," he said, then he slapped her hard with the flat of his hand before she could move out of reach. That was something he liked to do occasionally—leave a hand print on her backside just for the hell of it. He liked to see how long the imprint lasted.

Without saying a word, Angie stepped into the shower, pulled the door shut, and turned on the water full blast, hoping the steaming water would somehow clear her head.

As a working whore in L.A., she had been busted more times than she could count—often enough to have learned the cops' tired right-to-remain-silent speech by heart. In fact, she could recite the whole thing from beginning to end without any prompting.

But now we were talking about murder, and this was far more than just a right to remain silent. Silence was now an absolute necessity. Not only would anything she said be held against her, in the wrong hands, it could also prove deadly.

Silently, standing under the running water, Angie Kellogg began to cry, because, for the first time since that long-ago night in Battle Creek, Michigan, when her father's unspeakable violation had turned her little-girl world upside down, she was utterly terrified.

![chapter decoration] **NINE**

COMING DOWN Tombstone Canyon with Jennifer in the back seat of Ken Galloway's Bronco, Joanna guiltily remembered their ten head of cattle for the first time. There was plenty of water for them in the stock tank, and she had fed them the night before, but between then and now she hadn't given them another thought. There was still some forage left over from the summer's rainy season, but not much. By now they were probably very hungry.

Joanna doubted her mother had thought about the cattle or made arrangements to feed them, either. And why should she? They weren't her responsibility; they were Joanna's. Eleanor had made it abundantly clear that she was a confirmed town-dweller who had little patience with Joanna and Andy's "cockamamie" decision to take over what remained of the Brady family holdings.

Preoccupied with berating herself over neglecting the cattle, Joanna barely noticed when

Ken turned off the highway onto Double Adobe Road. Then, as they crossed the first cattle guard onto High Lonesome, her heart filled with sudden dread. Traveling down the dirt road, they were fast approaching the bridge, the place where she had found Andy lying wounded and dying in the sand. Concerned not only about what she might see but also her reaction to it, Joanna breathed a sigh of relief when she realized that in the deepening twilight nothing at all was visible. For now, at least, she didn't have to look at whatever physical evidence remained of that horrible ordeal.

"Somebody's here," Jennifer announced when they caught sight of lights from the house glimmering through the surrounding mesquite. A hundred yards into the ranch proper, Sadie appeared in the slice of headlights ahead of them, racing toward the Bronco at full throttle. Jennifer rolled down the window and called to her, urging the dog to keep pace. When they pulled into the yard, two extra vehicles were parked next to Joanna's Eagle in the brassy glow of the solitary yard light—Grandma and Grandpa Brady's Honda and Clayton Rhodes' ancient Ford pickup.

Clayton Rhodes, a wizened eighty-six-year-old neighbor from up the road, stood on Joanna's back porch with his thumbs hooked through his belt loops. When Ken Galloway's car stopped in front of the gate, Eva Lou and Jim Bob Brady, Andy's parents, came out through the backdoor and joined him. By then Sadie was barking and running around the Bronco in madly joyous circles. As soon as the wheels stopped turning, Jennifer tumbled out of the truck and threw herself at the dog.

For a moment all the adults stood still, watching the antics of the girl and the dog, then Eva Lou hurried forward to greet Joanna while the two men hung back. Tears streamed down the older woman's round cheeks as she gathered her daughter-in-law into her arms.

"I can't believe it," she murmured over and over. "I just can't believe it."

Joanna was glad to see Eva Lou. Her relationship with Andy's mother was far more cordial than with her own. The elder Bradys were rock-solid, salt-of-the-earth-type people whose very presence comforted her.

"How did you hear?" Joanna asked, pulling back from Eva Lou's embrace. "Did my mother call?"

Eva Lou shook her head, and wiped her tears on the tail of her borrowed apron. "Jimmy and I were on our way home from Tulsa when a police car pulled us over in Lordsburg. At first we couldn't figure out why they were stopping us, if Jimmy was speeding or what. But then the officer told us what had happened. It was such a shock. Someone from the sheriff's department here must have called over to Lordsburg and asked them to keep a lookout for us.

"When he told us we were already too late, we just pulled over on the side of the road and bawled like a couple of babies. That young officer was so nice. He waited right there with us and wouldn't let us leave town without buying us a cup of coffee."

Ken Galloway had walked up beside the two women and stood there awkwardly, holding Joanna's single suitcase. "Should I take this on inside?" he asked.

Joanna nodded. "Yes, please. Come on, Jenny," she called to her daughter. "Leave Sadie out here for now. She's way too excited to be in the house. Come inside and get her food ready."

"Oh, we've already fed the dog," Eva Lou said quickly as they trooped toward the house. "After Lordsburg, we didn't see much point in going on to Tucson. We thought we'd just come on over here and look after things for you. But Clayton got the jump on us. He was here and had the cattle fed and watered. He was about to take Sadie home with him to feed her as well."

Joanna stopped in front of Clayton Rhodes, a man who had befriended several succeeding generations of owners on the High Lonesome Ranch. A lifelong resident of Cochise County, Clayton Rhodes was bowlegged and bent, with a limp that came from some long ago bronco-riding mishap. Clearly a relic from an earlier age, he was a genuine, old-fashioned cowboy who had spent much of his life in the company of livestock. Small children were drawn to him because of his ability to tell tall tales, and they were fascinated by the set of ill-fitting dentures he usually carried in his shirt pocket, but Clayton Rhodes was terrifically shy around adults.

"Thanks so much, Mr. Rhodes," Joanna said. "It was very thoughtful of you to stop by and look after the animals."

He shied away from her thanks like a spooked pony. "Nothin' to it," he mumbled reticently, tipping his hat and edging off the steps toward the safety of the gate. "Nothin' to it a-tall."

On the top step of the back porch, Joanna paused long enough for Jim Bob Brady to enfold her in a bearhug, then they went on into the kitchen. The room was warm and inviting, filled with the enticing aroma of Eva Lou Brady's mouthwatering, baking-powder biscuits. On the counter a newly made pot of coffee was just finishing brewing.

"I didn't know if you and Jenny would be hungry," Eva Lou was saying, "but biscuits and honey are always good, even when people can't think about eating anything else. Would you like a cup of coffee, Ken?" she asked, taking the suitcase from his hands. "It's fresh."

Ken Galloway shook his head. "No, thanks. Appreciate the offer, but I'll just head on home."

"Now, Mama," Jim Bob Brady warned. "Don't go pushing food and drink on people. They just this minute stepped inside. Give them a chance to catch their breath."

Joanna looked at her father- and mother-in-law with a combination of appreciation and amazement. That afternoon she had lost a husband and Jenny a father, but these two wonderful old people had lost a son—their only son. And yet, here they were only a few hours later, bustling around, pitching in, and taking care of everybody else. It was astounding and yet so like them. Jim Bob and Eva Lou Brady were the exact antithesis of her own mother. That was one of the things Joanna liked about them.

"Well," Eva Lou said, ignoring her husband's caution. "Are you hungry?"

"I am," Jenny declared.

Joanna shook her head. "Not me. I'm more dirty than hungry. I want to take a shower."

With her suitcase in hand and still carrying the precious plastic bag holding only pitiful reminders of the man who had owned its contents, Joanna made her way through the kitchen and dining room and on into the bedroom. Just walking into that now too-familiar room took her breath away. Everything there reminded her of Andy, from the rolltop desk with its broken, patched-together chair, to the frayed cowboy hat that he wore around home, to their bed. Especially the bed. She couldn't face it. She dropped the plastic bag on the desk, then, gulping for air, she grabbed her robe and retreated into the bathroom.

There she clambered into the old-fashioned, claw-footed tub with its make-do shower and turned on the water full blast. She stood under the water for a long, long time, letting the steamy spray mingle with the tears on her face while the roar in the pipes muffled the sound of her sobs. Usually, Joanna was conscientious about taking three-minute showers. This time, she came to her senses only when all the hot water was gone. By then she was no longer crying. It was as though the well of tears inside her had finally run dry.

She toweled herself off and felt a surprising rush of gratitude that she was doing so in the familiar surroundings of her own bathroom in her own home. At least that part of her life was the same, and it would continue to be so. In Tucson, at the hospital, she had focused totally on dealing with the immediate problem of paying the hospital bill, but now she realized that through the insurance she owned, life insurance on both of them which Milo Davis had encouraged them to buy and helped them keep, she and Jenny would be able to stay in their own home for as long as they wanted. In fact, she could probably pay Eva Lou and Jim Bob off completely if she wanted to. But if the choice lay between having the house paid for and having Andy back . . .

Hastily pushing that thought aside, she tied the belt on her robe and emerged from the bathroom with a towel wrapped around her wet hair. In her absence, both Eleanor Lathrop and Marianne Maculyea had appeared. They, along with Jenny and the Bradys, were seated at the dining room table. For a few moments, Joanna stood silently in the hallway door without anyone noticing her.

Hollow-eyed, Jenny sat listening while her Grandmother Lathrop recounted her version of her son-in-law's death while the Bradys, too, heard the story for the first time. Eleanor, reveling in the attention of her audience, warmed to the telling.

"So when the doctor came back out," she was saying, "I left Margaret sitting there watching television and went over to ask him how Andy was. I mean, Joanna had been gone for some time by then, and none of the rest of us had been allowed in to visit. The doctor said that everything was just fine, that we shouldn't worry about a thing, but then, a few minutes later, some kind of alarm went off. After that there were all kinds of people rushing in and out of the room. I've never seen anything like it, but by then it was too late. They just couldn't bring him back."

Jim Bob Brady nodded solemnly and patted his wife's hand while she wept quietly into a hanky. Jennifer pushed back her chair and hurried to Eva Lou's side where she clung to the old woman's neck and helplessly patted her shoulder. By then Jenny was crying, too.

"Sounds like everybody did just about everything they could do," Jim Bob observed. "Some things can't be helped, now can they."

Looking from one face to the other, he happened to glance up and see Joanna hovering dry-eyed but grim-faced in the background. "Are you all right, Joanna?" he asked.

She wasn't all right. In fact, she was furious. She hadn't wanted Jenny to be subjected to her Grandmother Lathrop's version of things, but it was too late now. The damage, if any, was already done.

"I'm okay," Joanna answered. "Just a little tired, that's all."

The old man hurriedly started to rise to his feet. "We can get out of your way and head on into town right now if you like," he said.

"No. Don't rush off. We need to talk, all of us." She glanced at Marianne. "What are you doing here, Mari?" Joanna asked, not unkindly. "Jeff told me you had a board meeting."

"I skipped out," Marianne answered. "When I told them I was coming here, everyone understood."

Joanna took a seat at the head of the table, effectively shutting down Eleanor's story before she could embellish it any further. "As long as Marianne's here, we could just as well start making plans for the funeral. I understand Norm Higgins is waiting to hear from us in the morning so he can move forward on the arrangements. How soon can you schedule it, Marianne? What about Saturday?"

Reverend Maculyea shook her head dubiously. "That may be too soon, what with the autopsy and . . ."

"Autopsy?" Eva Lou echoed in dismay. "Do you mean to tell me that they're doing an autopsy on my boy? Why on earth would they need one of those?"

"They're routine, Mrs. Brady," Marianne explained. "When someone dies within twenty-four hours of being admitted to a hospital, an autopsy is pretty much standard procedure. They call them coroner's cases."

Eva Lou Brady remained unconvinced. "I don't care what they call them," she insisted. "From what I've heard, everybody knows Andy died of a gunshot wound. I don't see any good reason for them to go cutting him up that way, no reason at all."

"Can we do it Saturday at the church?" Joanna put in, wanting desperately to steer the discussion away from the subject of autopsies, "I'd really like to have the funeral as soon as possible. I want to get it over with."

Marianne made a note in her calendar. "I'll check on it in the morning."

"Will I be able to come?" Jennifer asked. "I've never been to a funeral before."

"You'll be there," Joanna told her. "You and I will be there together."

For the next two hours or so, the five adults huddled over the dining room table, choosing music and scripture passages, selecting people to give eulogies and to serve as pallbearers. It was a painful but necessary process. With every small decision, Joanna felt the reality of it inevitably settling into her soul. Andy really was dead.

By nine, suffering from emotional overload, Jennifer put herself to bed. Jim Bob and Eva Lou left for home in town around eleven, and Eleanor Lathrop followed suit a few minutes later. When Joanna went into the bedroom to check on Jenny, she emerged in time to find Marianne setting two ice-filled glasses and an unopened fifth of Jack Daniels on the dining room table.

"Where'd that come from?" Joanna asked, staring at the bottle while Marianne Maculyea twisted open the top.

"I'm not naming any names," the pastor returned, "but one of my most faithful parishioners gives Jeff and me one of these every Christmas whether we need it or not. And don't think I'm not grateful. I could never afford to buy this stuff on my salary. We save it for special occasions, and this seems special to me. I figure if anyone ever needed a drink, you do tonight. Here."

Marianne Maculyea handed Joanna a glass filled with amber liquid, took hers, and held it up in a toast. "To Andy," she said.

Joanna nodded. "To Andy," she repeated, and took a long sip, feeling the whiskey warm her throat and chest as she swallowed. Tears brimmed in her eyes and she sank into the nearest chair.

"How do I go on?" she asked. "How do people do it?"

Marianne sat down next to her and put a hand on Joanna's. "They do it one day at a time," she answered softly. "Or one minute at a time when the going's really tough. They do it with the love and help of people who care about them, and with love and guidance from the Big Guy upstairs."

Joanna stared down into the depths of her glass. "I couldn't talk to Jim Bob and Eva Lou about all the rumors," she said brokenly. "They have a right to know about them, I guess, that they're claiming it's suicide, the supposed illegal dealings with Lefty . . ."

"And the gun," Marianne added.

Joanna's head came up. "Gun? What gun?"

"You mean no one's told you about that?"

"Marianne, nobody's telling me anything more than they absolutely have to," Joanna returned.

"It's a rumor, too. I heard it from Deena O'Toole, and she heard it from her former mother-in-law. According to Gertrude, the *federales* are requesting ballistics tests on Andy's .357."

"Why?"

Marianne Maculyea paused before she answered. "They think it's the same gun that killed Lefty."

Joanna sat in stunned silence while Marianne poured more Jack Daniels over their melting ice.

"So what are we going to do about it?" Marianne asked.

"Do?"

"That's right—do. Jeff and I talked about it this afternoon while Jenny was taking a nap. We kept trying to reconcile all the things we'd heard about Andrew Brady in the last twenty-four hours, all these rumors, with the man we knew—the man who taught Sunday school and cleaned up after potlucks."

Joanna raised her eyes until they met and held Marianne Maculyea's serious, gray-eyed gaze. "And what did you decide?" Joanna asked.

Marianne raised her glass and finished off the drink. "That somebody's lying," she answered cheerfully. "All we have to do now is figure out who."

She got up then, picked up her glass, and carried it into the kitchen. "I'm going home now," she said, gathering her purse and keys. "You've got to be dead on your feet. We'll thrash this all out tomorrow. In the meantime, try to get some sleep."

Coming back to Joanna's side, she gave her a quick hug. "Will you be all right here by yourself?"

"Go on home," Joanna answered dully. "I'll be fine."

For some time after Marianne Maculyea drove

out of the yard, Joanna continued sitting at the table. Weary beyond all reason, she knew she needed to go to bed. Twice she got up and started for the bedroom and twice she turned back, unable to open the bedroom door.

Tired as she was, she couldn't bring herself to step inside the room that had once been her haven from the rest of the world. How could she possibly lie down on her side of that double bed, the one she and Andy had slept in all their married life? How could she put her head down on a pillow when the one next to hers would still be laden with Andy's distinctive scent? How could she go near a closet where his dirty clothes would still be lying in a haphazard pile on the floor and where his freshly ironed shirts and pants would still be hanging on his side of the closet waiting for him to come put them on?

No. The bedroom was definitely off limits, but Marianne Maculyea's whiskey was having the intended effect on Joanna's fatigued body. Finally, barely able to put one foot in front of the other, she shambled to the linen closet and dragged out one of Eva Lou's heavy, hand-crocheted afghans. Still wearing the terrycloth robe, Joanna turned off the lights, wrapped the afghan around her, and lay down on the living room couch.

As soon as she lay down, she knew it had been a mistake to turn out the lights. In the darkness, the house seemed oppressively quiet. Joanna started to get up and turn them back on, but just then Sadie came over to the couch and sniffed curiously at the afghan-wrapped cocoon. For some time the dog stood with her soft chin resting on Joanna's shoulder. Finally, voicing her objection in a huge sigh, Sadie flopped down on the floor next to the couch.

That night Joanna Brady fell asleep to the comforting rumble of Sadie's steady snores. In the face of that impossibly empty silence, the dog's company was a vast improvement over being alone.

 **TEN**

JENNIFER AWAKENED her mother early the next morning. At seven o'clock the child was already up and dressed. "Am I going to school?" she asked.

Lying on the couch, it took Joanna a moment before she was fully awake and functioning enough to realize where she was and why Jennifer was asking.

Fighting off despair, Joanna looked at her daughter. "There's lots to do. We have to finish planning Daddy's funeral today."

"But it'll be boring," Jennifer objected. "Besides, all the other kids will be in school. I already missed yesterday. Can't I go? Please?"

Joanna was torn. Inarguably, it would be easier to do things without having to worry about Jennifer, but as a mother, she wondered about the propriety of Jenny returning to school so soon after her father's death.

"If you really want to go, I suppose it'll be all

right," Joanna agreed finally. "But I'll take you. I'm not sending you on the bus. Have you had breakfast?"

"Not yet," Jenny said.

Joanna heaved off the afghan. "You go eat. I'll get dressed."

After another quick shower to subdue her hair, Joanna found that in the daylight, the bedroom wasn't quite as bad as it had been at night. Just inside the bedroom door she discovered the Arizona Inn shopping bag. She had no idea how it had ended up there; perhaps her mother had brought it along with her from Tucson. In any event, once dressed in a sweatshirt and ratty jeans, she took her work boots out of the bag and carried them along with her to the kitchen.

She found Jennifer in the breakfast nook reading the cereal box and crunching down a bowl of Cheerios. "I made coffee," Jenny said. "I hope it's not too strong."

Joanna paused long enough to pour a cup. It was strong, all right, but Joanna took it without complaint and without watering it down, either. She dropped her boots on the floor and settled down opposite her daughter. Jenny looked up at her questioningly.

"Are you mad because I'm going to school?" she asked.

Joanna shook her head. "I'm not mad at anybody," she said.

"Something like this never happened to me before," Jennifer continued. "I don't know how to act."

Joanna managed an affectionate smile. "At times like this, it's probably best to do whatever feels right. If you feel like going to school, go. How does that sound?"

"Fine," Jennifer nodded, then added, "Grandpa's here."

Joanna looked around. "He is? Where? When did he get here?"

"While you were in the shower. He said he'd be out in the barn getting hay for the cattle."

Joanna hunched down and began to pull on her boots. "Why's he doing that?" she flared. "I can feed cattle, for Pete's sake. I'm not helpless, you know."

Jennifer shrugged. "He said you have enough to worry about right now, so he's taking care of the animals."

"Well, he shouldn't!" Joanna exclaimed indignantly, straightening up and heading for the door.

"Maybe it seems right to him," Jennifer observed, without looking up from her cereal bowl. "Maybe it's what he feels like doing."

Joanna stopped at the door and looked back at her daughter, struck by the adult wisdom in her child's words. Sometimes Jennifer amazed her.

"Maybe you're right," Joanna said. "Finish your breakfast and brush your teeth. I'll go see if Daddy Jim needs any help. When we finish, I'll take you to school."

By the time Joanna went outside, though, Jim Bob Brady had already finished with the cattle and was coming from the barn to the house. He looked far older and more stoop-shouldered than

Joanna remembered. There had always been a re-
markable physical resemblance between Jim Bob
Brady and his son. As the old man walked toward
her now with the early morning sun on his face,
Joanna felt a sharp pang of loss. She would never
have a chance to see how Andy would look at that
age, to watch how his hair might grow gray or see
how sunlight and hard work might have etched
lines into his smooth features.

"Done already?" she asked.

Daddy Jim nodded. "It wasn't much."

"Would you like some coffee? Jenny made it."

The old man sighed. His eyes were puffy and
red-rimmed from lack of sleep. "No, thanks," he
said. "Reckon I'd better head on home. Mama's
taking this real hard. I shouldn't leave her alone
for very long at a stretch."

"Is she all right?" Joanna asked. "She seemed
okay last night."

Jim Bob shook his head. "You know Eva Lou,"
he said wearily. "She's fine as long as she's busy
doin' for somebody else, but this morning, I think
it finally hit home, what with the rumors and all."

"You've heard them, too?" Joanna asked. She
had hoped to spare her in-laws from some of the
ugliness, but that was impossible. They lived in
the town. They had eyes and ears.

Daddy Jim shrugged. "Heard some of 'em last
night right here from old Clayton Rhodes. I didn't
pass 'em along to Mama, though, 'cause I was
afraid they'd like to kill her. Wouldn't you know
somebody called her up bright and early this
morning to talk about it? And it was on the TV

news as well. To hear them talk, it's like it's all cut and dried, like Andy's guilty as sin when he's not here to defend himself. It don't seem fair to me that you're innocent until proven guilty 'less, of course, you're dead. Then all bets are off. I'll tell you what, it's about to break Eva Lou's heart. I mean, it's bad enough for him to be dead, but this . . . Damn!"

The old man strode away from her a few paces and swiped savagely at his eyes with his shirt sleeve. In all the years she'd known him Joanna had never seen her father-in-law shed a tear.

After a time he straightened his shoulders and drew a deep breath. "Where's it gonna end, Joanna?" he asked, walking back to her. "You hear all these terrible things, all these lies. It don't seem possible that they're talking about my boy, about my Andy, about him killing somebody in cold blood, about him taking money from drug dealers and all. But nobody's standing up for him, either. No one's yelling from the rooftops that Andrew Roy Brady never did any such thing!"

"I am," Joanna said quietly.

Jim Bob Brady looked at her earnestly. "So you don't think he did all those things, either, do you?"

"No."

"But what do we do about it?"

"Try to prove they're wrong," Joanna answered.

"How?"

"I don't know. By going to the bank and finding out where the money came from to buy my ring, for one thing," she replied. "By finding out exactly when Lefty O'Toole was murdered and by showing conclusively that Andy was nowhere around when that happened."

"Have you seen this note they keep talking about?" Jim Bob asked hoarsely. "The suicide note?"

"Not yet, but I will. He wouldn't do that, Daddy Jim."

"Don't you think I know that?" Jim Bob Brady returned. "Don't you think I know my own son well enough to say he'd never do such a thing, never leave his wife and child to make it on their own?" His voice cracked and he stopped for a moment.

"But how do you convince somebody else?" he continued. "I called Dick Voland last night after Mama fell asleep. I called then because I didn't want her knowin' what I was up to. I asked him straight out about hirin' a private investigator to look into this matter. Do you know what he says to me? He tells me to save my money and not bother. They must think they've got a pretty good case."

"Except for one small thing," Joanna asserted vehemently. "Andy didn't do it. He wouldn't kill another human being, not unless his very life depended on it, and maybe not even then."

The dim light of hope seemed to switch back on in Jim Bob Brady's eyes. "Do you think we'll we be able to prove it, Joanna?" he asked. "Will we be able to get anyone else to see it our way?"

The old man's tremulous hope caused a sudden stiffening in Joanna's spine. "We're going to try," Joanna responded. "We're going to use every trick in the book."

Jim Bob Brady shook his head. "I can't tell you what it would mean to Mama, if you found out Andy didn't do all those awful things," he said.

For a moment, neither of them spoke, then he went on. "Thank you, Joanna. You do whatever it is you need to do, and don't worry about the stock. Clayton and I talked it over last night. He says he'll come over of an evening, and I can handle mornings. That way you won't have to worry about it."

"Daddy Jim," Joanna objected firmly. "I appreciate the offer, but these cattle are not your problem. Jennifer and I can take care of things around here."

"Maybe so," Jim Bob Brady agreed. "In fact, I don't have a doubt in the world. The point is, you shouldn't have to. Not right now. Besides, bein' back out here takes my mind off my troubles, helps me think about other things."

If that was true, if coming out to do chores was therapeutic, Joanna could hardly tell him no. "All right," she conceded reluctantly, "but promise me that you won't work too hard, that you won't overdo it."

"I promise," he said quickly. "I may look old and all wore out, but I can still heft me a mean bale of hay now and then."

Behind them the screen door on the back porch banged open. "Mom," Jennifer said, "are you ready? It's getting late."

"She wants to go to school today," Joanna explained, worried that her father-in-law might take offense. "I told her it was up to her, that I'd take her in if she wants to go."

"I'm headed that way myself, Jenny," Jim Bob Brady said, speaking to the child over her mother's head. "Your mom's real busy. Go get your stuff. I'll drop you off on my way back home."

Jennifer dashed back into the house. The old man stepped closer to Joanna. This time, when he spoke, it was almost a whisper. "I don't mean to pry, Joanna, but are you and Jenny gonna be all right as far as money's concerned?"

He asked the question awkwardly, as though he knew he had no right to ask but found himself powerless in the face of his agonizing need to know.

"We'll be fine, Daddy Jim," Joanna answered. "I work for an insurance company, and Milo saw to it that we owned some. There'll be money from that and from Social Security as well. You don't have to worry on that score."

He sighed with relief. "I'm real happy to hear it. Maybe it'll help me sleep a little better tonight, but then again, maybe not."

Once more the screen door banged. Jennifer appeared between them carrying a lunch bag and a stack of books. Jim Bob Brady patted her shoulder fondly. "I suppose we'd best be getting along. Otherwise, you're gonna be tardy."

Jennifer headed toward the Honda, but despite his words, Jim Bob made no move to follow. He stood with both hands shoved deep in his pockets.

"You know," he said thoughtfully, "Mama and me were both pretty upset way back then when you and Andy turned up pregnant and all. We thought you was too young and crazy to get married and make it work, to make a go of it, but you did, by God.

"You were still just a kid, Joanna, but you made him a hell of a good wife. You helped him with school and made him grow up in a way Mama and I never could have. I want you to know right now that you're as much a daughter to me as Andy ever was a son, and I don't want you to forget it. If you and Jenny need something, anything at all, you come to me first, you hear?"

Joanna nodded wordlessly, her eyes filling with tears.

"Good," he said. "I just wanted you to know."

With that, he pulled his hand from his pocket and held it out to Joanna. It was an odd, surprising gesture. After all he'd said, she expected a hug, but Jim Bob Brady came from stern, dryland farming stock where physical displays of affection didn't come easily.

Joanna reached out to return what she thought was a proffered handshake. Instead, he placed something in her upturned palm and pressed her fingers shut around it.

Startled, Joanna opened her hand and looked. There, neatly folded into a tiny square, lay a piece of paper money. She unfolded it, thinking it might be a ten or a twenty. Instead, she found it to be a single hundred dollar bill.

"There's more where that came from," Jim Bob Brady declared in a forceful whisper.

With that, her father-in-law turned and strode

away. Blinded by tears, Joanna stumbled back into the kitchen, sank into the breakfast nook, put her head down on her arms, and bawled her eyes out, grateful that there was no one else around the house to see or hear her do it.

It was some time later before she managed to pull herself back together enough to get up and pour a second cup of coffee. She supposed it would be like this for some time—one step forward and two back, then she'd be fine for a while until something set her off again. In her present condition, kindness was almost more difficult to handle than anything else.

The fit of crying had passed and she was just beginning to work on a complex TO-DO list when the phone rang. Afraid it might be her mother, she almost didn't answer. Finally she did.

"Mrs. Brady?" a man asked. The voice sounded familiar, although at first Joanna couldn't place it.

"Yes."

"Dr. Sanders," he announced. "From University Hospital."

"Oh, yes," she said, thinking she must have failed to fill out one of the billing forms properly. "What can I do for you, Dr. Sanders?"

He paused. "This may sound funny, Mrs. Brady, but with all due humility, I'm a good doctor and an excellent surgeon. When you asked about your husband's prognosis yesterday morning, I gave you the worst possible scenario. I always do that as a matter of course, so that families have a chance to work backwards from there. I couldn't predict the eventual outcome of the possible paralysis, but from the family's standpoint, a partial recovery would have been better than no recovery at all, if that's what you're prepared for. Does that make sense?"

"Yes."

"I usually take Wednesday afternoons off. If I had thought your husband's condition was that critical, I never would have left the hospital. That's why I wasn't there when your husband's status deteriorated so rapidly. Now, I'm trying to make sense of what happened."

"They scheduled an autopsy," Joanna said.

"I know. Actually, I've already seen it. The preliminary results are inconclusive. With the kind of extensive injuries your husband sustained, I would have expected to find a stray blood clot that had come loose and made its way to either the heart or lungs, but the medical examiner found nothing of the kind. She's ordered a full battery of toxicology tests, but those take time."

"Toxicology?" Joanna asked. "Why that?"

"Because," he answered, without really addressing the question. "The reason I'm calling you right now," he continued, "is to see if you noticed any change in your husband's condition the last time you saw him."

"No. None. I was away from the hospital, too, when it happened. Have you spoken to the other doctor?"

"What other doctor?" Sanders demanded sharply.

"The one who stopped by just before Andy

went into cardiac arrest. My mother said he told her everything was fine."

There was dead silence on the other end of the line. "Mrs. Brady," Dr. Sanders said slowly. "I have your husband's chart right here in front of me. There's no indication of a doctor's visit after my last rounds at 11:30 A.M. just before I left for the day. Did your mother mention a name?"

"No, but she did say she talked to him when he came back out to the waiting room. He told her there wasn't anything to worry about."

"Has she spoken to the police about this?" Dr. Sanders asked.

"The police? Why would she?"

"She'd better," Dr. Sanders said quietly. "Someone posing as a doctor would explain a lot."

"What are you talking about?" Joanna asked.

"As I said, we can't be positive until after the toxicology report, but once you've seen one or two O.D.'s you know what they look like."

"O.D.," Joanna repeated. "As in drug overdose? How could that be? You mean someone accidentally administered the wrong thing?"

"I'm not saying anything of the kind," Dr. Sanders returned. "This so-called doctor your mother told you about wasn't a doctor at all."

The room spun around her. Joanna gripped the counter top in order to maintain her balance. "He was an imposter then?"

"Yes. I don't know about the bullet wound. I'm saying that I think there's a good possibility you were right. Those powder burns on your husband's hand and fingers may or may not have been faked, but at the time of his death, your husband was in no condition to self-administer a lethal dose of anything."

"You're saying he was murdered after all," Joanna managed.

"Damn right!" Dr. Sanders returned forcefully. "To be perfectly frank, Mrs. Brady, my initial interest in the autopsy was strictly from a medical malpractice standpoint. A patient was dead and I wanted to know, for my own benefit, if I was in any way liable. But after our conversation I wanted to call you right away and let you know what's going on. I would imagine the Tucson police will attempt to get in touch with your mother."

"I'm sure they will," Joanna agreed.

When she hung up the phone, Joanna didn't waste a moment before dialing her mother's number herself, but there was no answer. Eleanor Lathrop was already up and gone. Joanna was disappointed, but there was one small consolation. If she couldn't find her mother, neither could the Tucson police.

ELEVEN

AFTER A virtually sleepless night, Angie Kellogg staggered out of bed. She didn't want to be anywhere near Tony when he woke up. She didn't want him to touch her.

Angie was a survivor. She had avoided the pitfalls of drug use, not out of some sense of superior morality but because she saw for herself, time and again, that drug-using hookers died with astonishing regularity. And so far, she had managed to elude AIDS as well. Tony had insisted on having her tested before he'd take her to bed. Once he'd reassured himself that she was clean, he'd taken steps to make sure she stayed that way. It was funny that a cold-blooded killer would himself be so frightened of death. This morning Angie Kellogg wished she could give him a good healthy dose of clap just to get his attention.

On her part, she had allied herself with Tony Vargas when he was the only way out of what would otherwise have been a life-or-death situation. And now, ten months later, here she was in another one.

The day before, when Tony had left the house after watching the noon news, Angie had guessed what he'd be about. Now, knowing for sure, she was sick with revulsion. And fear. She wasn't sure of all the legal ramifications, but she was convinced that somehow, by knowing and keeping silent, the law would deem her an accomplice, if not before the fact then certainly after.

If the cops ever did manage to catch Tony and charge him, if Tony took a fall, so would she. When it came to dead cops, she knew she'd be sucked into the vortex right along with Tony. In fact, out of sheer spite, Tony would probably drag her down right along with him.

But fear of Tony and fear of the consequences weren't all that had kept her from sleeping. The other cause of her insomnia was guilt, the sure knowledge that by doing nothing, by not acting on her suspicions, she had played an unwitting part in the death of that sheriff's deputy.

After the terrible things her father had done to her, Angie had both blamed and hated herself. She had allowed self-condemnation to become the central issue of her life, distorting and dictating her every action, but compared to what she felt now, Angie's previous self-hatred had been little more than a child's puny effort. Nothing in her whole life had shamed her the way Andrew Brady's death did. He was dead because of her, and Angie Kellogg was suddenly drowning in self-loathing.

Pulling on her robe, Angie hurried to the vestibule. For an extra tip from Tony each month, the paper boy dropped their newspaper directly through the otherwise unused mail slot beside the front door. Angie retrieved the newspaper, then hurried toward the kitchen, reading as she went.

The latest crisis in the Mideast had bumped the Andrew Brady story off the front page, but it still had plenty of play. She read every word of the three-column article, trying to understand exactly what had happened. Angie was startled to realize that Andrew Brady's newly widowed wife, whose tenth anniversary had been the day before his death, was only a few years older than she was. The newspaper reported that they had a nine-year-old daughter. Knowing that only made Angie feel worse.

After reading the paper, she carefully put it back together and returned it to its place in the vestibule. It was better for her if Tony didn't realize she actually read newspapers in general and today's in particular.

Feeling anxious and ill at ease, Angie meandered into the living room. The two roadrunners were out cavorting in the back yard, but today she paid no attention. For weeks she had beguiled the time with half-formed daydreams about the kind of house she'd buy for herself some day, if she ever got the chance. Not one like this one, huge and spacious and uncaring where everything—from linens to silverware—was included in the rental. This place was elegant but impersonal in the same way hotel rooms were, and Angie had had a belly-ful of hotel rooms.

Angie wanted out of the life, permanently, and she wanted something more besides—a place of her own, small but cozy, with dishes and furniture and curtains that all carried her own particular stamp on them. She'd put up bird feeders all over the backyard—a yard with a single tall, shady tree. And she'd plant a garden, one thick with flowers and vegetables both.

Except, today she couldn't summon the daydream. Joanna Brady—the wife of the dead deputy—hadn't bothered Angie when she didn't know about her existence, but now she could think of nothing else. Andrew Brady was dead at thirty-two, Joanna Brady was a widow at twenty-seven, and it was all Angie's fault.

She sat there now, staring blindly out the window, struggling with her conscience and with what she should do. Her problem now was two-fold. Not only would she have to escape Tony, but she would have to elude the law as well. And whatever she did, it had to be soon. She had checked in the closet, had opened the latest brief-case she found there and seen the money. Getting away from Tony would take money, but those money-filled briefcases didn't stay in the closet for more than a few days at most, once they appeared. So speed was essential as far as the availability of money was concerned.

It was also the key to survival. Angie understood that if Tony had even the slightest glimmer that she knew the truth about him, that he wouldn't hesitate to kill her. Every time he looked at her, she was petrified that her face would some-how betray her, giving away to him the thoughts she meant to keep hidden in her head.

If she was going to get away, it would have to be soon, before Tony learned her secret, while she could still take his money and use it as a grubstake. But regardless of how much money there was, she doubted there would ever be enough for her to get away from him completely. The only way he'd ever leave her alone was if he was dead or in jail. Dead didn't seem likely, and thugs like Tony got out of jail all the time. And as soon as he got out, she knew he'd be after her. He'd be vicious as a bulldog, and just as relentless. She didn't dare think about what he'd do if he ever caught her.

If she did come up with a plan for getting away, she'd have to come up with a foolproof plan for getting rid of Tony as well. She couldn't see herself holding a gun on him and pulling the trigger, but she needed something every bit as permanent as a well-placed bullet, something that wouldn't land her in jail as well.

"Angie," he bellowed from the other room. She jumped as though she'd been shot. He was awake early and wanting her. Lost in thought, she hadn't even heard the click of the cigarette lighter.

"Did you start the coffee?"

"Not yet. I will in a minute."

"Bring me the paper," he ordered, "and turn on the TV set in here. I wish to hell I'd asked for that television repairman to come today instead of Sat-

urday. This worthless little set sucks. It's so goddamned small a man could go blind just trying to
see what's on it. And hurry up with the coffee."

FINISHED ORGANIZING her list, Joanna had
started to gather her keys and purse when Sadie,
her canine early-warning system, began to bark.
Joanna checked outside just in time to see two Cochise County sheriff's vehicles stopping in front of
her gate. Two men walked toward her back door—
Chief Deputy Richard Voland and Ernie Carpenter, Cochise County's chief homicide detective.

Joanna knew Dick Voland pretty well. Not so
Ernie Carpenter. Around the department he had
the unenviable reputation of being an unbend-
ing, humorless prig who nonetheless usually got
his man. In a world of bola ties and Stetsons, he
was the only officer on Walter McFadden's staff
who consistently showed up for work wearing
knotted ties and three-piece suits.

Andy hadn't particularly liked the man, and
neither did Joanna. Aloof and rigid, a stickler for
rules, Carpenter seemed to hold himself above it
all, from interdepartmental politics to volleyball
games at the annual picnic at Turkey Creek. Moments earlier, Joanna might have dreaded seeing
Detective Carpenter, but now, full of this latest bit
of information from Dr. Sanders, she was eager to
tell what she knew. Quieting the noisy dog, she
closed Sadie in Jenny's room and then hurried
back to the kitchen to open the door.

"Good morning, Joanna," Voland said, politely tipping his hat. "Hope we're not catching you at a bad time."

"No. Come on in."

From the distressed looks on their faces, it was apparent that neither one of the officers relished the coming encounter. The death of a fellow officer was always hard on all concerned. Thinking it would ease the situation, Joanna blurted out her news from Dr. Sanders. "Andy's surgeon from Tucson just called. He told me he thinks Andy was murdered."

To her surprise, neither Carpenter nor Voland seemed much interested in her news. "Really," Carpenter mused. "What makes him say that?"

"He saw preliminary results from the autopsy. They don't have a toxicology report yet, but Dr. Sanders seems to think Andy died of a possible drug overdose, that someone slipped Andy something lethal right there in the hospital under everyone's very noses."

Carpenter shook his head and smiled indulgently. "That's all very interesting, Joanna. Sounds like something straight out of a soap opera to me, but we have to take these things one step at a time. We need to ask you a few questions if you have time."

She nodded. Looking at the two burly men looming over her in the kitchen, Joanna knew they wouldn't be well suited to the tight-fitting benches of the breakfast nook. "Come on into the dining room," she said.

As they seated themselves around the table,

Dick Voland seemed especially uncomfortable. "I hate to bother you at a time like this. I'm sure you're real busy today, but since we couldn't visit with you yesterday . . ."

"It's all right," Joanna assured them, determined to be cooperative and do what she could to help. "I understand you've got your jobs to do. And after talking to Dr. Sanders, I'm ready to talk. Would anybody like coffee?"

Both men shook their heads in silent unison. Their joint refusal unnerved her a little. It wouldn't have hurt them to observe some social niceties, and it puzzled Joanna that they both seemed to give so little credence to Dr. Sanders' mind-boggling news.

"What's really going on?" she asked.

"Suppose we cut directly to the chase, Joanna," Ernie Carpenter said at once. "Can you tell us where Andy was weekend before last?"

She answered without hesitation. "Payson. Outside of Payson, actually, visiting with a friend. Floyd Demaris is his name, but everyone calls him Pookie. He and Andy graduated from the police academy in Phoenix together, but Pookie got shot while he was still a rookie. He's in a wheelchair and back living with his folks. He always loved the outdoors. Once each September, before it got too cold, he and Andy would go camping."

"And, as far as you know, that's what they did?" Detective Carpenter asked.

"As far as I know?" Joanna echoed. "You're saying Andy didn't go there?"

Sitting with a Cross ever-sharp pencil poised

above a blank page in a meticulously kept notebook, Ernie Carpenter abruptly changed the subject. "How many guns did Andy own?"

"Two," Joanna answered. "The .38 Chief and his .357."

"So you're aware he had two separate weapons?"

"Of course, I'm aware of that," Joanna returned shortly. "Guns were the tools of Andy's trade. Those are the kinds of things married couples usually know about each other. He carried the .357 with his uniform and wore the Chief with civilian clothes because it's so much smaller and easier to carry."

"So you would have expected him to take the Chief with him for the weekend rather than the .357?"

"That's right."

"Didn't you find it odd that he always left one or the other of those two weapons in his locker down at the department?"

"What's odd about it?" Joanna asked.

Carpenter looked her right in the eye. "I take mine home," he said.

"Do you have any little children at home?" she returned.

"Not anymore."

"We do. The day Jennifer was born Andy spent most of the day in the waiting room of the County Hospital with the distraught parents of a little girl who'd been playing with her father's pistol. Remember that?"

Both officers nodded. "She died, didn't she?" Detective Carpenter asked.

"That's right, she did. And it made quite an impression on Andy and me. He always said keeping track of one handgun was trouble enough. He didn't want to risk having two in the house at the same time. None of this was exactly a state secret, so why all the questions about Andy's guns? What do they have to do with the price of peanuts?"

Carpenter dropped his gaze as he made a quick notation in his notebook. "I'm sure you've heard by now about Lefty O'Toole's death, haven't you?"

"Yes, but . . ."

"We have the ballistics tests back," Carpenter continued. "We've confirmed that Lefty was shot with bullets fired from Andy's .357. We're estimating time of death as some time the weekend before last. That's only a best-guess estimate, nothing definitive."

"That's when Andy was in Payson," Joanna supplied.

Ernie Carpenter raised his eyes and met Joanna's. "He wasn't," the detective said. "Somebody else told us he was supposed to be there, so we did some checking. I've already spoken with Mr. Demaris. Andy called and canceled the trip late Thursday afternoon. He said something important had come up here at home and he wouldn't be able to make it."

"But . . ." Joanna began.

Detective Carpenter silenced her with a dismissive wave of his hand. "When he left here on

Friday afternoon, did Andy say anything to you to the effect that he had changed his mind and was going somewhere else?"

"No."

"And he stayed away the whole weekend, just as he would have if he really had made the trip to Payson?"

Joanna's stomach muscles tightened. Before, what she had heard about the investigation had been so much hearsay. Now there could be no doubt that Detective Ernie Carpenter was trying to implicate Andy in Lefty O'Toole's death. As the questions droned on, the investigator continued to show absolutely no sign of interest in Dr. Sanders' allegations. Hadn't he listened to her? Maybe she hadn't said it clearly enough.

"How much do you know about your husband's business dealings?" Carpenter went on. His questions were professional and gratingly dispassionate.

"I know everything," Joanna maintained. "I keep the books. We sell a few head of cattle now and then. I can show you in black and white that what we make doesn't amount to that much money."

"Do you own any property other than your place here, something Andy might have liquidated without your knowledge?"

"No. None at all."

"Did a relative of his die recently?"

"No. Why?"

"Mrs. Brady," Ernie Carpenter said slowly, "Andy was a colleague of mine. I'd like to find some legitimate source for the nine-thousand-five-hundred-dollar cash deposit he made into your joint checking account on Monday of this week. Do you have any idea where that money might have come from?"

Joanna was astonished. "How much?"

"Nine-thousand-five-hundred even," Carpenter repeated. "Sandy, down at the bank, said he brought it all into the branch in a stack of cash on Monday afternoon. He showed up with it just before closing time."

Shaken, Joanna found it difficult to speak. "But that's almost ten thousand dollars. I can't imagine where Andy would lay hands on that kind of money."

"Could he have borrowed it from his parents?"

"No. The Bradys don't have it, and he wouldn't have borrowed it from them even if they did."

"So you have no idea where this money came from?"

"None at all."

"Have there been other occasions when unexplained money has turned up in your account?

"No. Absolutely not." Joanna turned to Dick Voland who had maintained a strict silence during the entire interview process.

"How can you sit here and let him ask questions like this?" she stormed. "You worked with Andy, Dick. He wasn't like this, and you know it. He never did anything crooked in his life."

Voland shook his head but without offering any consolation. "Let him go on, Joanna. It's the only way we're ever going to get to the bottom of this."

"Did Andy ever mention Lefty O'Toole's name to you?" Ernie asked. "Were you aware of any ongoing relationship?"

"No!" Joanna answered.

"Had you two suffered any financial reverses lately?" he continued. "Were you behind in your mortgage payments?"

"No, not at all. We were doing fine."

"How did he act the past few weeks? Was he depressed for instance, anxious or upset?"

"No. Exactly the opposite. If anything, he was excited. He enjoyed campaigning, and that surprised him. It surprised us both. He wasn't depressed at all."

"Did he leave anything here that might have explained what happened? Any kind of note, a message?"

"There was a note with the flowers and ring, but that wasn't a suicide note if that's what you're implying."

"Could I see it?"

For the first time, Joanna remembered that Andy's forgotten roses had been left in the ICU waiting room, but she had stuffed the note in a pocket of the dress where she had discovered it when she finally slipped off her soiled clothing.

"It's in the bedroom," she said. "I'll go get it."

Joanna retrieved the note, handing it over to Ernie Carpenter who studied it for some time. "What's this about ten years?" he asked.

"We couldn't afford a ring when we got married," she answered.

"You didn't mind him spending three thousand bucks on one now?"

For the first time that morning, Joanna looked down at the glittering diamond on her finger. "He didn't ask me, Ernie," Joanna told him. "It was a surprise.

Carpenter nodded. "All right. According to Hiram Young, Andy paid for it on Tuesday afternoon with a personal check written on your joint account."

"Doesn't that tell you something?" Joanna asked. "If it were dishonest money, wouldn't he have hidden it from me, put it somewhere else rather than in our joint account?"

"That's one interpretation, I suppose," Carpenter admitted.

"Give me another one," Joanna retorted, her temper rising. Up to now, she had been patient, but now she was fast losing it as the questions moved away from mere intrusion to violation. She understood full well what another possible interpretation might be.

Carpenter was busily closing his notebook and putting it back in his pocket. "I'd rather not say at this time," he said.

"You don't have to mince words with me, Detective Carpenter," Joanna said coldly. "Adam York of the DEA already spilled the beans. Whatever it is, all of you seem to think I'm in on it, don't you."

"Joanna," Dick Voland put in, "nobody said anything like that."

"But everybody's hinting, and I'm damned sick of it."

Ernie Carpenter was studying her face with undisguised interest. "One more thing, Joanna. This may be painful for you, but I have to ask. Has there been any prior difficulty with other women in Andy's life?"

Joanna stared hard at the detective's impassive face, and her eyes narrowed when she finally understood the full implication behind the question. Her voice lowered.

"Whatever makes you think there's one now, Detective Carpenter? Get the hell out of here, both of you, and don't come back. I've had enough."

They stood up, headed for the door, and let themselves out. Joanna had planned on asking Dick Voland to be a pallbearer at Andy's funeral, but right then, she couldn't bring herself to do it.

TWELVE

STILL OUTRAGED at Detective Carpenter's blunt insinuation of infidelity, Joanna churned gravel in the yard as she headed for town. Navigating as if on rails, the Eagle followed its usual route straight to her office with Joanna so engrossed in inner turmoil that she barely glanced at the now-empty wash as she sped along High Lonesome Road.

The Davis Insurance Agency, originally a father-and-son operation, had been a fixture on Arizona Street for thirty years, and the latest in Milo Davis' long succession of Buicks always occupied the front corner parking place. As office manager, Joanna usually parked in the spot next to his, but today that place was taken by a silver Taurus with government plates.

Adam York from the DEA. What the hell is he doing here? Joanna wondered. She pulled into the nearest parking place, several spaces away, and stormed into the office.

Lisa Connors, the receptionist, looked up in surprise when Joanna appeared at her desk. "Joanna, I'm so sorry about Andy, but I didn't expect to see you today. What are you doing here?"

Joanna ignored the question. "Where is he?" she demanded.

"The guy from the DEA?" Joanna nodded. Lisa rolled her eyes and gestured toward Milo's private office. "He's been in with Mr. Davis for half an hour or so. You still haven't told me what you're doing here," she continued. "Mr. Davis said you'd be out for at least a week."

"I just stopped by for a few minutes," Joanna answered. "There are at least three applications that should have gone out yesterday, and they all need special underwriting memos. I'll be leaving again as soon as those are taken care of."

The phone rang. While Lisa answered it, Joanna hurried to her own desk, picked up the files, and quickly began keying the necessary memos into her computer, all the while conscious of the unintelligible rumble of voices emanating from behind Milo's closed door. She completed writing the memos and was printing the last of the three when the front door opened and Eleanor Lathrop burst into the room. She rushed past Lisa's desk and came straight to Joanna, reproach written on her face.

"I was driving past and saw your car outside. What in the world are you doing at work today?" Eleanor demanded. "What will people think?"

"I have a job," Joanna returned evenly. "People will think I'm doing it."

Through the years Joanna had learned to shrug off most of Eleanor's constant criticism. She had trained herself to disregard her mother's steady barrage of pointed remarks which covered everything from Joanna's poor choice of husbands to the fact that her daughter insisted on working outside the home. Oblivious to current economic reality, Eleanor Lathrop made no bones about disapproving of working mothers—all working mothers. She maintained that God intended for families to live within their means, and "means" meant whatever the husband brought home, regardless of how much or how little that might be.

This time Joanna wasn't quite strong enough to simply ignore the jibe, and her cool reply left Eleanor flustered. "Well, if you're here, where's Jenny? With the Bradys, I suppose?"

"She's at school," Joanna answered.

The look of aghast dismay that flashed across Eleanor's face was almost worth the price of admission. Joanna bit back a smile while Eleanor clutched dramatically at her throat.

"No. That can't be."

"It is. I gave her a choice," Joanna returned. "I told her she could either go to school or stay home, it was up to her. She chose to go."

"Children Jenny's age aren't old enough to have good sense. They have no business making choices like that. How could you . . . ."

Just then the door to Milo's office opened and Adam York emerged, walked briskly through the reception area and out into the street.

"Excuse me, Mother," Joanna said. Abandoning

Eleanor to her uncharacteristic shocked silence, Joanna trailed York out the door, catching up with him in the parking lot when he stopped to unlock the Taurus.

"What seems to be the problem, Mr. York?" she asked.

He turned toward her with a startled expression on his face. "I didn't expect to see you here today," he said.

"Neither did anyone else," she returned crisply. "What I want to know is, why are you here? Are you here checking on me or my husband?"

"We're conducting an investigation," he said in an answer that was less than no answer at all.

"What exactly is it about us you'd like to know, Mr. York? Maybe, if you asked me directly, I could tell you what you want to know. You'd get your information right from the horse's mouth instead of sneaking around behind my back."

"It's no big thing really," York acknowledged with a shrug. "Routine inquiries about your insurance situation, although I must say your friend Mr. Davis wasn't particularly helpful."

Joanna squared her shoulders. "There is such a thing as client confidentiality," she declared. "It's no wonder Milo wouldn't tell you anything. He can't, but I can. What would you like to know, Mr. York? That I'm the owner and beneficiary of a $150,000 policy on my husband's life? I am. The policy is seven years old, five years beyond the two-year contestability period. In other words, the death benefit is payable regardless of cause of death."

York looked at her under raised eyebrows. "Including suicide?"

She nodded. York removed a small notebook from his coat pocket and made a quick notation. "What about accidental death?" he asked.

"That too," Joanna replied. "The accidental death benefit doesn't apply in the case of suicide but it does for homicide."

"Oh, I see," York said. "How interesting." He acted as though that bit of information was new to him, although Joanna was certain he knew better. For a long moment they stood together in the parking lot while York seemed engrossed in studying what he'd written in the notebook. Finally he glanced up at her.

"Three hundred thousand dollars," he mused shrewdly. "That seems like a considerable amount of insurance for someone in your financial situation, doesn't it, Joanna?"

Her green eyes narrowed dangerously. "Mr. York," she said tersely. "I work for a company that *sells* life insurance. If I sold Tupperware, I might own more Tupperware. If I sold Mary Kay Cosmetics, I might wear more makeup. There's also a policy on me that would have gone to Andy had our situations been reversed."

York shook his head and pocketed the notebook. "If you'll pardon my saying it, Joanna, I'm somewhat surprised you can talk about all this in such a cold-blooded manner."

He had started opening the door. In a burst of fury she slammed it shut under his hand. "What exactly is *that* supposed to mean?"

"Sorry, if I offended you," he apologized.

"The hell you're sorry! You're implying that I had something to do with Andy's death, aren't you."

York looked at her in mock bemusement. "Did I say that? I don't remember mentioning anything of the kind."

Some women become shrill when they're angry or upset. Joanna Brady's voice dropped to an icy whisper. "I'd check with the Tucson police, if I were you, Mr. York. Check out the preliminary autopsy results. When you do, I believe you'll find you owe me an apology."

He frowned. "How is it that someone like you has immediate access to those kinds of reports?" he asked.

"It doesn't matter how," she countered. "What matters is that I do!"

With that, she spun on her heels and marched back into the office where she found her mother standing by the window, peering through the blinds at the Taurus backing out of its parking place.

"Who's that man?" Eleanor asked. "Is he really with the DEA?"

"That's what he says," Joanna answered grimly, "although I'm not so sure he's telling the truth."

"Why was he here? What did he want with you?"

"That I couldn't say, but don't be surprised if he comes back asking to talk with you."

"Me?" Eleanor echoed. "What would someone from the DEA want from me?"

Suddenly aware of a pounding headache, Joanna pressed her fingers to her throbbing temples. "Listen to me, Mother. Do you remember telling me about a doctor, one who went into Andy's room just before he died?"

"There were so many," Eleanor responded dubiously.

Joanna shook her head. "No, you mentioned one in particular, one who came through the waiting room and told you everything was fine just minutes before the alarms went off."

"Oh, him," Eleanor breathed.

"Yes, him. What did he look like?"

"Margaret and I were watching television. I'm not sure I remember."

"Try," Joanna urged. "Did he introduce himself? Was he wearing a name tag?"

"How do you expect me to come up with those kinds of details? After all, I only saw him for a minute or so."

"It's very important," Joanna said with dogged patience. "Can you tell me anything at all about him—what he looked like, what he was wearing? How did you know he was a doctor?"

Eleanor closed her eyes as if trying to picture the man. "He had on one of those long white coats, the kind all those doctors wear."

"And a stethoscope? Did he have one of those?"

"Maybe, maybe not." Eleanor shrugged. "I don't remember."

"What did he look like?"

"Oh, for heaven's sake, Joanna! I already told you. I only saw the man for a minute. What does it matter?"

"It matters a great deal, Mother," Joanna insisted firmly. "Try to tell me what he looked like. I've got to know."

"All right. He wasn't very tall, and a little on the heavyset side. He looked like a Mexican to me. Dark hair, wavy dark hair."

"Glasses?"

"No, but brown eyes. Definitely brown eyes."

"Anything else?"

"Lots of gold in his teeth. You know, gold crowns. You don't often see that kind of dental work in a man that young."

"How young?"

"Forty, maybe even forty-five. It's hard to judge men's ages. I don't understand what's going on. Why are you asking me all these questions?"

"Mother," Joanna said, "there's a good chance that man wasn't a doctor at all, that he was just pretending to be one to gain access to Andy's room. He may have gone in there and given Andy something."

Eleanor's eyes widened. "Like poison or something? You're not saying that he killed Andy, are you? You mean I was actually carrying on a conversation with a murderer?"

"All I'm saying is if someone from the Tucson Police Department calls and asks you about this, tell them exactly what you told me."

"Oh, I will. I certainly will." Suddenly Eleanor

stood up and started toward the door, moving with a whole new vigor and sense of purpose.

"And, Mother," Joanna added, before Eleanor made it all the way out of the room. "It might be better if you didn't talk to anyone else about this, unless it's someone in an official capacity."

"Of course not," Eleanor agreed emphatically. "I wouldn't think of it."

Joanna shook her head as she watched her mother walk away. Cautioning Eleanor Lathrop not to gossip was almost as good as telling her not to breathe.

With her mother gone, Joanna quickly finished clearing off the top surface of her desk, then she stood up and went to Milo's door. Apparently lost in thought, he sat with his back to his desk, staring out the window. At sixty-three, Milo Davis was completely bald. Only the very top of his perpetually sunburned head was visible over the top of his executive chair.

Joanna announced herself by tapping lightly on the door frame, then she stepped over the threshold into his office, pulling the door shut behind her. When he swiveled around to face her, Milo Davis's usually engaging grin was missing.

"Hello, Joanna," he said somberly. "Sit down."

She eased herself into one of the two client chairs in front of his desk. "Please don't say you didn't expect to see me today," Joanna began. "Three people have already given me that same line. I just stopped by long enough to complete those three underwriting memos."

Milo nodded. "Thanks for taking care of them.

You're absolutely right. They shouldn't have been left hanging for a whole week. Chances are I wouldn't have remembered them, either. I'm so used to you taking care of those kinds of details that I just don't think about them anymore."

For a moment he examined her face. "How are you doing, really?" he asked.

"Really?" Joanna shrugged uncomfortably and bit her lower lip. "Okay, I guess. It's all so sudden."

Milo nodded. "It's going to be hard as hell, Joanna," he said kindly. "And it's going to take time. This is a terrible tragedy, not just for you and Jenny, but for the whole town. Feelings are running high. Don't be surprised if folks choose up sides and throw stones."

"What do you mean?"

"It's times like this when you find out who your friends really are, Joanna, and I want you to know you can count on me. Is there anything I personally can do?"

She looked him squarely in the eye. "There is, Milo. Tell me what's going on. I was here when Adam York came out of your office. What was he doing here? What did he want? Was he asking you about Andy's and my insurance?"

Milo Davis frowned. "Not really, although I guess that was part of it. I didn't tell him much, but I'll have to eventually. He threatened to come back with a court order to examine my records, and my guess is he'll make good on it."

"What kind of records?"

"Payroll. Sales records. He wanted me to tell

him exactly how much you make, to the penny. He asked about both of you, but it seemed to me he was actually more interested in you than he was in Andy."

"Why me? Did he say?"

"I tried to press him on that, but he got real cagey about then." Milo's face was shadowed with concern. "My guess is that he's looking for extra cash, unexplained expenditures that are over and above what you and Andy could afford on what you both make. My guess is that he thinks you're involved in some kind of drug dealing."

"That's preposterous!" Joanna exclaimed.

"That's exactly what I told him."

Joanna took a deep breath. "I caught up with him in the parking lot, and he gave me some kind of song and dance about insurance fraud. But the DEA's conducting a war on drugs not insurance fraud."

"Damn!" Milo thundered. He slammed one meaty fist down on his desk top so hard that his crystal paperweight—a prize from the home office for some long-forgotten sales campaign—skittered dangerously close to the edge. Joanna caught it and returned it to its rightful place.

For almost a minute the room was silent. "He's a formidable adversary, Joanna," Milo said at last. "Formidable and smooth. He's one of those operators who, once he decides to send someone up the river, probably has enough horses behind him to pull it off. I'd be very careful around him if I were you."

"I'll be careful, but I'm going to stop him."

"How?"

She shook her head. "I don't know yet. First I have to find out why he's after me. He must have something that makes him believe I'm involved. I just can't for the life of me think of what it might be."

"He did ask me about that ring of yours," Milo said thoughtfully. "The one Andy gave you for your anniversary."

"You knew about that?" Joanna asked in surprise.

"You're the only one in the office who didn't. Andy brought it by to show to me as soon as he picked it up from Hiram. He wanted us to put a jewelry rider on your homeowner's policy. He asked me to handle it personally so you wouldn't find out about it.

"I told York flat out that I thought he was barking up the wrong tree concentrating on that ring. If Andy'd had anything to hide, he would have been a hell of a lot more secretive about it than he was. As far as I can tell, he told everybody in town but you, and that's as it should be."

Hearing Milo talk about the ring brought it back to Joanna's attention. She twisted it on her finger. "What else did you tell him?" she asked.

"Mostly just general stuff. I told him Andy grew up in my Boy Scout troop, from the time he was a little shaver with a crew cut in Cubs right up through him getting his Eagle badge in high school. I told him Andy was one of the finest young men to ever grow up around these parts. I told him both of you were fine, upstanding, honest, hardworking young people."

"Tell me again exactly what he wanted to know about me."

"How long you've worked here, whether you've taken any long vacations, that kind of thing. I told him you've been here for over ten years now, since before Jennifer was born. In fact, I gave him a whole earful on that score, about how you worked for me and put both Andy and yourself through school at the same time. I told him how you used to commute back and forth to Tucson three days a week. I think he was impressed. He should have been.

"And just before he left, I told him that this smear campaign about you and Andy had by God better come to a stop. It's absolutely unconscionable."

Joanna's eyes brimmed with tears. "Thanks, Milo," she murmured.

"You don't have to thank me. It's the truth. I told York that, and I said the same thing to Jim Bob Brady when I ran into him at the post office at little while ago. These so-called experts from out of town come waltzing in here in their fancy cars and throw their weight around, when they don't know up from down about what's really going on. And it sounds to me . . . ."

There was a sudden urgent tapping on the door. Lisa stuck her head inside. "There's a phone call for you, Joanna. Nina Evans from school. I tried to handle it myself, but she insists on talking to you personally."

Joanna's heart went to her throat. "The principal? Is something the matter with Jenny?"

Lisa nodded reluctantly. "They've got her in the office. Something about fighting."

"Jenny? Fighting? That doesn't sound like her." Joanna hurried to the phone. "This is Joanna Brady."

Mrs. Evans sounded relieved. "I'm glad you're there. We need you to come take Jenny home right away. She's totally out of control, and I don't think she ought to be in school today."

"What's wrong?"

"She got in a fight at recess."

"Jenny never gets in fights."

"Tell that to the two boys she lit into on the playground." Mrs. Evans returned. "One of them had a bloody nose, and the other's at the emergency room right now because of his thumb. She dislocated it. I'm surprised she didn't pull it completely out of the socket."

"I'll be right there."

Joanna put down the phone and turned to see Milo Davis, standing in his doorway. "What's the matter?" he asked.

"It's Jenny," Joanna replied. "She seems to have dislocated a little boy's thumb in a fight at recess."

Suddenly Milo's broad face broke into its usual wide grin. "Sounds like a chip off the old block. That stunt with the thumb, it's the same one D. H. taught you way back when he wanted you to be able to tell the boys no and mean it, isn't it?"

Joanna nodded.

"And it's the same trick you pulled on Walter McFadden yesterday in the hospital."

"Who told you about that?"

"Walter did. This morning at breakfast over at Daisy's. That's one thing I appreciate about Walter. Good sense of humor. Likes a good joke even when it's on him."

"I've gotta go," Joanna said, heading for the door.

She left the office shaking her head. That was the problem with living in a small town. For good or ill, everybody knew far too much about everybody else's business.

Dislocated thumbs included.

THIRTEEN

ANGIE HANDED Tony his newspaper and coffee. She watched while he searched out the same article she had read earlier that morning. Now he devoured it with avid interest. While Tony was preoccupied, Angie slipped out of the room and the house. Out in the backyard, disregarding the mid-September chill, she slipped off her robe and eased her body into the pool. For twenty minutes she swam one lap after another in the long, narrow pool. The steady series of measured strokes worked some of the kinks out of both her muscles and her nerves. Physical exercise was the only way she knew to hold the terrible anxiety at bay.

At last, physically and mentally exhausted, she climbed out of the pool and lay in the sun to dry. She was lying there half-asleep when the phone rang. Forbidden to answer it under any circumstances, she fully expected Tony to pick it up, but he must have been in the shower. Instead, the answering machine clicked into action. For some unaccountable reason, Tony had left the speaker option switched on, allowing Angie to hear the tinny voice.

"Tony," a man said. "I've got to see you right away. The usual time and place. It's urgent. I think somebody saw you." That was all. The man hung up leaving no name or phone number. Obviously Tony would know who it was and how to get back to him.

Pulling on her robe, Angie hurried inside. She squeezed fresh grapefruit and put Tony's breakfast on the table. By the time he came out of the bedroom, she ducked past him into the bathroom.

"There's a message on the machine," she told him. "It must have come in while I was in the pool."

Filled with an uneasy and unexplained dread, Angie showered hurriedly. When she turned off the water, she could hear him rummaging around in the bedroom. Peering in the mirror, she saw that an open suitcase lay on the bed and he was heaving clothing into it. Her heart constricted. If he was packing up to go, that meant the money would go with him. She had missed her chance.

"Are you going someplace?" she asked innocently.

"We both are," he said. "I'm going out. While I'm gone, I want you to pack."

"Pack?" she repeated.

"What are you, stupid? Yes, I said pack."

"Where are we going?" she asked. "For how long?"

She looked at him, trying to assess his mood without giving away the fact that she knew something she shouldn't. He glowered at her. "A week. Ten days. Take enough clothes for that and leave the rest."

She might have believed him, if she hadn't heard the message, if she hadn't known something was wrong. No, they were leaving for good. What they left in the house would only delay anyone starting a serious search. It was a time-honored way of skipping town without sounding the alarm for someone who might not want you to leave or, more likely, someone who was hot on your trail. Angie had pulled it a time or two herself.

"How soon will you be back?"

It was an innocuous enough question, but it seemed to drive Tony into a rage. "How the hell should I know? An hour, three? All you have to do is be ready when I get here."

He stalked from the room without even bothering to hit her on his way past. She followed him, expecting that he'd go by the hallway closet and pick up the briefcase, but he didn't. He went out through the door that led to the garage, locking the deadbolt behind him.

With the bath towel still wrapped around her, she hurried on out to the patio and stood listening, straining to hear the garage door open and close and for the tires to crunch down to the end of the gravel driveway. When she was sure he was gone, she raced back into the house and wrenched open the door to the closet. The briefcase was still on the shelf. Hardly daring to hope, she lifted it down. It was still heavy. Maybe she wasn't too late. With trembling fingers, she worked the lock. It took three or four tries before the lid popped open. The money was still there. She could do it.

She had thought about running away often, fantasized about it for months. If she was ever going to do it, now was the time to put her plan into action. Later she would figure out exactly what to do after she was free of him, but for now, escape was the only issue. If she didn't get away clean before Tony came back to get her, she never would.

She closed the briefcase and hefted it with one hand. It was heavy, but manageable if she wasn't carrying much else. On legs frail as toothpicks she raced back down the hallway to the bedroom. There, forcing herself to calm down, she went into the bathroom for a self-inflicted make-over. She applied her makeup unerringly and pulled her blonde hair up on top of her head. Then she dressed in a stylish red silk jumpsuit with a matching hat which she wore at a rakish angle.

From the back corner of her closet, she pulled out one of the few possessions that had made the transition from L.A. to Tucson—an old, frayed straw beach bag. She emptied the money into it except for a selection of bills, large and small, which she wadded into her pocket. On top of the money, she loaded in two pairs of shorts and two nondescript shirts as well as her makeup kit and a pair of thongs. She zipped the bulging beach bag shut and placed it inside a medium-sized, tapestry-covered suitcase.

She took the briefcase back to the entryway closet and then walked through the living room. For only a moment, she felt a twinge of regret. Angie Kellogg had been a prisoner here, but it had been a very nice prison, a comfortable one, better than any place she had ever lived. At times, when Tony was out of town, she had almost been able to pretend it belonged to her. Now she found herself dreading leaving it. Prison or not, at least it was familiar. She was plunging off into the unknown.

It wasn't until then that she ventured into Tony's office. What she wanted was there, concealed in the top drawer of his locked desk. Using a nail file, she quickly picked the desk lock and removed the little black leather-bound notebook. It seemed like such a small thing, really, hardly worth the trouble, but Angie knew instinctively that the collection of names and addresses and phone numbers contained inside it was her one real insurance policy, her ticket out. She hadn't quite thought through how she could use such a thing, but she understood beyond a doubt that the notebook was valuable. Somewhere there was a willing buyer for such an item, and once she found him, Angie Kellogg could probably name her own price.

With the book safely in her purse, Angie made one last tour of the house to see if there was anything else she wanted to take. Picking up her worn copy of the *Field Guide to North American Birds*, she slipped that into her purse as well. For her personally, that was the single item in the entire house that she couldn't bear to leave behind.

Finally, after checking in the phone book, she called a cab. Taking a deep breath, she gave the dispatcher the address of a neighboring house, one three doors down the street which she had memorized for just such an emergency. When he asked where she was going, she told him the airport.

As Angie put down the phone, wild trembling once more reasserted itself. She had irretrievably set her plan into motion. If Tony came home and caught her now, she was doomed for sure.

Clutching the suitcase, her beach bag, and a pair of three-inch, red high heels, she hurried out of the house and dashed across the backyard to the place where the dry wash ran under the fence, the place where she had watched the rabbits come and go, and had envied them their freedom. She had measured the opening with her eyes, but she had never dared approach it with a measuring tape for fear Tony might catch her at it and guess her intentions.

Weak with relief, she found it was easy to push the suitcase, hat and high heels through the high spot under the fence. It was much harder to wiggle under it herself. Once, as she squirmed along, she felt the fabric of the pantsuit hang up on the bottom of the fence, but she managed to free herself without tearing the delicate cloth. At last she found herself standing upright outside the fence, brushing sand and gravel from her clothing and hair and laughing uproariously. She had done it. Despite all of Tony's deadbolts and alarms, despite all his precautions, Angie Kellogg was out. The funny little rabbits had shown her the way.

She may have been out, but she wasn't home free. Even now, Tony might drive up and catch her waiting beside the road. Resolutely, she crammed her feet into the heels and went tripping across the rough terrain that led to the road and to the house where she was supposed to meet the cab. If anyone saw her like this—and she hoped someone would—they were bound to remember. That was the whole idea. She wanted them to notice. It was important that Tony pick up the trail and follow her—up to a point.

Her feet were out of practice wearing high heels, and she was limping by the time she reached the place where she was supposed to wait. The cab arrived after what seemed like an eternity, although Angie's watch said that only twenty minutes had elapsed. "Where to, lady?" the driver asked.

She threw herself into the back seat, letting her head fall as far back as possible so her face was less visible to other cars they might meet along the way.

"The airport," she said. "As fast as possible. I've got a plane to catch."

The cab driver took her at her word and drove to Tucson International at breathtaking speeds. "What airline?" he asked her, as they approached the terminal.

"United," she said, hoping that was an airline that actually flew into Tucson. She breathed a sigh of relief when she saw the airline's sign in the departing passenger lane.

"Are you gonna check your luggage?" the cabby asked.

"No. There's not enough time."

Angie Kellogg had been to O'Hare once, and she had been a regular commuter to L.A.X. She was shocked at the size of Tucson International. It was tiny by comparison.

Once she was in the terminal, she scanned the listed departures. The next plane scheduled to depart was one for Denver that was due to leave within fifteen minutes. With an astonishingly expensive one-way ticket in hand, one she purchased with a fistful of Tony's cash, she headed for the gate. This was the part she wasn't quite sure about.

The flight was already boarding when she reached the gate. She hurried inside and found her seat. Then, when the flight attendants were coming down the aisles, closing the over-head luggage doors in preparation for departure, Angie suddenly leaped to her feet, grabbed her bags, and with one hand covering her mouth, bolted for the door. The flight attendants were only too happy to let her go. After all, the flight would be busy enough without taking along a passenger who was clearly too sick to fly before the plane ever left the runway. When she wasn't in the jetway by the scheduled departure time, the attendants didn't spend any time waiting for her, either.

Angie didn't stop running until she was inside the stall of the nearest ladies' restroom. There, she stripped out of the pantsuit and hat in favor of a T-shirt, shorts, and thongs. She pulled off the single identifying luggage tag and left the suitcase in the locked stall by slipping out under the door when the coast was clear. With her purse inside, she carried only the shabby beach bag. She shoved her former finery into the nearest trash container then set about letting down her hair and scrubbing off the deftly applied makeup.

Angie Kellogg had entered the restroom as a distinctively dressed fashion plate. She left twenty minutes later disguised as a dingy young woman who might have been a harried housewife or an impoverished graduate student. With the addition of a large pair of sunglasses, it was possible not even the cab driver who had picked her up would have recognized her, but Angie wasn't taking any chances.

She walked back out into the terminal and made her way to the arriving passenger entrance where a driver was loading a stack of luggage into a hotel van. The van said "Spanish Trail." Angie had no idea where or what the Spanish Trail was, but it was good enough to have a van, and that would take her away from the terminal.

"Room enough for one more?" she asked the driver. He was probably within months of being the same age as Angie herself, but he seemed much younger.

"You bet," he said, smiling and reaching for her bag. "For you we've got plenty of room."

Angie wasn't willing to let the beach bag out of her hand. "I'll carry this," she said. "It's not that heavy."

She climbed into the van and went all the way to the back where a businessman sat with his briefcase resting on his knees. In the middle seat sat an older couple. The man smiled appreciatively at Angie as she went by, and she returned the smile. When she sat down behind him, though, she saw him jump as his wife elbowed him viciously in the ribs and scolded him in an exaggerated whisper.

You're not working now, Angie reminded herself. Lay off. She was out of the life, and she wanted to stay that way.

As the van made its way through the city, Angie ignored her fellow passengers. Instead, she watched the scenery moving by outside the window, noticing how the desert seemed alive with vivid colors. The shadows on the pavement had hard, clear edges to them, and the silver-blue sky seemed to stretch away into forever. For the first time in her young life Angie Kellogg was free to go and do whatever she wanted.

The Spanish Trail Inn didn't offer luxury accommodations, but it was far better than some of the flea traps Angie had frequented in her time. At the front desk there was a bit of a hassle over her renting a room because she carried no ID, but eventually Angie was able to jump that hurdle, registering under her old name—Annie Beason. Desk clerks had never been impervious to her charms, and it pleased her to know they still weren't. After picking up a newspaper from the stand near the front door, Angie was happy to let the van driver, who doubled as the bellman, carry her suitcase upstairs to her room.

"Will you be staying long?" he asked.

"I don't know," Angie returned seriously. "If I like it well enough, I may just stay forever."

Alone in the room, Angie closed the curtains, kicked off her shoes, and lay down on the bed. Annie Beason. It was strange coming back to that old, nearly forgotten name. Just thinking about it caused a stirring of memory and speculation. What would have happened to Annie Beason, if she had stayed in Battle Creek and in school, Angie wondered. By now, she might even have been graduating from college, if she had gone to college, that is. But then again, with her parents, that probably wouldn't have been possible. According to her father, boys were the ones who needed college. For a man, that was the only sure way out of the blue-collar jungle, but why would a girl need an education?

Why indeed? There were times, over the years, when Angie Kellogg had imagined what she would do with her life if she ever managed to slip her leash and escape the watchful eyes of her various pimps. Now, though, the issue of starting over in a new life was no longer a matter of idle imagining. Sitting up, Angie switched on the bedside lamp and reached for the newspaper. With the air conditioner turned up full blast, she thumbed through the paper to the help wanted ads.

Within minutes it was clear that there were hardly any openings for someone with her lack of skills and background. The office jobs all required at least "60 wpm," and she couldn't type any wpm. There were jobs for experienced fashion merchandisers. She was experienced in merchandising, all right, but not in the fashion arena. One sounded promising. It called for a motivated self-starter interested in earning up to 40k per year. She was interested in earning that much money, but when she dialed the number listed in the ad, it turned out to be an automobile dealership. She hung up without saying hello. Angie Kellogg didn't know how to drive.

Chastened by the dawning realization of her limited employment options, Angie retrieved her beach bag from the closet, unloaded the money, and counted it carefully. Considering what she had spent getting here, including the cab fare, plane ticket, and hotel room, she must have started with exactly $50,000. That much money sounded like a nice round figure, and it seemed to be a fairly large sum, but Angie knew it wouldn't last forever.

She put the money back in the bag and dug out the notebook. It was soft, made of high-grade, leather cowhide, with Tony's initials—A V— embossed in gold in the lower right-hand corner. For a moment, she held it close to her face, breathing in the clean leather smell. She would have to make sure that particular item went to the highest possible bidder, whoever that person might be.

Angie put the notebook safely back in the bag along with the money. It was time to decide what to do. As soon as he realized she was gone, Tony would be out searching for her, and if the cops ever learned of her existence, they would be, too. And both Tony and the cops would be eager to lay hands on the money. The trick now was to find a way to immobilize Tony without getting caught herself. As she sat there thinking about it, Angie realized that there was probably only one person in the world who wanted Tony Vargas caught worse than she did, and that was Joanna Brady.

She picked up the phone and dialed information. While she waited for someone to answer, she almost hung up. It didn't seem likely to her that a cop would have his name and telephone number listed with information, but within seconds the mechanically reproduced voice was telling her "The number is . . . ."

Quickly she jotted it down then dialed it before she lost her courage. A woman answered. "Joanna?" Angie asked tentatively.

"No. This is her mother. Joanna isn't here right now. May I take a message?"

Angie put down the receiver without saying another word. Slightly discouraged, she slipped her shoes back on. Never trusting of hotel housekeeping folks, Angie took the beach bag with her when she went downstairs to have dinner. There in the restaurant, she treated herself royally at her first solitary dinner—prime rib, baked potato, and a wonderful salad. It was early, though, and the friendly waitress had plenty of time for idle chitchat.

"Here for a visit?" she asked.

Angie nodded. "My baby sister's getting married day after tomorrow," she said.

"Really. Whereabouts?"

"Some church up in the foothills," Angie answered evasively.

It was growing dark outside by the time Angie was delicately making her way through a fluted glass filled with scrumptious chocolate mousse. Only by accident did she happen to be looking out through the lobby door as Tony Vargas walked past on his way from the front desk heading for her room.

Angie was thunderstruck and terrified. Obviously, he hadn't fallen for the airplane ruse. Already he was here, hot on her trail. How had he done it?

The look on her face must have shown. The waitress hurried to her side. "Are you all right?"

With trembling hands, Angie groped in her purse for some money. She threw a twenty-dollar bill into the waitress's hand. "Keep the change," she stammered. "It's my boyfriend. He's come here looking for me. Please don't tell him which way I went. Is there a back way out of here?"

The waitress nodded. "Through the kitchen," she said. "This way."

FOURTEEN

WHILE ANGIE stumbled past the cooks in the kitchen, Tony Vargas stood outside the door to her hotel room. He had come home to an empty house less than an hour after Angie left there. After storming through the place looking for her, he turned to the hall closet and discovered that the money was missing. And the notebook as well.

That incredible bitch! After everything he had done for her, how could she do such a thing? How could she treat him this way? And whatever made her think she could possibly get away with it?

Since there was no soft flesh to pummel with his fists, no target present on which to vent his rage, Tony Vargas controlled it. Stifling his anger, he sat down at his desk and calmly made a few phone calls. For someone with his kind of connections, it was surprisingly easy for him to learn that a cab had come to this particular street if not to this exact address much earlier that afternoon.

The driver had picked up a fare and had taken her to the airport. Tony went to the airport as well. With little difficulty he learned that a woman matching Angie's description had purchased a one-way ticket to Denver.

Denver? Tony Vargas hadn't made it to the top of his profession by being stupid. As far as he knew, Angie Kellogg had no connections in Denver, none at all, so why would she go there? Further inquiry revealed that she had bolted off the plane moments before its scheduled departure, the tricky little bitch. Vargas congratulated himself on not falling for that old maneuver and busied himself with the hard, shoe-leather work of figuring out where she had gone instead.

It took several hours, but his careful search paid off when he talked to a cab driver who had seen someone who looked like Angie—girls that good-looking were few and far between—get into the Spanish Trail's hotel van.

He tapped lightly on the door to her room, hoping she wouldn't be smart enough to look through the peephole before opening it up, but there was no answer, no sound from inside. He knocked again, impatiently this time. He wanted to get to her and teach her a lesson she'd never forget, not necessarily here where other people might listen to the noises and object, but back home where there would be no interruptions.

When there was still no answer to his third knock, he shouldered his way inside. The room was empty. The light was on. The bed had been rumpled but not slept in. A newspaper lay in a heap beside the bed, but Angie wasn't there, and neither was his money.

Frustrated, he stood in the middle of the room and turned in a complete circle. The desk lamp was switched on. He went over and looked down at the stack of message paper. Sure enough, the faint impression of the number written on the missing top sheet was still visible to the naked eye. Gleefully, he pocketed the paper and rushed from the room. Moving at a fast jog, he headed back downstairs.

Through luck, determination, and perseverance, he had come this close to catching her. He wasn't about to give up now. And even if she escaped for the time being, he had that piece of paper in his pocket. He was almost sure that would at least give him a clue about where she was really going.

As Angie Kellogg darted through the steamy kitchen, she knew her life hung in the balance. She emerged in the poorly lit back parking lot next to a fetid Dumpster. At best, she had only a few minutes' lead. She was lucky someone hadn't sent him directly into the dining room after her. Once he located her room, it wouldn't take him long to guess that she hadn't left the hotel and was down eating dinner. After that it would be only a matter of minutes before he traced her to and through the restaurant. The waitress might not tell him, but someone else would.

Angie searched the parking lot for some avenue

of escape. Seeing none, she pounded her way around to the front of the building. The Spanish Trail sat on one side of the T at the end of South Fourth Avenue. It faced a short frontage road bordering the freeway. I-10's northbound lanes lay beyond a chain-link fence and down a steep embankment. Two blocks to the north was South Sixth and an overpass that would take her over the freeway. Angie ran that way.

She started across Fourth. Checking traffic as she ran, she noticed a noisily idling eighteen-wheeler parked along the street half a block or so back. In the dim glow of a street light she caught sight of a man out checking one of his tires. With one last panic-stricken glance back over her shoulder toward the hotel and without breaking her stride, Angie turned in that direction. She reached the truck just as he started to swing himself up into the open door of the cab.

"Please, mister," she shouted over the truck engine's uncompromising roar. "Give me a lift. My boyfriend's back there. If he catches me, he'll kill me."

Maybe the trucker believed her, maybe he didn't. After so many years on the road, one line sounds about as good as another, but for a change, the woman doing the asking was a real looker, and Dayton Smith didn't mind the company. "Sure, lady. Climb in. Which way are you going?"

Without answering, Angie Kellogg scrambled into the cab in front of him. "It doesn't matter," she said gasping for breath. "Let's just get the hell out of here."

Moving slowly and with maddening deliberation, the driver climbed up into the cab beside her, switched on the lights, released the emergency brake, and eased the truck into gear. Angie watched out the window until the truck's blue, United Van Lines trailer completely obscured her view of the hotel.

"Do you see anybody back there?" she asked, as the truck rounded the corner.

"Not so far," the driver returned.

In a moment, Angie, too, could see back to the hotel's well-lit entrance. No one appeared there before the truck slid out of view completely at the next intersection. "I think we made it," she breathed in relief, settling back into the truck.

The driver looked at Angie appreciatively in the glow of the streetlights as they waited for the light to change and allow them onto the South Sixth overpass. "You were kidding, right?"

"About what?"

"About him killing you. I mean, people say that all the time, but it's usually a joke."

"This is no joke," Angie answered. "I mean it. He really would kill me."

"Well," the driver said with a shake of his head. "Seems to me, that would be a real shame. My name's Dayton Smith, by the way, and as of right now, we're headed toward El Paso."

As he spoke, the light changed and the truck slid into motion. A few moments later, they were heading down a southbound on ramp.

Angie tried to look, but she couldn't see in the

mirror herself. "Is there anybody back there?" she asked nervously.

The driver shook his head. "Nope. Not a soul. Is that all right with you?"

"Is what all right with me?"

"El Paso. You still didn't say where you're going."

"El Paso's fine. As long as Tony's not around, one place is as good as another."

"That's his name, Tony?"

Angie nodded.

"What'd you do that got him so pissed off?"

"I ran away," she answered. "I knew that when he came home, he was going to beat me up, so I ran away."

"Did he do that often? Beat you up, I mean."

"Pretty often."

The truck driver squirmed in his seat as though the very idea made him uncomfortable. "I'm sorry," he said.

Startled by the tone of his voice, Angie Kellogg looked at the pudgy, balding man with some surprise. It sounded for all the world as though he meant it. He looked as though he meant it as well.

"Me too," she agreed. "I'm real sorry."

They had driven only a few miles when Dayton Smith turned on his directional signal and started down an exit. There were lights on one side of the freeway, but none on the other. Except for the area right at the exit, they seemed to be in the middle of nowhere. Angie's apprehensions rose. She was a city girl, a born street fighter, but alone in the desert, she would be no match for this heavyset man if he ever set out to harm her. Once the truck stopped, if he came after her, she'd have to run like hell.

"Hope you don't mind," the driver said apologetically. "This is a truck stop. It's called the Triple T, and it's the last decent place for a long ways. I usually stop here for a slice of deep-dish apple pie and to get my thermos filled. Care for a cup of coffee?"

Weak with relief, Angie Kellogg burst out laughing. "I'd love a cup of coffee."

When she climbed down from the cab, the desert air was chilly on her bare arms. She shivered and Dayton Smith noticed. "Don't you have a jacket or sweater?" he asked.

She shook her head. "I left all my clothes back at the hotel."

Smith climbed back into the cab, rummaged behind the seat, and emerged holding a blue nylon jacket with the United Van Lines logo and Dayton Smith's name emblazoned on the front.

"Here," he said, "put this on. It may be five sizes too big, but it'll be warm."

Inside the truck stop, they were ushered into the front section reserved for professional drivers. Several of the other truckers seemed to recognize Dayton Smith. Seeing Angie with him, they greeted him with knowing winks and conspiratorial nods, all of which made Dayton blush to the roots of his receding hairline.

"Where are you going, really?" he asked.

Angie had been thinking about the map she

had looked at in her room hours earlier. The vague outlines of a plan were beginning to take shape in her head.

"How far is Bisbee from here?"

Smith shrugged his shoulders. "A hundred miles, give or take. What's in Bisbee?"

The waitress brought coffee. Dayton and Angie sat for a few moments, studying each other across the counter top. For her part, Angie was evaluating Dayton Smith according to the only scale she knew—the scale of how to get men to do what she wanted. There was money in her bag, but she never even considered offering to pay him with that. Angie was accustomed to dealing with the world with only one form of currency—her body. Old habits are hard to break.

She figured Dayton Smith would be easy pickings. Men like him were usually duck soup in the hands of a real professional. They usually wanted whores to do the things their uptight wives at home wouldn't agree to on a bet, and Angie Kellogg didn't mind kinky up to a point. She knew instinctively that there was no way Dayton Smith would be as physically mean to her as Tony Vargas had been, but there was always a certain risk with straitlaced, upright men. They could be unpredictable at times. More than one prostitute had had her brains bashed in by fine, upstanding men caught in the throes of unreasoning remorse after happily screwing their brains out.

Then, too, there was always the possibility that Dayton Smith wasn't at all what he seemed. Maybe he was really a cutthroat in disguise, one who would strangle her with his bare hands and disappear with the contents of her beach bag.

"Why Bisbee?" he prodded a second time.

Angie fought her way out of her reverie. "I have friends there," she said. "They'd probably let me stay with them."

"Call 'em up," Dayton Smith said. "Have 'em meet us in Benson. That's on my way and it's only fifty miles or so from Bisbee."

"I can't call," she lied. "They don't have a phone."

"Oh," he said.

His pie came, topped with a scoop of vanilla ice cream. He cleaned his plate enthusiastically while the gold band on his wedding ring winked at Angie in the warm fluorescent light.

"You're sure you're not hungry?" he asked. "I'd be glad to buy if you're short of cash."

"I'm not hungry," she said. "Thanks."

When he finished eating and after the waitress brought his filled thermos, they headed out into the parking lot. There were dozens of other trucks scattered throughout the lot, and Angie realized at once that now was the time to act. If Dayton Smith went bad on her afterward, at least here she'd have a chance to call for help.

He took her hand and helped her up into the tall cab where she settled in the middle of the seat instead of staying on the far side. When Dayton climbed into the cab beside her, she didn't move away. Instead, she reached out and put one suggestive hand on his upper thigh.

"Would you give me a ride to Bisbee, even if

it's out of your way?" she asked. "I could make it worth your while."

He reached down and took her hand. Firmly, he removed it from his leg and placed it back in her lap. "Move on over," he ordered. "You're in the way of the gearshift."

For the first time in all the years since she left home, Angie Kellogg felt herself blushing. His turn down had made her feel like the two-bit whore she was.

"You mean you don't want me?" she asked incredulously. "I'm good. I'm real good."

Dayton Smith slammed the truck into gear. "I'll just bet you are," he muttered.

"Let me out then," she squawked at him. "I'll go back and find someone else, someone who does want me. I'm going to Bisbee, dammit, and I'm going there tonight."

"Settle down," he barked. "I didn't say I wouldn't take you, did I? Hell, girl, you don't have to fuck me just to get a ride. It's not that far, only fifty miles or so out of my way."

Angie Kellogg wasn't used to openhanded kindness. She blinked in surprise. "You mean you'll take me for nothing?"

"Not for nothing," he countered. "I like your company, and you look like you could use a little help. I've got a daughter of my own who's about your age. So sit back and relax. Next stop is Bisbee, okay?"

Grateful and mystified both, Angie Kellogg settled back into the seat while the huge truck rumbled swiftly through the starlit desert night.

"What's your name?" Dayton Smith asked eventually.

"Tammy Sue Ferris," Angie said without missing a beat.

"Well, Tammy Sue," Dayton Smith said, settling back into the driver's seat. "Tell me where you're from."

"California."

"How old are you?"

"Twenty-three."

His face had an otherworldly glow in the greenish reflected light from the dashboard. As Angie answered his question, she felt almost as though he weren't real, as though she was talking to some kind of ghost.

"And what do you do for a living?"

Somehow she no longer felt like lying. "Do you really want to know?"

"Yes."

"I'm a whore," she said unexpectedly, surprising herself. "I have been for ten years." If she thought her answer would shock him, it didn't.

"And this Tony character was your pimp?"

"More or less," she replied. "Tony doesn't fit into any definite categories."

"You're away from him now," Dayton Smith said forcefully. "Stay that way. Get a job, get married, have children. In other words, have a real life."

"I don't know how," she said in a small voice. "I don't know how to do anything else."

"I wasn't born driving this truck, honey," he told her. "I took lessons, got myself a license.

That's what you're gonna have to do, too. Go back to school and learn typing or shorthand or whatever it is they teach girls nowadays. Maybe even computers, but at twenty-three, you've got your whole life to live. Don't screw it up."

After that, they didn't talk much more. At ten o'clock, Dayton Smith helped Tammy Sue Ferris check into the last available room in Bisbee's Copper Queen Hotel. When she stepped away from the desk, Dayton was standing halfway across the lobby with both hands stuffed in his hip pockets. He smiled at her.

"You'll do fine," he said. "I'm sure of it." He reached out, took one of her hands in both of his, and shook it warmly. "You be careful of the people you meet and keep the jacket. You need it worse than I do. If you ever turn up in Dallas give me a call. I'm in the book. The wife and I would like to have you over for dinner. She cooks a mean fried chicken."

With that, Dayton Smith turned and shambled out the door, leaving Angie Kellogg alone. Riding up to the third floor in the creaking elevator, she found herself wiping tears from her eyes. Dayton Smith was probably the nicest man she had ever met, but she couldn't understand why watching him walk out the door and down the steps had made her cry.

FIFTEEN

THE LONG, polished hardwood hallway of Greenway School still smelled exactly the way Joanna remembered it—dusty and lightly perfumed with hints of sweaty-haired children and overripe sack-lunch fruit. Worried about her daughter, Joanna walked swiftly toward the principal's office. As far as Joanna knew, this was the first time Jennifer Brady had been sent to the office for even the smallest infraction.

Nina Evans, the five-foot-nothing fireplug of a woman who was the school principal, met Joanna in the hallway. "I'm glad I was finally able to locate you," Mrs. Evans said irritably. "I didn't expect to find you at work today."

School principals had never been high on Joanna's list of favorite people, and Nina Evans was no exception. Joanna found herself bridling at the apparent rebuke in the woman's tone of voice.

"What seems to be the problem?" Joanna asked.

"Oh, you know how children are," Nina Evans said quickly. "I'm sure the boys didn't mean any harm."

"Which boys?"

"Jeffrey Block and Gordon Smith. According to what I've been able to learn, they evidently started it. Regardless of provocation, though, I simply can't allow students to resort to violence. That's no way to teach problem-solving. It's a short step from that kind of youthful behavior to starting wars."

Joanna was in no mood to hear an educational lecture on the political correctness of nonviolence. "What provocation?" she asked.

"No doubt Jennifer was feeling sensitive," the principal continued, "and I don't blame her. It's always difficult for children to be in school after a traumatic event like this. In fact, I'm not at all sure it was wise of you to send her to school today, considering what she's been through."

With her arms folded smugly across her chest, Nina Evans stood looking up at Joanna. There could be no mistaking her attitude of reproach and disapproval. The two boys may have started the day's altercation, but Nina Evans was holding Jennifer primarily responsible. Somehow, the fight was all Jennifer's fault, and, through Jenny, ultimately Joanna's.

Battling to control her temper, Joanna felt her jaws tighten and her face grow hot. "I didn't *send* Jenny to school today," she said firmly. "She came today of her own accord, because she wanted to.

In fact, she begged me to let her. Now, tell me exactly what happened."

Nina Evans replied with a noncommittal shrug. "At morning recess the boys were evidently teasing Jennifer and saying naughty things to her. She waited until noon and then punched them out when they were all three supposed to be on their way to the lunchroom."

"Both of them at once?"

The principal nodded. "That's what I've been told. Jeffrey's parents took him over to the dispensary to have his thumb looked after. Gordon Smith's mother picked him up about half an hour ago. Jennifer's the only one still here. I didn't want to send her home with someone else without first having a chance to discuss the situation with you in person. It's far too serious."

"I want to see her," Joanna said. "Where is she?"

"In my office. You can go on in if you want."

In the fifteen years since Joanna's eighth grade graduation, the Greenway School principal's office had altered very little. Personnel changes had occurred because elementary school principals come and go, but the same gray metal desk still sat in one corner of the room with the same old-fashioned wooden bench sitting across from it.

On the wall above the bench hung the familiar, but now much more faded, print of George Washington. The print, too, was exactly the same. Joanna remembered the cornerwise crack in the glass. She remembered how she had sat on the wooden bench herself and craned her neck to stare up at George Washington's face on that long-ago spring afternoon when her fourth-grade teacher, Mrs. Fennessy, had sentenced Joanna Lathrop to a day in the principal's office.

Jennifer glanced up nervously as the door opened. Seeing Joanna, she dropped her eyes and stared at her shoes. "I'm sorry," she said at once.

Joanna walked across the room and sat down on the bench beside her daughter. "Tell me about it," she said quietly. "What did those boys say to you?"

For a time the child sat with her head lowered and didn't answer. Joanna watched as a fat, heavy tear squeezed out of the corner of Jennifer's eye and coursed down her freckled cheek before dripping silently off her chin.

"Tell me," Joanna insisted.

Jennifer bit her lower lip, a gesture Joanna recognized as being very like one of her own.

"Do I have to say it?" the child whispered.

"Yes."

"They said Daddy was a crook," Jennifer choked out at last. "I told them they'd better take it back, but they wouldn't, so I beat 'em up. Daddy wasn't even a black hat, Mom, so why would they say such a thing?"

Joanna draped one arm across Jennifer's small shoulder and pulled the child close. Milo had told her the town was choosing up sides. Now she understood far better what he had meant.

Unfortunately, some of the first stones thrown had landed squarely on Jenny.

"What happened to Daddy didn't just happen to us, you know," Joanna said slowly, groping for words. "We're not the only people who are trying to figure out what happened and what's going to happen next. Everyone else is, too. Those boys were probably just repeating things they had heard at home from their own parents."

"You mean everybody's talking about it? About us?"

"Pretty much."

"And they all think Daddy was a crook?"

It was hard enough for Joanna to cope with the flurry of disturbing rumors. It hurt her even more to realize that Jennifer would have to deal with them at her own level as well. She swallowed the lump in her throat.

"Not everyone believes that, Jenny," she answered quietly, "but some people do. You've got to try to not let it bother you."

"But it does," Jennifer whispered fiercely. "It really does. It made me so mad, I wanted to knock Jeffrey Block's teeth out. All I did was hurt his thumb."

For a moment they sat side by side without speaking. "But it isn't true, is it?" Jennifer asked forlornly, with a trace of doubt leaking into her questioning voice.

Joanna squeezed her daughter's shoulders and held her tight. "No," she declared, "but it's up to us to prove it."

"Can we?"

Joanna shook her head. "I don't know if we can for sure, but we're certainly going to try."

"And then those boys will have to take it back, won't they."

There was a tough ferocity about Jennifer's loyalty to her father that made Joanna smile in spite of herself. "Yes," she agreed. "They'll have to take it back, and so will Adam York."

"Who's he?" Jenny asked.

"Never mind," Joanna answered.

"Will I have to stay here in the office until the bell rings?"

"No. You're coming with me. I have lots of errands to run, and you'll have to come along." Joanna handed her daughter a tissue. "Here," she said. "Blow your nose and dry your face. Did I ever tell you about the time I got sent to this very same principal's office?"

Jennifer blew her nose with a bellowing, foghorn effect that belied her small size. "You?" she asked disbelievingly. "I didn't think you ever got in trouble."

"It was in the fourth grade," Joanna told her. "During arithmetic. The boy behind me was new to town. He didn't stay long, but I never forgot his name—Kasamir Moulter. He copied all the answers off my paper. Mrs. Fennessy gave us both F's."

"How come she did that? If he copied your paper, he should have been the one in trouble, not you."

"She thought I gave him the answers."

"Even though it wasn't true?"

"Even though."

"Couldn't you prove it was his fault?"

"How? It was his word against mine. Mrs. Fennessy believed him."

"That wasn't fair," Jennifer protested.

"Two against one isn't fair," Joanna countered.

Jennifer looked up at her mother for a long time before nodding in understanding. "I'm ready to go," she said. "Will I come back to school tomorrow?"

Joanna shook her head. "I don't think so. Mrs. Evans doesn't want you in school for a day or two. She seems to think you're a menace to society."

For the first time, a hint of a smile played around the corners of Jennifer's mouth. "I am, too," the child said stoutly. "I did it just the way you taught me. You would of been proud of me."

"Would *have*," Joanna corrected. "Come on."

They found Nina Evans in the hall. "I'll take Jenny home for now," Joanna told the principal. "And I may keep her home tomorrow as well, but when she comes back, you might spread the word that if anyone else hassles her about what happened, they'll end up dealing with me."

Holding Jenny by the hand, the two of them marched down the hall. "Where are we going?" Jenny asked in a small voice.

"Did you eat any lunch?"

"No."

"First we'll go by Daisy's and split a pasty," Joanna said. "Then we'll start working our way through the list."

Daisy Maxwell, the original owner of Daisy's Cafe, had been retired for twenty years and dead for ten, but the restaurant she started still reflected her initial menu as well as the ethnic diversity of Bisbee's mining camp origins when miners from all over the world had flocked to Arizona's copper strikes. Along with the usual standbys of hamburgers and sandwiches, Mexican food, Cornish pasties and Hungarian goulash were featured as daily specials at least once a week. Grits were usually available, upon request, with breakfast.

Between the two of them, Joanna and Jenny wiped out most of the huge platter-filling pasty with its flaky outside crust and steaming beef-vegetable stew interior. Afterward they made a series of stops—at the mortuary, the florist, Marianne and Jeff's—making sure the arrangements were solidified for the funeral on Saturday afternoon. They went by the Sheriff's Department and spoke briefly with Dick Voland and Ken Galloway, both of whom readily agreed to be pallbearers. Joanna had wanted to speak to Walter McFadden about doing a eulogy, but they were told he had taken the afternoon off and had gone home early.

Everywhere they went—in shops and offices, on the street—people stopped them to murmur their condolences and to ask if there was anything they could do to help.

"Most people are pretty nice, aren't they?" Jennifer commented after the fifth such encounter.

Joanna nodded. "Most of them are," she agreed.

It was late in the afternoon before they finally stopped by First Merchant's Bank. Sandra Henning, the manager, was working with one of the tellers when Joanna and Jenny walked into the lobby. She looked up when they came through the door and then looked away again, but not before Joanna noticed a deep crimson flush creep across Sandy's stolid features.

That's odd, Joanna thought. She and Sandy weren't especially good friends, but they had lunched together on occasion and had worked on various school and civic committees together. Joanna led Jenny over to the two chairs in front of Sandy's desk.

"We'll sit here and wait for Mrs. Henning to finish," Joanna said.

It was several minutes before Sandy Henning came out from behind the tellers' line. She approached her desk uneasily, nervously smoothing her skirt and putting her hands in and out of the pocket on her fuchsia blazer.

"I'm so sorry about Andy," Sandra Henning said as she eased her heavy bulk into her chair. "And the thing about the DEA, too. We had to give them the information they asked for, Joanna. They had a court order. My hands were tied."

"Don't worry about it, Sandy. I know how those things work, but I did want to talk to you, one bureaucrat to another, to see if you can help me figure out where that ninety-five-hundred-dollar deposit came from."

At once the flush returned, and the color of Sandra Henning's face soon matched the brilliant hue of her blazer. "You mean nobody's told you?"

"Told me what?" Joanna asked.

Sandy's eyes swung away from Joanna's face to that of the little girl who was sitting in the chair with her legs swinging free listening to their conversation.

"Why don't you go ask one of the tellers for a Candy Kiss, Jenny?" Sandra Henning suggested. "Peggy, the lady down at the end of the counter, usually has a dish of them at her window."

Jenny looked to her mother for permission. Joanna nodded. "Go ahead," she said, "then go on outside and wait in the car. I'll be there in a minute."

With a shrug, Jenny did as she was told. Both women watched until the child was safely out the door then Joanna turned back to Sandra Henning. "What is it?" she asked. "What aren't you telling me?"

Sandy ducked her chin into her ample breast. "When Andy brought the money in, Joanna, he had a woman with him."

"What woman?"

"I don't know. He never introduced us. Well, that's not exactly true. He told me her name was Cora."

"Cora who? I don't know any Coras."

"He didn't tell me her last name, Joanna, but . . . ."

"But what?"

"I thought somebody else would tell you," Sandy said miserably. "I didn't want to have to be the one."

A light came on in Joanna's head. "But you told Ernie Carpenter about her, didn't you."

"Yes. And the man from the DEA as well. They asked."

"Well, now I'm asking," Joanna said, fighting to stay calm. "Maybe you'd better tell me, too."

"She wasn't a nice woman, Joanna," Sandra said quickly. "And not from around here, either. We don't see women like that very often."

"Like what?"

"You know, short leather skirt, boots, big hair, lots of makeup. She was laughing and hanging on Andy, whispering in his ear."

"They came to the bank together?"

"No. Actually, she was here first. She drove up and waited outside. He came a few minutes later. When he got out of his truck, she hurried over to him, gave him a big hug and a kiss and the envelope."

"What envelope?"

"The one with the money in it. The ninety-five-hundred dollars in cash. They counted it all out together, right here at my desk."

Joanna took a deep breath. "I see," she said. Sandra Henning waited, as though she had no idea what else to say.

"You say she drove up to the bank?"

"That's right. In one of those cute little Geo Storms, one of the turquoise blue ones. It had Nevada plates. I noticed that much."

"How old was she?"

"Not very old. Early twenties."

Joanna nodded. She felt queasy. The lunchtime pasty that had tasted so good hours earlier was a leaden mass in her gut, groaning and wanting to rebel. It was all too much. Everywhere she turned, someone new was accusing Andy of something else. Could any of it be true? She had thought she knew Andy as well as she knew herself, but all around her were people telling her she was a fool, and blind besides.

A storm of tears came bubbling to the surface. Joanna wanted to duck out of the bank before they struck. She didn't want to make a scene in public, any more so than she already had.

"Cora," she murmured, standing up. "Cora from Nevada, a girl with no last name."

Sandra met Joanna's eyes. "I'm sorry," she said.

"Believe me," Joanna returned, stumbling blindly away from the desk. "So am I."

Outside, Jenny was waiting in the car. "What's the matter?" she asked, as soon as she saw her mother's face. "Did Mrs. Henning say something mean?"

"I'm okay," Joanna said.

"But you're crying."

"I'm all right."

Jenny settled back in the car seat and crossed her arms. "Are we going home now?"

Joanna gripped the steering wheel and

thought about the question. Finally she shook her head.

"No," she said. "We have to make one more stop along the way."

"Where?" Jenny asked.

"Before we go home, we're going to go see Sheriff McFadden."

✺ SIXTEEN

WALTER McFADDEN'S house sat at the top end of Arizona Street, less than half a block from where town gave way to open desert. Usually he wouldn't have been there at five o'clock, but Dick Voland had already told Joanna that today McFadden had gone home early. When the Eagle turned onto Cole Avenue, his Toyota was parked in the carport behind the redbrick house.

As Joanna stopped near the back gate, she saw a bright yellow Frisbee come sailing off the shaded front porch and fly along just under the eaves of the house. At almost the same instant, a dog launched itself into the yard from three steps up. The dog chased the Frisbee and overtook it halfway across the back yard, leaping up and snagging it out of the air in a graceful, four-foot arch. With the Frisbee clenched tightly in its teeth, the dog tore back toward the front porch.

"Good catch," Jennifer commented. "I wish Sadie did that good with Frisbees."

"*Well*," Joanna corrected without thinking. "I wish Sadie did that *well*."

Walter McFadden stood up and sauntered off the porch to greet them, carrying an open can of Coors, a Silver Bullet, in one hand. He walked over to the gate with the dog at his heels.

"Howdy, Joanna, Jennifer. What can I do for you?"

"Can we come in?"

"Sure."

Stories about the sheriff's ugly mutt were legend in Bisbee. The dog, an improbable mixture of half-golden retriever/half-pit bull, had been destined for destruction before Walter McFadden had come to the animal's rescue. As a puppy, the dog had belonged to an escaped felon who was discovered and apprehended while living in an abandoned shack up in Old Bisbee. When the man was picked up and sent back where he belonged, the dog, a starveling pup, was sentenced to death and would have been put down if the sheriff, newly widowed and terribly lonely, hadn't intervened.

"Are you sure the dog will be okay?" Joanna asked.

The sheriff grinned. "He's fine. You don't have to worry about Tigger. He may be ugly as all sin, but he's real sweet-tempered."

Jennifer, following her mother into the yard, peered critically at the dog and made a face. "He *is* kinda ugly, isn't he?" she agreed. "Why'd you name him Tigger? After Winnie the Pooh?"

Walter McFadden smiled and nodded. "That's right. How'd you know?"

"When I was little," Jenny said, "*Winnie the Pooh* used to be one of my favorite books."

"It still is one of mine," McFadden said, "although I don't have anyone to read it to now that my own little girl is all grown up."

"What kind of dog is it?"

"I always say that Tigger's a pit bull wearing a golden retriever suit," McFadden replied seriously. "I'm not sure which was which, but either his daddy or his mama must've been a pit bull. That's where he gets the square nose and that godawful circle around his one eye. The rest of him's pretty much golden retriever. I don't know where the jumping comes from."

"Can I try throwing for him?" Jennifer asked.

McFadden glanced quizzically in Joanna's direction, and he picked up on her almost imperceptible nod. "You bet," he said. "As much as you like. There isn't anything Tigger likes better than having someone new throw the Frisbee for him. You do that, while I talk to your mama."

McFadden handed the tooth-pocked Frisbee over to Jennifer and then led Joanna up onto the porch and motioned her into the old-fashioned metal lawn chair. "Care for a beer?" he asked. Joanna shook her head. "Is something the matter?"

"I found out where the money came from," she said. "Sandra Henning down at the bank told me."

"The woman, you mean?"

Joanna nodded, and McFadden took a long

swig of beer. "Doesn't mean much," he said. "Question is, where'd she get it? The money, that is. And nobody's been able to track her down so far, either."

"Why didn't you tell me about her?" Joanna asked.

"Fact of the matter is, I didn't know about her myself, not until I got back home yesterday afternoon. The DEA guys turned most of that stuff up when they got the court order to look at your account. My department's been playing catch-up ball ever since."

"So everybody in town knew about her but me," Joanna commented bitterly.

"Maybe there's not that much to know," McFadden suggested.

"And maybe there is," Joanna returned. "What's Ernie Carpenter after really, Walter? Andy's dead. It's bad enough to lose him, but is anyone interested in finding out who killed him or are they just interested in dragging his name through the mud? If Andy was having an affair, it hurts, hurts like hell to find out about it now. I would a whole lot rather not have known about it at all, but to my way of thinking, that doesn't matter nearly as much as who killed Andy and why. Those preliminary autopsy results . . ."

"Whoa, down, Joanna. Let me tell you something. You're hurting. We all understand that. As Andy's widow and as D. H.'s daughter, everybody's trying to give you the benefit of the doubt, but . . ."

"Benefit of the doubt?" Joanna exploded. "What does that mean?"

"Joanna, no matter who you are, you can't go around the system. I don't know how you laid hands on those preliminary autopsy results—that's Pima County's problem not mine—but you've got no business interfering with this investigation. You're going to have to step back and let people like Ernie Carpenter do his job."

"Ernie Carpenter isn't investigating Andy's death nearly as much as he's investigating what he believes Andy did wrong. There's a big difference."

"See there?" McFadden pointed out. "You're doing it again."

"And what about Adam York? What's his game?"

"Federal drug enforcement's no game," McFadden reasoned seriously. "If you think it is, you're crazy."

"Right, but if Adam York's busy waging a war on drugs, why's he nosing around town asking questions about me? This morning when I tackled him about it, he gave me some lame song and dance about possible insurance fraud, but as you just told me, that's not his job. So what's going on? There must be some reason he's after me specifically, and I want to know what it is."

McFadden shook his head. "Look, Joanna, theoretically, York and I are on the same side of the fence, but the Feds are under no obligation to share their information with us, and they usually don't. If York's asking questions, he must have some good reason for doing so, but if you personally have done nothing wrong—and I can't imagine you have—then I'm sure it'll all get straightened out eventually."

"Me personally," she repeated, plucking the two most significant words out of McFadden's sentence and focusing in on those. "You said if I personally have done nothing wrong. What about Andy?"

McFadden raised the can of Coors and finished it. He dropped the empty can into a paper bag beside his chair while his somber gaze met and held hers. "I don't want to break your heart, Joanna," he answered quietly. "That's the last thing I want to do, but I'm not so sure about Andy."

Joanna's chest constricted. "And you won't tell me anything more than that?"

"Can't, Joanna. Sorry."

"There's a big difference between can't and won't, Sheriff McFadden," she said, standing up abruptly. "Come on, Jenny. We've got to go."

Jennifer dashed up onto the porch and handed the Frisbee over to Walter McFadden. "Tigger's one neat dog," she said. "Hey, Mom. Can we get a Frisbee so I can teach Sadie to catch like that?"

"We can try," Joanna said. With a curt nod over her shoulder to Walter McFadden, she led Jennifer back to the car. The sheriff watched them go, shaking his head as he did so.

"Come on, Tigger," McFadden said to the dog. "Let's go see about rustling us up some dinner." The two of them, man and dog, walked into the house together.

Joanna headed home. Jennifer, who had been laughing and running with the dog, was suddenly quiet and subdued. "Are you mad at me?" she asked.

"Mad? Why would I be mad at you?"

"I was having so much fun, I almost forgot," Jenny said.

Joanna shook her head. "No. If I'm mad at anybody, I'm angry with myself."

"Why?"

"For not taking my own advice. I told you not to let what people say bother you, but I'm letting it bother me."

"Sheriff McFadden said something?"

"Everybody's entitled to his opinion," Joanna said tightly.

When they pulled into the yard at the ranch, with Sadie running laps around the Eagle, Eleanor Lathrop's Chrysler was parked by the gate, and Clayton Rhodes' Ford pickup was down near the barn.

"You go on inside and let Grandma Lathrop know we're home," Joanna said. "I'll go see if Mr. Rhodes needs any help."

As she opened the car door, she heard the troublesome pump in the corral stock tank cough, wheeze, and finally catch. When she reached the corral, she found the ten head of cattle were already munching hay, while a steady stream of water flowed into the metal stock tank. Clayton Rhodes was standing there watching the tank fill when she came up behind him. He jumped when she spoke.

"You and Jim Bob don't have to do this, you know," Joanna said.

Clayton Rhodes turned around to face her, cupping one hand to his ear. "What's that?" he asked. Without teeth he spoke with a decided lisp.

"You don't have to do this," Joanna repeated loudly enough to compensate for both the old man's deafness and the noisy rattle of the pump's motor. "You and Jim Bob are doing way too much. Jenny and I can handle the chores ourselves, really."

Clayton shrugged his bony, stooped shoulders. "It's no trouble," he said. "I figure I could just as well be doing something useful of an evening."

He turned back to the pump and studied the flow of water into the metal tank. "Didn't put in much gas," he added. "Should fill up the tank without running over. You won't have to come back out and turn it off. I started the pump out in the back pasture on my way over."

"Thank you," Joanna said. "I had forgotten about that one completely."

"Other people haven't," Clayton Rhodes observed with a frown. "From the footprints and tire tracks around it, I'd say somebody's been having a regular convention."

"Hunters?" Joanna asked.

He shrugged. "Maybe, but why hunters would be out tramping around in street shoes is more than I can figure."

Street shoes? Joanna wondered.

Finished with the chores, Clayton Rhodes wiped his hands on his worn overalls and started toward his truck with Joanna and Sadie both trailing along behind.

"I don't understand," Joanna said. "Why would someone in street shoes be out in the middle of my back pasture?"

"Kinda makes you wonder, don't it," Clayton nodded.

Suddenly Joanna remembered to mind her manners. "Won't you come on up to the house for coffee. If there isn't any ready, it'll only take a few minutes."

"Nope, but thank you just the same," he said, as they reached Clayton's ancient Ford with its much-replaced wooden bed. "Think I'll head on home." For a moment he stood with one hand on the door handle as if trying to reach some decision. "You know," he said finally, "I worry about you and Jenny being out here all by yourselves."

"We're all right," Joanna said. "For right now, there are plenty of people in and out. Besides, we've got the dog."

Clayton looked down at the hound and shook his head. "This worthless old thing?" he said disparagingly, ruffling the dog's floppy ears. "Why, she'd as soon lick somebody to death as bite 'em. She didn't even bother to bark at me when I showed up here a while ago.

"I'm serious as hell about this, Joanna. With that there new prison down at Douglas and with wetbacks coming across the line the way they do nowadays, a person needs to be ready to defend himself. Maybe some folks are buying off on that suicide story, but it seems to me as if somebody was mad enough at Andy to take a shot at him. And now we've got a pack of strangers hanging out in your back pasture. Nosiree, I don't like this a-tall. You got yourself a gun there in the house?"

Joanna shook her head. "Andy had guns, two of them, but we don't have either one of them anymore."

The old man nodded sagely. "That's about what I figured. You do know how to use one, don't you?"

She nodded. "My dad taught me when I was a girl. It's like riding a bicycle, you never really forget the basics, but maintaining any kind of accuracy takes constant practice, and I haven't fired a gun in years."

"Then I'd get myself some practice if I were you."

With that, Clayton Rhodes wrenched open the creaking door and reached across the truck's threadbare seat. He opened the glove box and pulled out a small bundle which he handed over to Joanna. From the feel and the shape of the surprisingly heavy package, Joanna knew she was holding a gun wrapped in an old pillowcase.

"Here," he said. "This here used to be Molly's before she up and died on me. I never liked leaving her out here all by herself, either, so she kept this in her apron pocket just in case. Never had to use it, thank God, but we had some good laughs about her bein' a pistol packin' mama."

He reached in his pocket and pulled out a box of ammunition. "You'll need this along with it."

Joanna started to object, to say that she couldn't

possibly accept it, but the old man silenced her with a wave of his hand. "Humor a butt-sprung old man, will you?" he said, climbing up into the truck. "You hang onto it as a personal favor to me."

He turned the key in the ignition and the old engine coughed to life, then he looked back at Joanna. "Deal?" he said through the permanently opened window.

She nodded. "Deal," she said, "but only as a personal favor."

As he drove out of the yard, Joanna realized that in all the years she had known Clayton Rhodes, this was the most she had ever heard him say. Only heartfelt concern for her and for Jenny had propelled him beyond his usual reticence. She headed for the house both humbled and grateful.

Joanna Brady was riding an emotional roller coaster. Inside the house her gratitude toward Clayton Rhodes quickly turned to irritation with her mother. Just inside the back door she stumbled and almost fell over Eleanor Lathrop's pride and joy, her Rainbow Water Vacuum, which was parked there in the dark. The kitchen was a shambles. Every inch of countertop was covered with the contents of Joanna's kitchen cupboards. Eleanor herself, perched precariously on a stepladder, was busily scrubbing down the topmost shelf directly over the sink.

"Mother, what in the world are you doing?" Joanna demanded.

"Cleaning the cupboards," Eleanor replied. "You know as well as I do that the ladies from the church are going to be all over this house for the next few days, and I don't believe this kitchen has been properly cleaned in years."

The phone rang just then and Jenny leaped to answer it. "Brady residence," she said. "Jennifer speaking." After that she said nothing, and a moment later, she hung up the phone.

"Who was that?" Joanna asked.

"I dunno," Jenny answered with a shrug. "Whoever it was hung up."

"Don't pay any attention to the phone," Eleanor said. "It's been ringing all day. Come over here now, Jenny, and start handing up things from that stack over there. That way I won't have to climb up and down so much."

Jenny hurried to help. Shaking her head, Joanna headed for the bedroom, still holding Clayton Rhodes's pillowcase-wrapped gift.

"Where are you going?" Eleanor asked after her.

"I think I'll go to bed," Joanna answered. "As far as I'm concerned, if the ladies from church want to come to my house and examine the kitchen cupboards with a fine-toothed comb, they deserve whatever they find."

SEVENTEEN

STILL CRADLING Clayton's unexpected package as well as her purse, Joanna slammed the bedroom door shut behind her and then stood leaning against it, hoping to cool off. She was amazed by the intensity of the anger she felt toward her mother. She wanted to go back out into the kitchen and scream at Eleanor to get down off the damn ladder and leave her kitchen the hell alone. But that had never been her way where Eleanor was concerned. Instead, following her father's lead, Joanna had always avoided direct confrontation, going around her mother rather than through her.

To be fair, the rules of the game were somehow changing, and Eleanor had yet to figure it out. In the past, right or wrong, Joanna would have swallowed her anger, returned to the kitchen, and helped her mother put things right. But tonight she didn't. If she had wanted the kitchen cleaned right then, she would have done it herself. Instead, Joanna Brady had other concerns.

Like coming to terms with this room, for instance. Twice now, she had raced through it as though the space was full of demons. Now, she needed to find a way to stand here and look around at the familiar furniture, seeing it as a stranger might and trying to decide if it was, indeed, still the same place it had been two days earlier. Now, with Andy gone and the rest of the world conspiring to rob her of his memory, she wondered if there would ever again be a time when she could be comfortable in this room. Or would she forever feel as alien in this place as she did in this instant?

Walking haltingly, like someone uncertain of footing on rough terrain, she made her way to the bed and sat down on the edge of it. Gingerly she began unwrapping the layers of faded pillow case surrounding the gun until at last a Colt .44, naked and deadly, lay in her hand. Remembering Molly Rhodes's voluminous aprons, Joanna could see how the gun would easily have fit into one of her pockets. And living out on the Rhodes place through the years, Joanna could see how Molly might have needed to take a shot at an occasional chicken-stealing coyote or at a rattlesnake that might choose a spot under the clothesline to sun itself.

But Clayton Rhodes wasn't thinking about either rattlesnakes or coyotes when he gave the gun to Joanna. And now that she was holding the weapon in her hand, Joanna wasn't either.

For a few moments it was almost as though Joanna's father himself was standing there in the room with her, reminding her of all the old lessons—how she should never handle a gun of any kind without knowing for sure whether or not it was clean and loaded. She checked. The answer was yes as far as the cleaning was concerned, but the weapon wasn't loaded.

Joanna loaded it herself, taking bullets from the box Clayton Rhodes had given her, then she hefted the .44 in her hand, gauging the weight of it, fingering the grip, remembering the importance of balance and the necessity of the two-handed, spread-footed stance her father had taught her. And she recalled how he'd patiently worked with her, teaching her how to handle recoils—to expect them and flow with them rather than fighting against them.

In remembering D.H. Lathrop's lessons, Joanna missed him anew with almost the same force as she missed Andy. A wave of grief that was also physical pain washed over her.

Resolutely, she stood up and tried to think of something else. Clayton was right. She would have to practice in order to regain some of her former proficiency, and that wouldn't be tonight. Probably not in the next few days, either. In the meantime, she needed a safe place to keep the weapon, a place where Jenny wouldn't accidentally stumble across it.

Kicking off her shoes, Joanna got up and padded over to Andy's rolltop desk. It was locked, but the key was in its usual place in the pencil cup on top. Joanna turned the key in the lock and shoved up the lid, thinking the small drawer at the back of the desk would be a good place to keep the gun, but when she opened the drawer and tried to put the gun inside, it wouldn't fit. Something else was in the way.

Exploring the drawer with her fingers, she drew out a small address book. It was Andy's—she recognized it instantly—but she was surprised to find it there. He usually kept it with him, and she would have expected it to be with the packet of personal effects she had been given in the hospital.

She put the gun and the extra ammunition in the drawer in place of the address book, closed the top of the desk, locked it, and put the key in the pocket of her jeans. Then, taking the book with her, she started to return to the bed.

On the way, a piece of paper slipped out from between the leaves and fluttered to the floor. Joanna scooped it up and unfolded a piece of rich, creamy white stationery with the Ritz Carlton logo emblazoned across the top. In the upper right-hand corner the date was listed as September 10.

Dear Andy,

I've been thinking about your offer. It's hard to get to be my age and realize you've been a first-class asshole all your life. Thanks for giving me a chance to make the world a better place, if not for me, than maybe for my kids and yours.

There are a few things I need to straighten out before

I can leave here. When I get those cleared up, I can meet
you in Nogales or Tijuana, wherever, and we'll go to
York then. Together we ought to be able to make it stick.
I guess I don't need to tell you that if anybody finds out
about this I'm a dead man. And so are you.

Be careful,
Lefty

Joanna read the note through several times in
rapid succession. Each time another little piece of
understanding slipped into place. Without telling
her, Andy had been in touch with Lefty O'Toole.
Why had he been so secretive? She had thought
that she and Andy had a good marriage, that they
had shared almost everything, yet here was another proof, almost as damning as Sandra Henning's, that Andrew Brady's sharing with his wife
had been woefully incomplete.

In the note, Lefty had warned Andy to keep
whatever was going on between them a secret.
Andy had certainly complied with that request, at
least as far as Joanna was concerned, she thought
angrily, but someone else must have guessed or
found out. Whoever that person was, Joanna was
convinced he was responsible not only for Lefty
O'Toole's murder but for Andy's as well.

It wasn't until the third reading that the name
"York" registered. Andy and Lefty had been planning to go to York. That would have to be Adam
York with the DEA. Who else could it be? But
why, Joanna wondered. Were they going to tell
York something about someone else, or was York
himself the source of the problem? The DEA

agent's attitude toward her had been a puzzle from the start. What could explain his antagonistic suspicion of her when Joanna knew she had done nothing wrong?

Sitting there, she tried to remember what had happened in each of her encounters with the man. What if he was the one who was actually behind all this and his questions about possible insurance fraud were only a device to throw suspicion in someone else's direction. He had been with her at the Arizona Inn at the exact moment of Andy's death, but he had also been lurking around the waiting room off and on all morning. It would have been simple for him to alert an accomplice that Joanna was leaving for a time, thus clearing the field for the real killer, the man with the gold in his teeth.

So what did an ordinary citizen do if they suspected a federal peace officer of wrongdoing? Did you go to the local authorities, someone you knew and trusted like Walter McFadden or Ken Galloway? Did you tell them what you knew and hand over your evidence, or did you go looking for someone else, someone further up the DEA chain of command and report your suspicions to him?

Regardless, Joanna knew there was nothing to be done about it tonight, and until she chose a definite course of action, it was important that Lefty's letter, a vital piece of evidence, be kept in a safe place. Her first instinct was to lock it away in the desk drawer along with the gun, but that seemed too obvious. Besides, even with the desk locked, she wasn't sure it would be safe from Eleanor's prying eyes. In the end, she took the only reasonable course of action and placed the carefully folded paper in the side pocket of her purse.

Then, she picked up the address book once more. No matter how much it hurt, it was time to find out. For years she and Andy had argued over his unorthodox filing system. They kept separate address books because he, without a truly bureaucratic mentality, kept things filed under first names rather than last. With trembling fingers, she turned to the "C" page, and there it was, at the very bottom, the single name Cora with two phone numbers, both with Nevada prefixes.

Fighting back tears, Joanna copied them onto a note pad she carried in her purse. She was just fastening the purse shut when the phone on Andy's night stand rang shrilly. The noise startled her, and she jumped involuntarily before picking up the receiver. "Hello."

There was a slight pause. For a moment Joanna thought it might be a crank call with no one on the line, but then a woman spoke. "Joanna Brady?" the caller asked hesitantly, speaking in little more than an exaggerated whisper.

Joanna strained to hear, trying to recognize if the voice belonged to someone she knew. "Yes," she answered. "This is Joanna. Who's this?"

"You don't know me," the woman replied, "but I need to talk to you about your husband."

Instantly Joanna's whole body went on full red alert. Here was a strange woman who wanted to talk to her about Andy. The voice sounded young and undeniably sexy. Could this be the same woman Sandra Henning had told her about, the one who had come into the bank, hanging on Andy's arm and counting out all that money?

"What's your name?" Joanna asked.

"Tammy Sue Ferris," the woman said, this time with no hesitation whatsoever.

Sure it is, Joanna thought, but if this was Cora, it was probably better not to accuse her of lying, not just yet. "What about my husband?" Joanna asked guardedly.

"I believe I know who killed him," Tammy Sue answered.

Not trusting her ears, Joanna couldn't stifle a sharp intake of breath. "What did you say?"

"I said I think I know who killed him," Tammy Sue replied. "In the hospital."

A storm of questions roared through Joanna's head. "Who is it?" she demanded. "And how do you know about that? Do you work in the hospital? Are you a nurse? Have you talked to the police?"

"I can't go to the police."

"Why not?"

"Because if I do and Tony finds out, he'll kill me."

"Who's Tony?"

"The man who killed your husband, Mrs. Brady."

The killer had a name and this woman knew it? "Tell me who he is. How do you know he did it? Did you see him?"

"Not personally, but I know he did."

"You've got to talk to the police," Joanna insisted. "Where are you? I'll call and have someone come talk to you right away."

"No, please. No police!" the woman returned. "If you call the police, I'll disappear. You'll never hear from me again."

Joanna was afraid the woman would hang up on her. Even if the woman on the phone was the same woman who had been with Andy in the bank, she was also the first person, other than Joanna herself, to insist that Andy had been murdered. She couldn't afford to frighten Tammy Sue Ferris away.

"What do you want then?" Joanna asked. "Why are you calling me?"

"I want you to help me work a deal."

"What kind of deal?"

"With the cops."

"What kind of deal?" Joanna repeated.

"I have something of Tony's," Tammy Sue explained. "Something important that the cops are going to want."

"That's simple enough," Joanna said. "Why don't you just take it to them?"

"I want them to buy it. I need the money."

"Wait a minute. You're saying you have an important piece of evidence, and you expect to be paid for it?"

Although the young woman seemed to be speaking in dead earnest, for some reason Joanna found the whole scheme wildly implausible. Maybe Tammy Sue Ferris was a mental case.

"This is Cochise County," Joanna said, "a place where budget cuts are the order of the day. I don't think you'll find many likely buyers."

"Oh, they'll buy, all right. Once they know what I have, somebody will be willing to buy, but I have to stay alive long enough to negotiate. That's where you come in."

"Me?" Joanna echoed. "What does any of this have to do with me?"

Tammy Sue Ferris took a deep breath. "I already told you. Tony's a killer. If you can put him in prison for killing your husband, then he won't be able to come after me. That's the only way I'll be safe, if Tony's dead or in jail."

Suddenly Joanna could see that it had everything to do with her. If the woman was telling the truth, if this Tony really was Andy's killer, then there was nothing she wanted in the world more than putting him in jail. But how could she determine whether or not Tammy Sue was on the level?

"If you didn't see him do it, how do you know this Tony's responsible?" Joanna asked.

"He got paid for it," Tammy Sue answered. "And when he saw on the news that your husband wasn't dead . . ."

"He got paid to do it? Why would someone pay to have Andy killed?"

"That's what Tony does for a living. He kills people."

"But who does he work for?"

"I don't know, not for sure. Drug dealers most likely. They've got plenty of money."

Joanna's mind was awhirl. Some things in Tammy Sue's wild story made sense in a way that Joanna desperately wanted to believe, and yet, she couldn't escape the sense that she was somehow being suckered. She wanted to be smart about all this, to walk into whatever it was with her eyes open.

"Are you going to tell me about the money?" she asked.

This time the sharp but unmistakable intake of breath was on the other end of the line. "How do you know about that?" Tammy Sue managed. "Maybe I was wrong. I never should have called."

Joanna could tell that her lucky guess about the money was causing Tammy Sue to lose heart. "Please, don't hang up," Joanna put in quickly. "Maybe we can work something out. Where are you?"

"But if you know about the money . . ."

"That doesn't matter. You're right about me. There's nothing I want more than putting this Tony, whoever he is, away. Where are you? Let me come see you. We'll talk. I do know people around here. If you can help me find Andy's killer, if you can help me put him where he belongs, then I should be able to help you with your problem."

"And you won't tell the cops about me?" There was something vulnerable and plaintive in the way Tammy Sue asked the question, something that reminded Joanna of junior-high-school-aged girls, telling one another tales of adolescent love and swearing each other to secrecy.

"Were you ever a Girl Scout?" Joanna asked.

"No."

"I was, and I give you my word of honor that I won't tell the cops. Where are you?"

"At a place called the Copper Queen."

"You're here in Bisbee? Why didn't you say so? I can be there in ten minutes. What room are you in?"

"Four twelve."

Joanna didn't want to give Tammy Sue time to change her mind. "Stay right there," she said. "I'll be up as soon as I can."

She slammed down the phone and leaped to retrieve her shoes. Just then there was a tentative knock on the door, and Jenny popped her head in.

"Grandma Lathrop wants to know if you want some cocoa and toast."

"No. I've got to go back uptown."

"Can I go along?"

"No. I'll have to go alone. Ask Grandma if she can stay here with you until I get back."

"I'll go ask."

Jenny disappeared while Joanna tracked down another denim jacket, a new fleece-lined one that she had given Andy the previous Christmas. Andy wouldn't be wearing it now, but putting it on made him feel closer to her somehow in a way Joanna couldn't explain. She picked up her purse then stood in the middle of the room, looking at the desk, torn by indecision.

All her life she had lived in a small town, insulated from some of the harsher realities of life in other places. But this past week violence had touched her life and home. Her husband was dead, murdered, and she was going to meet with a woman, a stranger, who claimed to know Andy's killer. Clayton Rhodes had given her a gift, a weapon, an equalizer, that could help deal with any number of unexpected contingencies. Could she, in good conscience, afford to thumb her nose at his gift?

Shaking her head, Joanna went back to the desk, extracting the key from her pocket as she did so. Once the loaded .44 was out of the drawer, she stuck it into her purse which, in its own way, was every bit as spacious as Molly Rhodes's apron pockets. She was well aware that she had no permit to carry a concealed weapon, but, considering the circumstances, that was a risk she'd have to take.

The gun had no more than disappeared into the purse when Jenny returned. "Grandma says she'll stay, but she wants to know where you're going."

The house was one of the old Sears Craftsman homes, a Somerset, that had come West by rail in the early teens—precut and premilled, ready to be assembled. By current standards, the two-bedroom house may have been small, but it did have both a front and back door. The front door was seldom used on a day-to-day basis, but it was available. Maybe the rules between Joanna and her mother still hadn't changed all that much.

Slinging the purse over her shoulder, Joanna headed for the front door with Jenny trailing along behind. "But you still haven't said where you're going," the child objected.

Joanna stopped, leaned down, and pulled Jenny to her in a brief but fierce hug. "Tell Grandma that I'm going out to see a man about a white horse."

Jenny frowned. "You're going to buy a horse in the middle of the night?"

Joanna laughed. "Not really. It's what Grandma always used to tell me when I was your age."

"But what does it mean?"

"It means that where I'm going is none of Grandma's business."

With that, Joanna hurried out of the house. Sadie tried to follow, but Joanna shooed the dog back inside and locked the door. Not wanting to waste a moment, she ran to the Eagle, jumped in, and gunned the motor when she started it.

The absolute irony of the situation wasn't lost on Joanna Brady. Here she was, racing off to a clandestine meeting with a woman who had most likely been her husband's mistress. Yet she was rushing to get there and feeling good about it besides, because Joanna knew instinctively that Tammy Sue Ferris or whatever her name was had the information Joanna wanted. At last she was going to get some straight answers, and answers, no matter how hurtful, were better than the terrible pain of not knowing, of being left totally in the dark.

Rushing to her appointment, Joanna was in such a single-minded hurry that she didn't even notice the car with its lights off that was parked a dozen yards or so north of the ranch turnoff on High Lonesome Road. And when she paused briefly at the stop sign at Grace's Corner, if she saw the vehicle pull out of High Lonesome Road onto Double Adobe Road behind her to come racing after her, she didn't pay any attention.

She didn't notice, but she should have.

EIGHTEEN

MELVIN WILLIAMS, although a relative new-comer to Bisbee, had made it his business to meet as many of the townsfolk as possible. He and his wife, recent purchasers of the Copper Queen Hotel, were able to eke out a respectable enough living from that aging dowager of a place only so long as they did most of the work themselves. Melvin handled the front desk, Kitty managed the restaurant, and Gary, their son, ran the bar.

As a result, Melvin himself was manning the front desk when Joanna Brady, after lucking into a parking spot directly out front, came dashing into the hotel. Instead of waiting for the creaking elevator, Joanna headed directly for the red-carpeted stairway.

"Can I help you?" Melvin asked.

Joanna shook her head. "I'm on my way to see Tammy Sue Ferris," she said, hurrying by. "I already know the room number."

Halfway up the first flight of stairs, however, she looked up in time to see Adam York coming down. She stopped short, trying to conceal her confusion and dismay.

It shouldn't have been that much of a shock to find him there. After all, if the DEA agent was in town conducting an investigation, there weren't many places to stay in Bisbee besides the Copper Queen. But how could she maintain any kind of composure in the presence of someone she was almost sure was a crooked cop and possibly a murderer besides? Not only that, if Tammy Sue became aware of York's presence and identity, she might erroneously assume Joanna had brought him with her.

"Hello, Joanna," York said, cordially enough. "Were you looking for me?"

Hardly, she thought. "An old friend came to town for the funeral," she replied, thinking on her feet as she continued on up the stairs. "With all the other people around, this may be the only chance we'll have to visit by ourselves."

"You still haven't told me how you happened to know about those autopsy results," York said from behind her. "Do you maintain some kind of private information line in and out of the sheriff's department?"

Joanna stopped at the landing, turned, and looked back down at him. "Why are you so interested in my sources, Mr. York? It seems to me you should be more interested in finding the person or persons who murdered my husband."

Melvin Williams looked around uneasily,

hoping none of his other guests would overhear. This kind of conversation wasn't exactly good for business.

Adam York, however, didn't seem the least concerned if the whole world listened in. "I understand your mother may have something to tell us in that regard, but I haven't been able to locate her. You wouldn't happen to know where we could find her, now would you?"

Joanna studied the man, trying to assess who and what he was. What kind of secret, three-way connection had linked this man to Andy and Lefty O'Toole? Two of the three were now dead. Was Adam York also marked for death, or was he the one behind the other killings?

Either way, Joanna didn't much want him anywhere near either Eleanor or Jenny. To keep from betraying her real feelings, Joanna dredged up her best flip answer.

"I'm not my mother's keeper," she said frostily and stalked on up the stairs. She listened for footsteps on the stairway behind her, but Adam York made no move to follow.

With no further difficulty, Joanna located room 412 and knocked on the door. From inside she could hear the blare of a television set. She knocked again, more firmly this time. Finally the door opened to reveal a pajama-clad middle-aged man holding a can of beer in his hand.

"Whadyya want?" he demanded.

Joanna had not expected to find a man in room 412. "I'm looking for Tammy Sue Ferris," she stammered uncertainly. "I was told this was her room."

"You were told wrong," the man returned. "Nobody named Tammy's in here," and he slammed the door shut in Joanna's face.

Stunned, she stepped back and stood in the corridor, staring at the closed door in front of her, unsure how to proceed. Had she remembered the number wrong? And if she went back down to the desk to check with Melvin Williams, would Adam York still be in the lobby?

Discouraged, she started back down the hall. As she walked past the next room, the door swung open and a woman stepped into the corridor. "Joanna?" Tammy Sue Ferris asked.

Joanna nodded, and Tammy pulled her inside the room. "I was afraid someone might follow you."

With the makeup scrubbed off her face and with her mane of blonde hair pulled back in a ponytail, Tammy Sue's looks didn't at all match up to Joanna's expectations. Sandra Henning had described a regular harlot. This girl looked like someone barely out of high school.

"No one followed me," Joanna said, "but I ran into a DEA agent on the stairs. Adam York. Did you know he was here?"

The golden tan on the woman's face faded to white. "You didn't tell him, did you?"

"No, I didn't tell him," Joanna said. "I gave you my word."

"What's he doing here then?"

"Actually, he's trying to find a way to pin my husband's murder on me. You and I both know that's not true, so let's get down to business. If you want me to help work this deal, as you put it, then I've got to know what's going on."

Joanna paused, gathering her courage before she asked the next question, dreading what the answer might be. "First of all," she said slowly, deliberately, "tell me how you knew Andy."

The woman Joanna knew as Tammy Sue Ferris looked genuinely thunderstruck. "Your husband? I didn't know him at all."

Joanna crossed her arms and stared implacably at the other woman. "Look, Cora. Let's get one thing straight. If you want me to help you, you're going to have to tell me the truth."

"Cora?" Angie echoed. "Who's Cora?"

"And while we're at it, you'd better tell me about the money as well. I want to know where it came from. Otherwise, I'm walking out the door this very minute and calling Adam York. You can work out your own deal with the DEA."

Tammy Sue Ferris/Angie Kellogg sank down on the edge of the bed. This wasn't the way she'd expected the meeting to go. She had thought Joanna Brady would be eager to work with her, that the woman would be eternally grateful for any kind of help in nailing her husband's killer. But with the DEA lurking downstairs, and with Tony Vargas out there somewhere looking for her, Angie had to decide. Should she trust this angry red-haired woman standing there in front of the door asking crazy questions, or should she push her out of the way, bolt from the room, run like hell, and hope for the best?

"Where'd the money come from?" Joanna was asking.

Feeling trapped, Angie decided to quit lying. There didn't seem to be any point. "I stole it," she answered. "I stole it from Tony."

"I thought you told me you had evidence, something the cops wanted."

Angie shrugged. "I have that, too, but I took the money because I need a way to live until I can get a job. If I go to the cops and they find out about it, they'll take the money away from me the same as Tony would."

"How much did you steal?"

"Fifty thousand, I guess."

"And why'd you give ten of that to Andy?"

"I didn't give any of it to your husband," Angie insisted forcefully. "How many times do I have to tell you? I never even met the man. How could I give him money? Besides, I didn't steal it until after he was already dead."

Joanna felt as though she was spinning in dizzying circles. None of this made sense. She took a step closer to the other woman. "Your name's not really Tammy Sue anybody, is it! Tell me your real name, lady, or I swear I'm out of here."

"Angie," the woman replied. "My name's Angie Kellogg."

"Not Cora?"

"Not Cora."

"And where does this Angie Kellogg live?" Joanna asked sarcastically.

"Tucson," Angie replied dully. "At least that's where I lived until yesterday."

"You're lying. You live somewhere in Nevada."

"I'm not. I swear to God. What good would it do me to lie? I've been in Nevada only once in my whole life. Tony took me to Vegas. Wait, I'll show you."

Angie got up, dragged a beach bag out of the closet, and rummaged through it until she found a small, worn book, a bird book. Opening it, she took out what appeared to be a postcard. It was a picture of two people standing in front of a horseshoe-shaped container, the inside back wall of which was covered with money.

"That's us," Angie said, "Tony and me. We had our picture taken in Vegas at the Horseshoe."

She handed the picture over, and Joanna studied it. It was sepia rather than color or black and white, so colors were difficult to judge, but the man standing next to Angie matched Eleanor's description—middle-aged, verging on heavy set, Hispanic features, and dark wavy hair.

"May I keep this?" Joanna asked.

Angie shrugged. "I don't care. Anyway," she continued, "I lived with Tony in Tucson until yesterday. And now he's after me. He would have caught me, too, if some nice truck driver hadn't given me a ride here."

"And why exactly did you come here? Was it just to see me?"

Angie nodded and hung her head. "I thought we could figure out a way to catch him," she said.

"A way to put him in jail without me having to testify against him. And I have this book. Sort of a record book that Tony kept. I thought maybe somebody would want to buy it."

"Show it to me," Joanna ordered.

"I can't," Angie replied.

"Why not?"

"I left it in the safe at the desk, just in case," Angie answered.

"I'll go down and pick it up," Joanna offered.

Angie shook her head. "No, I told him to only give it to me. If you didn't tell the DEA guy about me, he won't know who I am." She got up and reached for the beach bag.

"Oh, no," Joanna said. "Leave that here. It's my only guarantee that you'll come back."

TONY VARGAS had run into a stumbling block. Following the speeding Eagle into town, he was primarily concerned with closing the distance between the two vehicles as he came around a long, flat curve by an immense, dark hole in the ground that was actually an abandoned open-pit copper mine. Tony Vargas had no way of knowing that Bisbee locals had good reason for calling this particular stretch of Highway 80 "Citation Avenue," but he was about to find out.

"Fuck!" Vargas exclaimed, pounding the steering wheel when the flashing red lights came on behind him. As a professional, Vargas prided himself with never returning to the scene of the crime, but Angie's theft of his precious book had forced him to break his own cardinal rule.

Panicked, it was all he could do to keep from reaching for the gun he wore. He wanted to pull it out and blow the interfering son of a bitch of a cop off the face of the earth. Instead, cursing his own bad luck, he forced himself to calm down.

He fumbled in the glove compartment to find the registration and extracted his driver's license from his wallet. Tony Vargas had an unending supply of fake IDs, but he always kept one legitimate set of papers. It took effort to make sure the current set of paperwork—driver's license, registration, and insurance forms—all checked out. Traffic cops liked it better that way.

"Evening, sir," the young police officer said cheerfully. "Mind stepping out of the car?"

Vargas did as he was told. Concealing his inner turmoil, he did his best to remain affably contrite while the cop checked both his ID and registration. As far as the police officer was concerned, he, too, was equally agreeable.

"You were doing eight over, so I'm only issuing a warning," the cop said, as he set about writing it up. "We like tourists around here, and we want you to come back, but we also want our visitors to drive safely."

"You're absolutely right, officer," Tony Vargas replied with real conviction. "I won't let it happen again."

When the cop finished, Tony thanked him politely then took his copy of the citation back to the car. Only when his hand was out of sight behind the car seat did he wad the paper up into a furious ball and drop it on the floorboard. Then, signaling carefully, and obeying every posted speed limit sign, Tony Vargas went hunting for Joanna Brady.

He drove into the mouth of Tombstone Canyon, the bottom of what's known as Old Bisbee. He followed the winding main drag up through the commercial district until businesses gave way to a residential area with houses stacked improbably on either side of the narrow street.

She has to be here somewhere, Tony thought grimly. The town isn't that big.

A mile or so up the narrow canyon Vargas came to a wide spot in the road where he was able to make a careful U-turn around what was evidently some kind of statue. Then he retraced his route back down through the business district a second time. Most of the way the commercial area was no more than a single street wide. But this time, as he drove back down, he came to a level spot in the road where he could see another small section of business off to the left.

Expecting to have to comb the entire area, he turned left and left again. And there it was—Joanna Brady's Eagle—parked directly in front of a place called the Copper Queen Hotel.

"Hot damn!" The Copper Queen was just the kind of place Angie would go, thinking she'd blend into the woodwork. What did that stupid bitch know about life in small towns?

Vargas had to drive on up the one-way street

before he, too, was able to find a parking place. Once parked, he didn't approach the hotel directly. Instead, using a roundabout route, he made his way down to a small city park. From there he tried to reconnoiter. The hotel seemed to be three or four stories high with the entrance and lobby situated between a dining room on one side and a bar on the other. At ten o'clock there were only one or two late diners left in the dining room, but the bar seemed to be serving a modest crowd.

The bar offered the best opportunity of getting inside the hotel without anyone noticing him, so Vargas gravitated in that direction. He had no way of knowing for sure if Joanna Brady was actually inside the hotel, and there was only a remote chance that Angie was there as well. The trick now was to find out for sure.

After years of leading a charmed existence, Tony felt his life unraveling. He had meant to use that damn book as his own ace in the hole if he and his employers ever came to an unexpected and disagreeable parting of the ways. Now, though, by its very existence, the book had blown up in his face. If he didn't get it back before it fell into the wrong hands, then Tony's very survival would be in question. The cartel had plenty of other high-priced, hired killers, ones who were every bit as thorough as he was.

Tony sauntered easily up the steps and peered in the windows. Three or four men were stationed at the bar. Several of the candlelit tables were occupied, but he saw no one who resembled either Angie or what he had glimpsed of Joanna Brady.

Opening the door, he walked the length of the L-shaped bar and took the corner stool at the far end. To avoid calling any unwanted attention to himself, he ordered a draft beer and paid when the bartender brought it. He was busily taking inventory of the people at the bar, when his heart almost stopped.

Tony Vargas prided himself on knowing all about his opposition. As far as he was concerned, the best way to play the game was for him to know exactly who he was up against, without the other team knowing Tony Vargas existed. So he was aware of Adam York's name and knew what he looked like as well.

What's York doing here, Tony wondered. If Angie was going to sell the book to the highest bidder, Adam York of the DEA was a most likely prospect, one who would be prepared to pay absolutely top dollar.

Clammy fear gripped his gut. There wasn't a moment to lose. Taking one more sip from his beer but leaving the half-full glass there on the bar to save his place, Tony headed for the restroom which was down a long hallway off the lobby.

There were several doors along the way. Unobtrusively, he tried each of them as he went. The third one opened on a small janitor's closet. Inside he found everything he needed, including a selection of oily rags and wrapped packages of paper towels. Pulling the paper towels out of their packages and wadding them into a loose pile on the floor, he stacked the oily rags on top and set fire to the mess with his cigarette lighter. Then, careful to wipe the doorknob clean of prints on his way out, he closed the door behind him and walked away.

Casually unhurried, he returned to the bar and finished his beer. Then, waving at the bartender, he wandered outside to wait. It wouldn't take long for the smoke alarms to go off. When they did, everyone in the Copper Queen Hotel would be evacuated.

If Angie Kellogg was in there, she'd turn up on the street sooner or later. Then, all he'd have to do was track her down and take her out.

NINETEEN

EMPTY-HANDED, Angie Kellogg came racing back to the room in a blind panic. "He's here!"

"Who's here?" Joanna asked.

"Tony. I saw him. As I was coming down the stairs, he was going into the bar. How did he get here? What am I going to do?"

There was no mistaking Angie's despair or her terror. She rushed to the window and looked out. Afraid she might climb out or jump, Joanna moved to restrain her. "Are you sure?" she asked. "How would he know to follow you here? You must have left some kind of trail, some clue."

"No, I didn't, I swear. But where can I go now? If he found me once, he'll find me again. You don't know what he's like." The words poured out in a blithering torrent.

"Calm down," Joanna said. "Let's think this thing through."

She tried to sound composed even though her

own mind was churning. There was a certain ominous symmetry in having both Vargas and York turn up in the Copper Queen at the same time. Were they both there looking for someone else—Angie, for instance? Or were they there to meet each other? As soon as that ugly thought occurred to her, Joanna felt physically sick.

She turned to Angie. "Did Tony ever mention Adam York's name to you?"

"The DEA agent?" Joanna nodded. "No, not that I remember. Why?"

"Did you read through Tony's book by any chance? See what was in it?"

Angie shrugged. "I glanced at it is all. Names, telephone numbers, dates, that kind of thing."

"Do you remember any of the names?"

"No. There wasn't enough time. I was too worried about getting away to pay that much attention. Why? What are you thinking?"

"Supposing Adam York's name is one of the ones listed in that book," Joanna suggested. "Supposing he's been working with Tony and the others all along. If that's the case, you and that book aren't just Tony's problem any more. If the drug dealers have a well-placed accomplice working in the DEA, they're going to move heaven and earth to keep him there. Not only that, if they realize you and I have made contact . . ."

A jangling fire alarm clanged noisily in the hallway outside the room, cutting Joanna off in mid-sentence. Angie jumped like a startled deer. Reflexively, she grabbed for her beach bag and started for the door.

"Wait," Joanna cautioned. "What if it's a trick?"

"A trick?"

"Maybe it's a false alarm. Maybe they're waiting for us downstairs."

"Oh, my God."

Joanna went to the door and opened it a crack. The alarm was directly across the hall and the shrill clanging was almost deafening. The man from room 412, still pulling on his pants, was scurrying barefoot toward the stairs. No one else was visible in the hallway, but with the door open, Joanna could smell the unmistakable odor of smoke. She turned back to Angie.

"It is a fire! Come on."

But Angie had retreated to the far corner of the room where she stood, clutching the beach bag and frozen with fear. "No," she whimpered. "You're right. It's a trap. He'll get me as soon as I step outside."

Joanna slammed the door shut and came back into the room. A blue United Van Lines windbreaker lay on the bed. Joanna plucked it off the bed, walked over to Angie, and handed it to her. "Put this on," she ordered. "We've got to get out of here!"

Still Angie didn't budge. Gripping both the jacket and the beach bag, she stood as if transfixed, unable to move. Joanna fought to appear calm. She spoke soothingly to Angie, persuading and cajoling, as she might have done with a terrified child.

"I won't let them get you, Angie. I swear. We can get out the back way, but we've got to hurry."

Through the open window came the confused sounds of an approaching fire truck mixed with what seemed to be a dozen garbled voices raised in excited shouts. Joanna darted into the tiny bathroom and wet two bath towels, then she raced back out to find Angie still hadn't moved.

"Put on the jacket, Angie," she ordered. "Now!"

Woodenly, Angie complied. Joanna passed her one of the towels. "No telling what it'll be like when we open the door. Hold this up to your face and hang onto my arm. Whatever you do, don't let go."

Dragging Angie along, they moved in tandem toward the door. Expecting the corridor to be filled with smoke or flames, Joanna was amazed when the hallway was relatively clear. Only a thin pall of smoke still hung in the air. The fire alarm on the wall continued its nerve-shattering clamor, but there was no sign of flames.

At first Joanna was reassured by the fact that the fire was probably already under control, but that didn't last long. Her second thought chilled her. If Vargas and York would go so far as to set fire to a hotel in order to flush out their quarry, then they would stop at nothing.

As they stepped into the corridor, Angie automatically turned toward the stairs. Joanna dragged her back and urged her in the opposite direction.

"Where are we going?" Angie protested.

"This way. There's a fire escape back here."

During their abbreviated honeymoon, Joanna remembered how she and Andy had tiptoed down this same hallway in the middle of the night for a two A.M. unauthorized session of skinny-dipping in the hotel's postage-stamp-sized pool. The space for the pool and surrounding patio had been carved out of a rock outcropping behind the hotel and was walled off by a combination of cliff and high stuccoed wall, but Joanna was sure she remembered a door in the wall, or maybe a gate.

With Joanna still leading the way, they reached the fire exit door and peered out into the darkness. They were standing at the top of a long and narrow, dimly lit ramp. Halfway down the incline, the ramp doubled back on itself before dropping down to the pool. The back side of the patio was sheer cliff, the other two were impassable walls.

"We're trapped," Angie wailed, shrinking back into the building.

"No, we're not," Joanna insisted determinedly. "This way."

She dragged Angie down the ramp to the place she remembered. There, at a landing where the ramp doubled back, a dilapidated door had been built into the stuccoed wall. Barely daring to hope, Joanna tried the handle. The door was locked, but the weathered door shuddered and creaked when she pushed against it. She tried again, shoving harder this time. The wood seemed to give way beneath her body. Strengthened by a surge of fear-summoned adrenaline, she threw herself against the door. This time it sprang open, spilling both women headfirst into an abandoned street above a weed-choked yard.

Gasping for breath, Joanna leaped up and attempted to prop the door back shut. Inside the hotel, the clanging alarm ceased abruptly, leaving behind a strangely pregnant silence. Joanna held her breath and tried to listen over the rush of blood in her own ears. Sure enough, on the far side of the hotel, between it and the Presbyterian church next door, she heard at least one pair of pounding feet.

Joanna hurried back to Angie who was on her hands and knees in the rocks, patchy weeds, broken glass, and blowing trash, searching for something.

"Come on," Joanna whispered urgently. "Someone's coming."

"My thong came off," Angie whispered back. "I can't find it anywhere."

"You'll have to go barefoot. Come on!"

She helped pull Angie to her feet. The woman was still clutching the beach bag. She may have lost a thong, but the money was still intact. Together they started across the broken pavement and the rough, uneven yard. They had gone barely two steps each when a broken bottle sliced into the bottom of Angie's leg. Gasping in pain, she stopped in her tracks. Joanna looked down in time to see a spurt of blood pour from her wounded ankle.

"It's not far," Joanna whispered. "Lean on me. We can make it."

Together they limped down the steep hillside to where a single frail streetlight dangled on a crooked pole at the top of a stairway. They paused momentarily at the top of the stairs. Below them they heard the occasional tires and saw the headlights of passing automobiles. There was still no sound of pursuit from behind. They might just make it.

"That's Brewery Gulch," Joanna said, whispering still. "If we can make it down there, we should find someone to help us."

They started forward again. Joanna looked back over her shoulder. They had delayed for only a matter of seconds at the top of the stairs, but a pool of blood was clearly visible on the rough concrete surface of the step. Even without someone chasing them, there wasn't a moment to lose.

In the old days Brewery Gulch had been a wide-open redlight district, complete with bars, gambling dens, and scarlet women. Joanna remembered her father telling stories about how, even in his time, Brewery Gulch had been a thriving beehive of activity. As they hurried down the stairs, Joanna fervently wished it were still so. In places like that, even a woman with a bloody foot could melt into a crowd and disappear, but the same economics that had closed down the copper mines had also emptied most of the bars along Brewery Gulch.

In the darkness behind and above them something heavy clattered to the ground. Their pursuer had discovered the door and knocked it down in his eagerness to come after them. The sound galvanized them both and they charged

out of the stairway onto the raised sidewalk of a
seemingly deserted street. Only two sets of neon
lights offered any hope of haven.

Leading Angie along, Joanna headed for the
closest one, a place called the Blue Moon Saloon.
They barged in through the door. The sound of
an approaching police vehicle entered the long
high-ceilinged room with them. Joanna quickly
shut the door closing out the noise.

Inside, the narrow room was smoky and dimly
lit. A carved wooden bar ran the entire length of
one wall. With the exception of the bartender and
two solitary customers seated at opposite ends of
the bar, the Blue Moon was empty. All three men
glanced up in surprise at the sudden appearance
of the two women who had stopped just inside the
door.

"Hey, ladies," the bartender called at once.
"You gotta wear shoes in here. The health department's already after my ass."

"Hey, Bobo," Joanna called. "Come quick and
give me a hand. She's bleeding to death."

Bobo Jenkins, the huge bartender who had been
the only black student in Andy's graduating class,
placed both hands on the bar then swung himself
up and over and came hurrying to her side. He
looked down at Angie's bloody ankle. "Sheeit, Joanna, what'd she do, try to cut the damn thing
off?"

"Somebody's after us, Bobo. We need your
help."

Without a word, he picked Angie Kellogg up
and carried her away from the door. He took her

to the far wall where, holding her on a raised knee, he opened a door that led to a small stock closet. He set her down on a bar stool.

"You wait here, honey," he said. "Nobody's going to find you here." With that, he hurried back to Joanna who was mopping up the blood with the wet towel she had somehow managed to hang onto.

"I'll handle that, Joanna. You go be with your friend. The door locks from inside."

Nodding, Joanna scurried away while Bobo took over the cleanup difficulties. "There are clean towels inside there," he called over his shoulder. "You're going to need them. And as for you," he said to the two men at the bar, "you two jokers may be too drunk to go chase the fire trucks, but you'd by god better be sober enough to keep your mouths shut, you hear?"

"You're the boss, Bobo," one of them returned. "Archie and me'll do whatever you say."

Bobo was on his hands and knees mopping up the last of the blood that had pooled on the floor in front of the door. "Fill those two ice buckets with hot soapy water and bring them over here, Willy. Hurry. Archie, you bring me the broom."

A tipsy eighty-year-old, Willy Haskins was surprisingly spry for his age and condition. He hurried around the end of the bar, filled two plastic buckets with detergent and water, and lugged them over to Bobo. The bartender took them outside. Within seconds the entire length of sidewalk in front of the Blue Moon Saloon was awash in wet, soapy suds. He left the broom out front as though he was in the middle of a routine, late night sidewalk cleanup.

Nodding in approval, Bobo hustled Willy and Archie back inside. "Looks like the next round's on the house," he told the two old men. Willy Haskins and Archie McBride nodded in happy unison.

Bobo laughed and shook his head. "In six years, that's the first time you two boys ever agreed with one another about anything. Keep your mouths shut when the time comes, and I'll buy you another."

Moments later, the door swung open and a man stuck his head inside and looked around, then he walked up to the bar and ordered a shot of tequila. "Did a woman just come by here?" he asked.

Bobo Jenkins pushed the man's drink across the bar, smiling sadly. "No such luck, Bud. You missing one? They've just had some excitement up at the hotel. Maybe's she's up there."

The stranger paid for his drink then chugged it. "She's not there," he said. "I already looked."

A toothless, gaunt old man was sitting next to him at the bar. "You say you lost your woman?" he asked loudly. "Me, too. I lost my wife a couple years back, and when I come in here and told Willy, you wanna know what this old geezer tole me? He says, 'Hey Archie, did you remember to look under the refrigerator?'"

At that both old men, the speaker and his equally aged counterpart at the end of the bar, burst into loud uproarious laughter. "You get it?"

he asked, holding his sides and wiping the tears from his eyes. "Maybe you'd better look in the same place."

"Yeah," the other drunk added. "Have another drink. Maybe she'll show up."

Slamming his shot glass down on the bar, the man got up and stalked out. Willy and Archie were still laughing. Bobo Jenkins wasn't. He'd been a bartender long enough to recognize danger when he saw it. He felt a trickle of cold sweat run down the back of his neck, but he made no effort to wipe it away.

Bobo walked over to the window and flipped over the closed sign, then he walked back to the bar. "I'm closing up, boys," he said. "It's motel time."

"Wait a minute," Archie said. "You promised us a drink."

"I promised you a drink if you kept your mouths shut," Bobo corrected.

Willy howled in outrage. "Why, Bobo Jenkins, you're a no-good lousy welsher."

Bobo shook his head. "I promised you a drink for keeping quiet. What I got was a damn stand-up comedy routine. So here's what I'm gonna do. Tonight, I'm shuttin' her down. You two are eighty-sixed. Come tomorrow, though, you boys show up at the regular time, and the entire evening's on me."

"No shit?" Archie asked hopefully. "You mean it?"

Bobo Jenkins nodded. "You bet your ass I do. Now you two get the hell out of here. And if you meet that bastard out on the street, you keep quiet or the deal's off. You dig?"

"Mum's the word," Willy said, climbing down from his stool and staggering toward the door. "Mum is definitely the word."

And Bobo Jenkins knew he had found the secret formula that would keep those two old codgers quiet no matter what.

🌵 TWENTY

BOBO AND Joanna's joint assessment was that the cut on Angie's foot required a doctor's immediate attention. Carrying her as effortlessly as if she were a doll, Bobo packed her out the door and across the street to the tiny lot where he kept his mint-condition El Camino. After placing Angie in the truck he hurried back to Joanna who was having difficulty working the troublesome lock on the Blue Moon's front door.

"Who the hell is that bad-ass bastard?" Bobo asked under his breath, as he took the key from Joanna's fingers and quickly finished locking the door himself.

"She thinks the man chasing her is the one who killed Andy," Joanna replied. "And he won't stop at anything to keep her from going to the cops."

"But why's he after you?"

Joanna shrugged. "I'm with her."

They headed for the car where a still-frightened

Angie sat huddled in the middle of the seat with her bleeding foot wrapped tightly in a thick swathe of towels. Bobo Jenkins was large enough that, with three people crammed together on the bench seat, it was all they could do to close the doors.

"I'd appreciate it if you wouldn't bleed on the carpet," Bobo said with a nod to Angie as he turned the key in the ignition. Angie looked up at him warily and tried to move closer to Joanna.

"Hey," Bobo said. "That was just a joke, trying to lighten things up. You go right ahead and bleed all you want."

Joanna recognized the old-time Bobo humor. He had always been the class clown, and evidently nothing had changed. When Joanna laughed, so did Angie. It didn't change a thing about their situation, but it did relieve the suffocating tension.

"What are we going to do?" Angie asked.

"Once you're under a doctor's care, I'm going to go see Walter McFadden," Joanna told her.

"The sheriff?"

"That's right."

"Are you going to tell him about me?"

"I've got to, Angie. It's too dangerous otherwise. There's no telling what they might do."

"They?" Bobo asked attentively.

"At least two," Joanna returned. "The one you met, Tony."

"Tony Vargas," Angie supplied.

"And a DEA agent named Adam York."

"Thanks for telling me," Bobo muttered. "It's nice to know who the hell's on what side."

Most of the police officers in the City of Bisbee

were still congregated around the Copper Queen Hotel, trying to locate two missing female guests who had disappeared in the aftermath of a minor fire. As a consequence, Bobo Jenkins sped through town at sixty or so miles per hour with no one pulling him over or raising an eyebrow. They made the three-mile drive from Old Bisbee to the Warren district in record-breaking time while Joanna quickly brought Bobo Jenkins up to speed on what had been going on.

"When they ask who you are," Joanna cautioned Angie as they pulled up to the emergency entrance, "give them some kind of phony name, and one that isn't Tammy Sue Ferris, either. Tell them you're Andy's cousin from Tulsa or Enid, Oklahoma, and that you're in town for the funeral. Got that?"

Angie Kellogg nodded. "Okay," she said.

Stopping the car directly in front of the entrance, Bobo again picked Angie up and bodily carried her inside. Joanna followed. Once the emergency room nurses had taken charge of Angie and rolled her away on a gurney, Bobo and Joanna were left waiting in the empty lobby.

"Lend me your car, Bobo," Joanna said quietly.

"So you can go see McFadden?"

Joanna nodded. "I'll come with you," Bobo offered.

"No, you stay here and keep an eye on her. If Tony somehow figures out she's here, I'm still afraid he might try something."

"In the middle of a hospital?" Bobo asked. "What is he, crazy or something?"

"Andy's being in a hospital didn't stop him before," she replied.

"Jeez!" Bobo exclaimed, then he frowned. "He wouldn't try to get to you through Jenny, would he?"

Joanna felt as though she'd taken a pounding blow to the midsection. "I never thought of that."

"Where is she?"

"At home, out at the ranch, with my mother."

"I'd get her out of there quick if I were you," Bobo warned. "Have them go someplace else until this all gets straightened out."

Joanna nodded even as she was turning in a frantic search for a telephone. She found a pay phone near the lobby. Bobo Jenkins supplied the necessary quarter. Joanna breathed a sigh of relief when Eleanor answered the phone.

"Where in the world are you?" Eleanor demanded. "It's late. I need to get home pretty soon."

"Is Jenny asleep?"

"Of course she is. Hours ago. And Ken Galloway is here waiting to see you. He came to pick up Andy's uniform and take it up to the funeral home. I thought you were going to do that this afternoon. It should have been done before this."

"Mother," Joanna said, "listen to me. I don't have time to deal with that right now. I want you to get Jenny up and bring her into town. Take her up to Jeff and Marianne's. I'll call on ahead and tell them you're coming. Bring Sadie, too. It'll make Jenny feel better if she has the dog with her."

"You want me to wake Jenny up in the middle of the night and drag her into town? Hasn't she been through enough?" Eleanor demanded. "That's the craziest thing I've ever heard of. And I don't want that filthy dog in my car."

"Mother," Joanna said slowly, "this time, we're doing it my way. I want both Jenny and Sadie out of that house, and I want them out now. If there's a problem with your car, I'll clean it up later, but I'm warning you. If you want to have a granddaughter when all this is over, one you can talk to and visit, then you'll do as I say."

Eleanor greeted her daughter's threat with a moment of shocked silence. "I don't understand any of this at all," she said at last. "What's going on, anyway? Where are you going to be?"

"I've got to go talk to Walter McFadden right away. After you drop Jenny off, you go on to your own place. When I can, I'll stop by and let you know what's going on."

"I should think so," Eleanor returned sourly.

Joanna hung up and borrowed another of Bobo Jenkins' quarters. She dialed Marianne Maculyea's number and was relieved when Marianne answered after only one ring.

"I'm calling to ask a favor," Joanna said. "I know it's late, but my mother and Jenny are on their way to your house right now. Mother's bringing both Jenny and Sadie. I need you to keep them overnight. I'll be there as soon as I can."

"Joanna, something's wrong. You sound funny. Are you all right?" Marianne asked.

"I will be eventually," Joanna returned. "I've gotta go."

"Are you sure you don't want me to go along?" Bobo asked when she put down the phone.

Joanna was filled with momentary misgivings. The world outside the brightly lit hospital corridor seemed dark and dangerous. Adam York and/or Tony might be lurking out there in the forbidding parking lot, waiting for her to set foot outside. And if something happened to her and to Angie both . . .

Decisively, Joanna reached down and fumbled in the side pocket of her purse. Leaving the purse sitting open on the floor, she located the two items she was searching for—Lefty's puzzling letter to Andy and the note pad containing the mysterious Cora's telephone number.

"Keep this for me, Bobo," she said, handing over Lefty O'Toole's letter. "If anything happens to me, I want you to turn it over to the authorities. You need to know that Vargas is really after Angie because of a book she stole from him, one Vargas used to keep track of his business dealings. It's in the safe up at the Copper Queen. If anything happens to her, the cops need to know about that, too."

"You really do think they're going to try coming after her, don't you?"

Joanna nodded grimly. "I sure as hell do."

She opened the note pad and stared down at the page containing Cora's telephone number. Finally, she tore it out and handed that to him as well. "You've heard about the money I suppose?"

"I've heard rumors," Bobo conceded, "but I'm not sure I believe any of 'em."

"This telephone number belongs to someone named Cora. She's most likely the woman who showed up at the bank with Andy the day he deposited the extra money in our account. Again, if anything happens to me, I want you to call this number and find out where that money came from. I don't care if she and Andy were having an affair or not. At this point, it doesn't much matter. But I want Jenny to know the truth about where that money came from and why. If it was from some kind of crooked dealings, so be it. Jenny needs to know that about her father. If not, she deserves to know that, too."

Bobo handed Joanna the keys to the El Camino while his dark eyes clouded with sympathy. "They've put you through hell, Joanna. I'm sorry."

She shook her head. "It's not so bad, Bobo," she replied. "At least I've got friends to help me."

Her purse had sat open on the floor. When she leaned down to pick it up, the .44 was clearly visible.

Bobo saw the gun without registering the least bit of surprise. "From what I've heard about these guys," he said, "I think I'd keep that thing handy. But if you need it, you'll be better off with it in a pocket rather than in a purse. In a pinch, it'll be a hell of a lot easier to get to."

With a nod, Joanna reached down, picked up

the gun, and shoved it deep into the pocket of her fleece-lined jacket.

"And if the doc doesn't want to keep Angie overnight, I'll take her home with me," Bobo continued. "That way you'll know she's safe, but you'll also know where to come looking for her."

Joanna reached up and gave him a quick, grateful hug. "I'll be back as soon as I finish up with Walter McFadden," she said.

From the hospital it was a straight shot down Cole Avenue to Walter McFadden's place. It was after eleven and no lights were showing when she pulled up outside the gate at the side of his yard. As she fumbled for the parking brake in the unfamiliar vehicle, a car with its lights on bright pulled up directly behind her and stopped. Temporarily blinded by bright lights followed by total darkness, she blinked once. In that brief instant of time, someone was beside the car door wrenching it open.

"Get out," a man ordered.

Joanna recognized Tony Vargas at once. She hadn't ever seen him in person, but his picture from the Horseshoe Casino was still in her pocket.

"Hello, Mr. Vargas," she said coolly, stepping out of the car to face him, refusing to look at the gun he was holding in his hand.

"You know who I am, then?"

Joanna was conscious of only one thought. She was standing next to Andy's killer. He was armed, but so was she. Thanks to Clayton Rhodes and Bobo Jenkins she had a loaded .44 in her pocket. That was something Tony Vargas probably wouldn't expect. Fighting off panic, she forced herself to hold his eyes with hers. She wanted his eyes on her face not her hands.

"When I get through with you, everyone else will too," she responded, deliberately taunting him.

A chillingly insincere smile flickered across Tony Vargas' broad features. "I wouldn't be so sure about that if I were you. Where's Angie? Where's my book?"

"Someplace safe. Someplace where you won't be able to find them."

Vargas turned his head slightly but without taking his eyes off her. "Hey, Ken, turn on the dome light in there, would you?" he asked.

Joanna glanced at the other car for the first time and was dismayed when she recognized it to be a Cochise County Sheriff's Department patrol car. The interior lights came on in the car and revealed Ken Galloway sitting in the driver's seat. Then something moved in the back seat. In a heart-stopping second, Joanna realized that Jenny was there, locked behind the metal mesh, waving at her through the window. Jenny and her mother both.

She turned back to Vargas in sudden fury. "What are they doing here?" she demanded.

He smiled again. "Don't get excited. You sell insurance, don't you, Mrs. Brady? And that's what they are. My insurance policy. You're going to drive this car to wherever you've hidden Angie. When I have her and my book, you're going to drive us to Ken's airplane down at the airport. Once we're safely out of here, then you get your mother and the little girl back, understand?"

Walter McFadden's back porch light snapped on. The door opened and Tigger came out first, followed by the sheriff himself, barefoot and wearing jeans and a T-shirt. He came limping down his back steps. "Who's out here?" he demanded. "What's going on?"

The interior light of the patrol car snapped off and Ken Galloway stepped out of the car. "No biggie," he said calmly, walking over to the gate. "We're just doing a little damage control."

"Damage control!" Joanna exclaimed, wondering if there was a chance the sheriff might have a weapon concealed somewhere on his body. "Walter, this is the man who killed Andy. They've got my mother and Jenny locked in the back of Ken's patrol car."

"Is that true, Ken?" McFadden asked. "About Jenny and Eleanor Lathrop?"

Ken shook his head. "It's like Tony was telling Joanna here. We're only using them for insurance. It's gonna get real rough around here, Walter. We've got a plane to catch, and there's enough room in it for three people—you, me, and Tony. We won't hurt Joanna or her mother or Jenny, either. But by the time they get loose, we'll be over the border and long gone."

Tigger came up behind Walter, tail wagging, and dropped the Frisbee at his master's feet. Seeing him, McFadden shook his head. "Go lie down," the sheriff ordered. The dog, disappointed, retreated to the back porch while Walter McFadden turned back to Ken Galloway.

"It's over then, isn't it, Ken, for all of us. But I'm not leaving. I've wanted it to be over for a helluva long time. I just didn't have guts enough to do anything about it."

With no further warning, McFadden flung open the metal gate, catching Ken Galloway by surprise and full in the midsection. The top brace of the gate slammed into his ribs, sending him reeling backwards toward the patrol car. When Vargas turned to help Galloway, Joanna saw her chance.

Throughout the confrontation, she had been edging her hand nearer the pocket containing the gun. Now her fingers closed around the grip of the .44. Carefully she thumbed back the hammer. At that close range, there was no need to aim the weapon or even bring it fully out of her pocket.

When she pulled the trigger, the roar of gunfire was deafening. The force of the recoil sent her spinning back against the roof of the El Camino. Tony Vargas groaned in surprise, doubled over, and crumpled to the ground.

Tony's gun fell from his hand, but it was still within reach. As soon as Joanna regained her balance, she kicked it under the car, as far as she could away from his grasping fingers. In the meantime, Ken Galloway had pulled his own gun from its holster and was holding it on Walter McFadden. Trying to watch both McFadden and Joanna, his head swiveled back and forth between them.

"Go ahead and shoot," Walter McFadden dared Galloway. "That way I'll have the monkey off my back once and for all." As he spoke, the sheriff was easing himself through the now-open gate, steadily closing the distance between himself and his renegade deputy.

"Stop right there, Walter," Galloway warned. "Don't come any closer."

"Actually," Walter drawled, "I do believe I much prefer shooting."

All the while the sheriff was moving inevitably forward as Galloway backed away. That's when Joanna realized what McFadden was doing. By pushing Galloway farther into the street, away from the patrol car, he was effectively easing Jenny and Eleanor out of the line of fire. Joanna moved with the two men, taking her part of the triangle along. Meantime lights were coming on all over the neighborhood.

"That way I won't have to stand around any longer, turning a blind eye to your slimy blackmail deals and murder for hire schemes," McFadden continued. "I'm looking forward to that, to not having scumbags like you in my life, Ken. Besides, if you do a good enough job, if your aim is good enough, there won't be enough of me left over to ship off to prison. I never did much like Florence, you know. It's too damned hot up there."

With that, Walter McFadden lunged forward, throwing himself toward Ken Galloway's gun. In the blazing hail of gunfire that followed, both men went down, first Ken Galloway and then Sheriff Walter McFadden.

Joanna heard sirens then. As close as they were, they must have been audible for some time before she noticed them. Still holding the gun, she hurried to where Ken Galloway lay moaning on the ground. She picked up his .357 and handed it over to the first neighbor who appeared on the scene.

"Watch him," Joanna ordered. "Don't let him move."

She rushed to Walter McFadden and knelt beside him. He was pressing his hand to his chest, a hand's breadth beneath his breastbone. Despite the pressure, blood still oozed up through his fingers.

"Good shooting, Joanna. But then your daddy always said you were a crack shot."

"Quiet," she said. "Listen to the siren. The ambulance is on its way."

"Morphine was the hook—that's what finally got me," he whispered. "When the pain got too bad, when Carol was crying for it in the middle of the night, I would've done anything to get it for her. One buy was all it took. As soon as I stepped out of line, the bastards had me."

"Shhhhh," she said, but he ignored her, although his voice was weaker now. She had to strain to hear him over the noise of arriving emergency vehicles.

"They blackmailed me, Joanna." He took a breath before he could go on. "I didn't know what all went on or who all was involved. My job was to walk around howdying people and being blind, deaf, and dumb to what was going on in my own department." He paused again. "Was Andy in on it?"

Tears were coursing down Joanna's cheeks. She bit her lip and ducked her head. "I don't know, Walter."

"I hope not," Walter McFadden muttered weakly. "For your sake and Jenny's, I sure as hell hope not."

And he was gone.

☙ TWENTY-ONE

JOANNA STOOD up. By then the place was crowded with Emergency Medical Technicians and City of Bisbee police officers to say nothing of dismayed neighbors who were struggling to come to grips with exactly what had happened.

Both Tony Vargas and Walter McFadden were beyond help, so all the lifesaving activity centered around Ken Galloway. Joanna walked past the flurry of activity to the patrol car. There, without anyone paying attention, she pressed the door lock and opened the door, freeing both Jenny and her mother. Once they were out of the vehicle, Eleanor and Jenny clung to Joanna as though fearing she might somehow disappear.

"Is Sheriff McFadden all right?" Jenny asked tearfully.

Joanna shook her head. "He's dead," she answered. "He died before the ambulance ever got here."

Bobo Jenkins turned up just then with Adam York in tow. Joanna took Jenny by the shoulders. "Go sit on the porch with Tigger," she said. "Stay out of the way. I'll be there as soon as I can."

Jenny tiptoed through the gate then ran to the back porch where she flung her arms around Tigger's neck. The dog, as ordered, was still lying down, waiting for a release signal from Walter McFadden that was never going to come.

"What should I do?" Eleanor asked meekly.

"Stay with Jenny, Mother."

Eleanor started after her granddaughter then paused. "It was him, wasn't it," she said. "The man with the gold in his teeth."

Joanna looked down at the lifeless body of Tony Vargas. She nodded. "It was him," she said.

Joanna had spoken gently to both her daughter and her mother, but when she turned to face Bobo Jenkins her face was full of barely repressed fury. "What's *he* doing here?" she asked, nodding toward Adam York who was off to one side consulting with several of the uniformed officers on the scene.

"I talked to the man, Joanna," Bobo Jenkins explained. "He followed the bloody footprints down the stairs from the hotel, put two and two together, and came to the hospital. He's on the up-and-up."

"Sure he is," Joanna returned with her eyes narrowing. "I'll believe it when I see it."

As if on cue, Adam York turned and caught her looking at him. He left the officers and walked over to where she was standing. "Joanna, are you all right?" he asked.

"I'm fine."

"Good."

"Look," she said, "you may have convinced my friend Bobo, here, that you walk on water, but I'm not buying it. Until I see some proof otherwise, I'm going to continue to consider you part of the opposition."

"Your husband got Lefty O'Toole to agree to come into the Witness Protection Program," York said. "Andy had contacted me and told me to expect Lefty within a matter of days. When it all fell apart, when Lefty showed up dead and then Andy suddenly laid his hands on a considerable sum of unexplained money, I figured the cartel had turned him. Then, when Andy was killed as well it made sense that there was some other traitor pretty close to home."

"You thought it was me?" Joanna asked.

York shrugged. "Why not? I was casting my net around and you turned up in it. You're right, I do owe you an apology, and not just over the autopsy results. I wouldn't be surprised to find that Ken Galloway was the one who typed the suicide note in Andy's file. We've known for years that Cochise County was a major conduit of the drug trade and we figured there had to be someone in law enforcement working with them, but it wasn't until Andy connected with Lefty that we figured we were going to get a break. Now, thanks to you, we finally know who some of those people were."

"If Lefty knew Galloway was involved, why didn't he warn Andy?"

"Maybe he did or maybe he didn't. It's possible he tried to and Ken intercepted the message. Andy and Ken were supposedly good friends, weren't they?"

"Supposedly," Joanna agreed, bitterly. "We thought he was a friend."

"With Lefty out of the picture, I figured the whole investigation was blown, but now, with this book . . ."

"What book?" Joanna demanded.

"Angie's book. She's scared to death and tired of running. I guess she finally decided she had to trust somebody. She spilled her guts about Tony and his little black book. She even suggested a possible deal."

"Angie trusted you?" Joanna asked sharply.

"Why not?" Adam York returned. "You don't think I'd cheat her, do you?"

"Until I read that book for myself and make sure your name isn't in it, I'm not trusting anybody."

York studied Joanna's face for some time before he nodded. "Considering what you've been through," he said, "that's probably a very wise position to take. By the way," he added, "are you aware that you have what appears to be a bullet hole in your jacket pocket? You may want to mention that to the crime scene investigators here. Otherwise, they're not going to understand some of the evidence they're looking at."

It was several hours later before anyone made

a move to go home. Marianne Maculyea had shown up in her 1967 sea foam-green VW Bug. Jeff Daniels, who kept the old Bug running perfectly, turned up in Joanna's Eagle, which he had hot-wired to bring down from the hotel. When it was time to go, Joanna loaded her mother into the car first and then went to find Jenny.

"What's going to happen to Tigger?" Jenny asked. "We can't just leave him here, can we?"

And, of course, the answer to that question was no. Jenny and Tigger rode in the back while a strangely subdued Eleanor rode in front. "Thank you for the ride," Eleanor said when Joanna dropped her off in front of her own house at four in the morning. "Thank you for everything."

Try as she might, Joanna could never remember hearing her mother saying those words ever before.

At home at last, Joanna was so tired she could barely walk. Without thinking, she went directly to the bedroom. Looking at it, she realized there would be times in the future when the memories of that bed would make sleeping there impossible, but now she was too tired. Joanna tumbled across it. With the comforting scent of Andy's pillow lingering in her nostrils, she was asleep within minutes.

She didn't stir again until almost ten that morning. When she went padding through the house to check on things, she discovered that both big dogs were curled up on Jenny's bed. They opened their eyes and looked at her, but neither Sadie nor Tigger made any effort to get down, and since Jenny was still sound asleep, Joanna left them there.

In the kitchen where she went to start a pot of coffee, Joanna discovered a note from Jim Bob Brady saying he'd been out to feed the cattle and also that one of Norm Higgins's boys had stopped by to see about picking up Andy's clothes for the funeral. Jim Bob had told him to come back later.

Steeling herself for the ordeal, Joanna went back to the bedroom to pick out Andrew Brady's clothing for the last time. She marched directly to his side of the closet. Norm Higgins had hinted that maybe, under the circumstances, it might be better if Andy were buried in civilian clothes rather than his uniform, but Joanna had decided otherwise.

One at a time she started sorting through the selection of carefully pressed clothing until she located Andy's newest dress uniform shirt, one that wasn't frayed around the cuffs and didn't have any cracked or chipped or missing buttons. She picked out trousers and socks and a full set of clean underwear. After all, Andy never went anywhere without clean underwear.

When the clothes were all laid out neatly on the bed she retrieved the plastic package she'd been given in the hospital and sorted through it until she found Andy's badge. Then, taking the badge and his best dress boots, she headed for the kitchen. There, drinking coffee and shedding quiet, private tears, she polished the boots to a high gloss and cleaned the badge with Brasso. When she finished, she took the boots and badge back to the bedroom and carefully pinned the badge to the pocket of the shirt, using the previously made holes in the material as a guide to placing the badge properly.

Seeing his clothes all laid out like that made her feel lightheaded. It was as though he had put them there himself and was in the bathroom taking a shower, getting ready to go to work. It was almost too much. Joanna was relieved to hear a car drive into the yard. It meant she had to pull herself together. Otherwise she would have drowned in self-pity.

Marianne Maculyea came in the kitchen door without bothering to knock. "Where's Jenny?" she asked.

"Still asleep," Joanna answered.

Marianne shook her head. "Poor little tyke," she said. "She must have been worn out. How about you?"

"I've been better," Joanna allowed. "How's Ken Galloway?" Part of her wanted him dead; the other part dreaded whatever investigation would inevitably follow.

"Still nip and tuck," Marianne answered. "They've flown him to Tucson now. He's at University Hospital under a heavy police guard."

Joanna shook her head. "It hurts so much," she said. "We thought he was our friend."

"I know," Marianne said. "The only way an enemy can betray you is by becoming your friend, but when friends . . ." She broke off, knowing that beyond a certain point, words are no comfort.

"I've been working on Lefty O'Toole's eulogy,"

she added, changing the subject. "I've spent the whole morning doing my homework. I've talked to Adam York. Bobo suggested I talk to him. It sounds to me as though Gertrude O'Toole was right after all, that Lefty really was getting his life turned around."

"You've been talking to York, too?" Joanna asked. "First Bobo and now you. Next thing you know, Adam York's going to be so popular around here that somebody'll run him for sheriff."

Marianne cocked her head. "No," she said slowly, "but he did have a suggestion in that regard."

"Oh, really?" Joanna snorted. "What's that?"

"You."

"Me?" Joanna echoed. "Are you kidding?"

"Nobody's kidding, Joanna. And he's not the only one who's mentioned it, either."

Joanna Brady shook her head. "Oh, no," she said. "Absolutely not. Not me."

"It's going to take a complete outsider to straighten up this mess, Joanna," Marianne said. "Someone who has nothing to gain by taking on the job."

"I've already got a job," Joanna reminded her.

"That's funny," Marianne replied. "It turns out that Milo Davis was one of the ones I heard talking about it over coffee just this morning."

"Do we have to discuss this now?" Joanna asked.

Marianne shook her head. "No. I stopped by to pick up Andy's clothes if they're ready."

Joanna nodded. "They're in the bedroom, laid out on the bed."

Jenny picked that precise moment to come dashing into the kitchen, trailed by the two dogs. Within minutes a carload of women from the church arrived with the beginnings of what would be several days' worth of casserole meals. Just when it seemed as though Joanna's home had turned into a complete circus, a silver-gray Taurus with government plates drove into the yard.

Not wanting to talk to Adam York in front of her other guests, Joanna hurried out to meet him. "What are you doing here?" she asked.

"I came to invite you to the unveiling."

"What are you talking about?"

"Your friends, Bobo Jenkins and Angie Kellogg, just went up to the hotel to pick up that book. I wanted you to be there when they brought it back so you'd be able to see with your own eyes that I'm not in it."

Joanna looked at him steadily. He met her gaze without faltering. "I really am a good guy, Joanna, and from what I've learned around town, I've pretty much figured out that you are too."

"I'll go tell Jenny that I'm leaving," Joanna said.

The Taurus sped down High Lonesome Road. "Is that where it happened?" Adam York asked, nodding at the wash beneath the bridge.

Joanna nodded stonily.

"I'm sorry," he said. "It's a terrible, terrible thing."

"Thank you," Joanna murmured.

They drove for a while in silence. "I've been thinking about Angie Kellogg," Adam York said at last. "She wants to sell me that book of hers."

"I know," Joanna responded.

"But if I do that, I'll have to go through channels and across desks. The book will end up in an official inventory somewhere, Angie becomes an official witness, a paid informant, and the money she has in that damn beach bag of hers becomes part of an official investigation as well. Since it's most likely drug cartel money, it would automatically be forfeit."

"So?"

"She came up with the idea on her own, and it seems like a good one. She gives me the book and I don't ask any questions about the money in her beach bag. The taxpayers aren't out any money, and I have access to Tony Vargas's clientele without anyone knowing I have it."

"I'll know," Joanna said.

"Is that a threat?" York asked.

"You could call it that."

"Listen, Joanna. There may very well be other crooked cops in that book, trusted officers in other jurisdictions, maybe even some in my own. This book, if it's kept under wraps, may be our one chance to clean house."

"And if you don't use it to do just that, you'll be hearing from me."

York laughed. "According to the rumors around town, I may be hearing from you anyway."

"What rumors are those?"

"I heard you're running for sheriff."

"You heard wrong."

"Oh," he said.

A moment later Joanna asked, "Why are you

telling me all this, about this under the table deal with Angie? Wouldn't you be better off with it just between the two of you?"

"Because she won't finalize the deal until you give the okay."

"And I'm not okaying anything until I see for sure that your name's not in that book."

York laughed again. "You really are one stubborn woman, aren't you, but believe me. My name's not in there."

They found Angie Kellogg with her foot still securely wrapped in bandages sitting on the tiny front porch of Bobo Jenkins' home in Galena Townsites, one of Bisbee's subdivisions. Galena was an area where look-alike homes had been built as company housing during Bisbee's mining heyday. After the mine closures in the mid-seventies, the houses, previously rented to employees, had been sold off at rock-bottom prices.

Angie was wearing what was evidently a pair of Bobo Jenkins' oversized sweats. The arms had been rolled up several times and the legs bagged out around her ankles like pantaloons. She was holding two books in her lap. One, black leather with gold-embossed letters on the front, looked like a date book of some kind. The other was the same shabby bird book Joanna had seen before. The well-thumbed field guide was open and Angie's face was alight.

"Bobo actually has a hummingbird feeder, right here by the porch," she said pointing. "Two of those cute little things were here just a couple of minutes ago. I've never been that close to hummingbirds. Have you?"

"Not that I remember," Joanna said.

"Did Mr. York tell you about my offer?" Angie asked.

Joanna nodded.

"What do you think?"

"I told him you shouldn't make up your mind until we checked to see if his name is in Tony's book."

"It isn't," Angie Kellogg said. "I already looked."

TWENTY-TWO

THAT EVENING, the visitation at the mortuary went on for hours. Joanna shook hands with what seemed like hundreds of people, all of whom came to express their condolences. It was a wary, reserved gathering. Everyone in town was still in shock over the revelations about Walter McFadden and Ken Galloway, and they were all leery about how many others of their law enforcement officers might be caught up in the dragnet.

Toward the end, when visitors were finally beginning to dwindle, a young woman breezed into the room, pushing a wizened, much older man in a wheelchair. The two of them came directly to Joanna.

"Hello," said the woman, holding out her hand. "You must be Joanna. I'm Cora, Cora Hancock. This is my Uncle Henry, Henry Adkins. I can't tell you how sorry we are. Andy was such a nice

313

young man. I just don't know when I've ever met anyone nicer."

Cora, Joanna wondered as her heart skipped a beat. She had planned to call that phone number in Nevada eventually—someday much farther down the line when she would be better prepared for what she might hear. But she had deliberately put it off for a while, until she felt stronger, until the raw wounds from the last few days had begun to heal. She had not expected to confront Cora, who seemed to have a last name after all. Yet, here she was, on Joanna's home turf—and with Andrew Brady not yet in his grave.

But Cora, with her bleached blonde hair and amazing makeup, looked every bit the fallen woman Sandra Henning had described, except for her laugh which was warm and irrepressible.

"When I heard the funeral was scheduled for Saturday, I told Uncle Henry that I didn't know if I'd be able to get off, since weekends are always the busiest time at Harrahs. Have you ever been to Laughlin, Nevada, by the way?" she asked, pausing minutely for breath. "It's just across the Colorado from Bullhead City."

Joanna shook her head. "Anyway, the director got somebody to fill in for me, so I told Uncle Henry we could come, and here we are. It's been a long drive, although not as long as it seemed the last time I made it."

Again she paused for breath, but Joanna was too dumbstruck to say a word. "That reminds me, did Andy get you that ring he was going to?"

Joanna held out her hand and finally found a way to speak. "This? He told you about my ring?"

"Oh, yes. There it is, just as pretty as he said it would be. And he told me about the rest of the surprise as well."

"What surprise?"

"About the money. He told me he wasn't going to tell you about it until your anniversary dinner because he was afraid you would make him take the ring back and remodel the bathrooms instead. He was such a wonderful man, such a nice man," she added breathlessly. "This is all so terribly sad that I think I'm going to cry." And she did.

Uncle Henry reached out and patted her elbow with one of his bony, gnarled old hands. "There, there," he said. "Don't take on so, girl."

Jim Bob and Eva Lou, en route to the door, happened by at that precise moment. Jim Bob stopped and looked down at the little old man in puzzled consternation, as if trying to remember the name of someone he knew.

"Henry?" he asked tentatively. "Is that you?"

Uncle Henry smiled broadly. "Jimmy B? I'll be damned. The last time I saw you, you were still in short pants. It's a shame that it takes such a sad occasion to get together after all these years. I mean, I barely remember what the original argument was about all those years ago, and now it doesn't matter."

"Uncle Henry?" Joanna asked.

Jim Bob nodded. "He's my mother's second-oldest brother. He and the rest of the family had a falling out years ago, when I was just a boy. Uncle Henry, this is Joanna, my daughter-in-law."

Uncle Henry nodded. "Glad to make your acquaintance, and this is Cora. She's actually my third wife's niece—my wife's dead now—but that's too confusing, so we just say she's my niece. She's a dancer during the weekends, but she helps out in the office during the week."

"Office?" Jim Bob asked. "What office?"

Uncle Henry waved impatiently. "Now that I'm too old and broke up to go out prospecting any more, I've got me a little one-man office in Searchlight. Sell a few things now and then, lease a few mineral rights here and there. That's where Andy's little windfall came from, by the way. Over the years, I'd put one of the grandnephews' names on a claim, and if that one came in, I'd send them the money. Told 'em not to say where it came from, of course. Didn't want 'em to get in trouble for having anything to do with an old black sheep."

Cora blew her nose. "You're not so bad for a black sheep," she said. "And none of those kids ever turned the money down, either."

"Including you," he said with a smile.

She nodded. "Including me."

"And you only give the gifts in cash?" Joanna asked.

Uncle Henry straightened in his chair. "Young woman, the Income Tax is the most abominable piece of illegal legislation ever palmed off on this land, but it exists. And to my mind, the only thing lower than a revenuer is a banker, so I try to conduct my business in a way that keeps those vermin out of it. If I give away less than ten thousand dollars at a time, nobody gets excited. And if I do it in cash, I don't have to deal with banks. If I have a gift to be delivered, Cora usually handles it for me on her days off from the casino. I don't like banks, but it's still a very bad idea to send that much cash through the mail, understand?"

"Yes," Joanna answered. "I believe I do."

"Where are you staying?" Jim Bob asked.

"Well, I had thought we'd stay at a place called the Copper Queen Hotel, but evidently, that's not too easy to get in and out of in a wheelchair, so we've got a couple of rooms at a place called the El Cobre Lodge."

Joanna was still trying to sort things out. "So the money Cora gave Andy was from some kind of mining claim?"

"Some guys out of Elko," Uncle Henry said. "They leased it for exploratory purposes, and I gifted half of what they paid to Andy. Those guys'll have six months with an option for six more after that. I can't tell if they're for real or not, but their money was good. If there's more coming, believe me, you and your little girl will get it."

"Thank you," Joanna said. "Thank you very much."

Not long after that, she headed home, glad to have escaped the crush of people in the mortuary, but knowing that back home at the ranch, there would be more of the same. And she was right. When she drove into the yard, she counted at least ten cars scattered here and there. Inside the house several of the ladies from the church choir were busily trying to find places in the burgeoning refrigerator for yet another donated covered dish.

Joanna paused in the kitchen long enough to pour herself a glass of white wine, then she wandered into the living room. It wasn't exactly a party. It was her home, but she wasn't exactly the hostess and she wasn't exactly a guest either. The women managing the kitchen were most insistent in telling her that she was expected to mingle and not lift a hand to do any of the work.

On the couch at the far end of the room she spotted Milo Davis sitting with Jenny. When she got close enough, she saw that Jenny had dragged out her old copy of *Winnie the Pooh* and was patiently explaining to Milo the origin of her new dog's name.

"Hi, Mom," Jenny said, when Joanna sat down on the couch behind her. "Mr. Davis never heard of Tigger before. Can you believe that?"

Joanna smiled and nodded her head. "I can believe it all right," she said.

"Did you try any of the lemon chiffon pie that Mrs. Davis sent over? It's my favorite."

"Maybe I'll have some later."

Eventually Jenny got up and wandered away. Joanna turned to Milo Davis. "They tell me you're promoting Joanna Brady as a candidate for sheriff. Are you trying to get rid of me?" she asked.

"That's not exactly what I meant," Milo returned. "It's just that sometimes the best man for a job is a woman, at least that's what my mother always used to say. I think she was a little before her time."

"Milo," Joanna said seriously, "I don't want to be sheriff of Cochise County. I happen to *like* selling insurance."

"Who else is going to do it?" he asked. "Look what you did the other night."

"What I did that night was personal, Milo. Jenny and my mother were at risk. My husband was murdered. Most people in my position would have done exactly the same thing."

Milo Davis shook his head. "What you did for this county was a lot more than settle a personal score. That drug business and the corruption in the sheriff's department must have been going on for years, and it would have kept right on if you hadn't taken a stand and done something about it. And who else knows more about the sheriff's department than you? One way or the other, you've been around it all your life. Maybe there are people who work there who've been around longer, but none of them can run, not right now because of the scandal. It's a wide-open race, Joanna, and we've got to have someone who's squeaky clean. You're it. You'll win hands down."

"Milo, I don't want to do this."

"Neither did your daddy when he took it on, Joanna, but it was a time very much like this, a time when the old administration needed to be swept out with a clean broom. This kind of thing never would have happened on old D. H.'s, watch, now would it?"

Joanna shook her head. "No," she agreed. "It never would have."

"Back then, in your dad's time, Kiwanis was the thing to do if you wanted to go someplace," Milo continued. "When he got elected, he joined up and never missed a single meeting until the day he died. We didn't have women in the club back then, and there was a whole lot more high jinks than goes on today. We all had a nickname for your dad, a secret nickname. Did he ever tell you about that?"

"No. Not that I remember."

"The whole time I knew him, he only went by his initials. We were always teasing him and telling him he needed to have a real name. Finally we gave him one. We told them that his real name was Desert Heat on account of him being a cop. It was kind of hokey, I guess, an in crowd joke, but he seemed to get a bang out of it."

Milo studied his listener's face, waiting to see if D. H. Lathrop's daughter would smile at the joke. She didn't. Joanna Brady was way beyond smiling.

"It seemed funny back then," he said with a sigh. "Maybe you had to be there."

By the time Joanna finished that one glass of wine, she had moved beyond her ability to socialize as well. She tracked Eleanor down in a small group in the dining room. "Are you going home tonight, or are you going to stay here?" Joanna asked.

"I thought I'd stay, if you don't mind."

"Do whatever you want, but I have to go to bed. I can't hold my head up any longer."

In the past, that kind of announcement would probably have provoked an argument on the impropriety of Joanna's abandoning her guests. This time it didn't.

"I'm sure you're tired," Eleanor said. "I don't think people will mind if you disappear."

Joanna headed toward her bedroom. She expected her mother to stay in the dining room chatting with the guests. Instead Eleanor followed Joanna into the bedroom.

"Can I talk to you a minute?"

Expecting another lecture, Joanna tried to hide the impatience in her voice. "What about?"

"Your father."

"Everybody seems to be thinking about him tonight."

Eleanor smiled. "He used to call you Little Hank just to drive me crazy. It did, too, I think. And then, when he taught you how to shoot a gun, my word, I wondered what the world was coming to."

Joanna walked over to the closet and began taking off her clothes. The blouse she was wearing was one of her favorites, but it buttoned down the back. Without Andy to help with the buttons, Joanna didn't know if she'd be able to wear it very often from now on. She worked her way down the row until she reached the button in the middle of her back, the one that was hardest to reach. Just then, Eleanor came over and unbuttoned it for her.

"It's hard to let go of a daughter," she said awkwardly. "Even when she's all grown up. Just wait until it happens to Jenny. You still think of her as a little girl in braids, and then one day, she's standing there doing something like washing dishes or canning peaches, and you know she's not little anymore."

"Mother," Joanna interrupted, but Eleanor shook her head.

"It didn't seem fair to me that when he had such a beautiful little girl your father still always wanted a boy. That's one of the things we fought about. He made you act like a boy, and I was always mad at him over it. But last night, Joanna, I saw he was right. If you hadn't been just the way your father raised you, I don't know what would have happened."

Joanna felt tears welling up in her eyes no matter how hard she tried to blink them back, but Eleanor didn't seem to notice.

"I've heard people talking around town today, at Helene's, when I went to have my hair done and in the grocery store. They're all saying you should run for sheriff."

"Don't worry, Mother. I already told Milo I wouldn't do it."

"But that's what I'm trying to tell you," Eleanor said. "I think you should. I used to believe that when your daddy died, it was all his fault. After all, since he was sheriff, he deliberately put himself in danger. I thought that he had wanted it somehow and that when it happened, it was sort of divine retribution. Over the years, I guess I've finally figured out that wasn't right.

"When it came time to bury him, I went ahead and let them dress him in his uniform even though I hated that uniform with an abiding passion. I did it that way because I knew it's what he would have wanted. I kept one part of his uniform back though, just one thing."

Eleanor Lathrop reached into her pocket and pulled out a tarnished silver star. "It's your daddy's badge, Joanna," Eleanor said softly. "I saved it for you because I thought you might want it someday. I'm giving it to you now because I think you've earned it."

With that, after pressing the badge into Joanna's hand, Eleanor fled the room.

Stunned, Joanna took the badge to the bed and sank down on it, examining the etched star in careful detail and marveling. After all those years, she was holding her father's badge. As she was growing up, if she could have had one thing that had belonged to her father, this would have been it, but that was always a secret, selfish wish, one she had never dared share with her mother. That would have been too disloyal.

Joanna stared down at the badge for a long, long time, until her eyes began to blur, then she reached over and picked up the phone. She had dialed the number so many times in the past few days that she knew it by heart.

The town mortician's newest son-in-law and newest employee was the one stuck with night duty. He was also the one who answered the phone.

"This is Joanna Brady," she said. "I'm calling to ask a favor. Andy's wearing his badge right now, but I'd like you to take it off and put it in an envelope for me. Would you do that?"

"Sure thing, Mrs. Brady. No problem."

"And put my daughter's name on the outside. Jenny. Jennifer Brady. She may want to have that badge someday as a keepsake."

"Right, Mrs. Brady. It'll be at the desk for you in the morning. Anything else?"

"No. That's all."

Putting the phone down and turning out the light, Joanna lay down crosswise on the bed and wrapped the heavy bedspread around her. She had been dreadfully sleepy earlier, but now sleep seemed far away.

Milo Davis, Marianne Maculyea, her mother— all of them thought she should run. All of them, including Adam York, seemed to think she could do it. Could she, Joanna wondered. Maybe. What would it hurt to try?

And moments later, while that embryonic thought still lingered in her head, and still holding tight to her father's precious badge, Joanna Brady fell into a dreamless but untroubled sleep.

She woke up in the morning with the sun streaming in through the window and with Jenny tiptoeing across the room to snuggle into bed beside her.

"What's this?" Jenny asked, seeing the badge in her mother's hand. "Is it Daddy's?"

"No," Joanna explained, "it was my daddy's, your grandfather's."

"Grandpa Lathrop's? But what are you doing with it?"

Joanna looked down at Jenny and suddenly knew what she had to do.

"Grandma gave it to me," Joanna said. "For right now, I'm going to put it away in my jewelry box. If I ever get it out again, it'll be time to put it on and wear it."

Jennifer Brady looked at her in wide-eyed astonishment. "For real? You mean you'd be sheriff?"

"I'd try," Joanna answered. "It would mean we'd have to go on with the election campaign only this time I'd be the candidate. It would mean that no matter how hard it was, we'd have to go out and do all the things we would have done if your daddy was still running. It would be hard work because now there are only the two of us. Would you be willing to help me? Do you think we could do it?"

"Yes." Jennifer Ann Brady answered without the slightest hesitation.

Joanna hugged her child close. "Well then," she said huskily, "I guess we'll have to try. If enough people in Cochise County want me to be their new sheriff, that's exactly what I'll be."

Here's a sneak preview of
J. A. Jance's novel

Available now
wherever books are sold

I AM NOT a wimp. Maybe that sounds too much like Richard Nixon's "I am not a crook," but it's true. I'm not. With twenty plus years at Seattle P.D., most of it on the Homicide Squad, and with several more years of laboring in the Washington State attorney general's Special Homicide Investigation Team, I think I can make that statement with some confidence. Usually. Most of the time. Right up until I got on the Mad Hatter's Tea Party ride at Disneyland with my six-year-old granddaughter, Karen Louise, aka Kayla.

She had been in charge of the spinning. She loved it. I did not. When the ride ended, she went skipping away as happy as can be toward her waiting parents while I staggered along after her. Over her shoulder I heard her say, "Can we go again?"

Then, stopping to look at me she added, "Gramps, how come your face is so green?"

Good question.

When Kayla was younger, she used to call me Gumpa, which I liked. Now I've been demoted or promoted, I'm not sure which, to Gramps, which I don't like. It's better, however, than what she calls Dave Livingston, my first wife's second husband and official widower. (Karen, Kayla's biological grandmother, has been dead for a long time now, but Dave is still a permanent part of all our lives.) Kayla stuck him with the handle of Poppa. As far as I'm concerned, that's a lot worse than Gramps.

But back to my face. It really was green. I was having a tough time standing upright, and believe me, I hadn't had a drop to drink, either. By then, though, Mel figured out that I was in trouble.

Melissa Majors Soames is my third wife. That seems like a bit of a misnomer since my second wife, Anne Corley, was married to me for less than twenty-four hours. Our time together was, as they say, short but brief, ending in what is often referred to as "suicide by cop." It bothered me that Anne preferred being dead to being married to me, and it gave me something of a complex—I believe shrinks call it a fear of commitment—that made it difficult for me to move on. Mel Soames was the one who finally changed all that.

She and I met while working for the S.H.I.T. squad. (Yes, I agree, it's an unfortunate name but we're stuck with it.) Originally we just worked together, then it evolved into something else. Mel is someone who is absolutely cool in the face of trouble, and she's watched my back on more than one occasion. And since this whole idea of having a "three-day family bonding vacation at Disneyland" had been her bright idea, it was only fair that she should watch my back now.

She didn't come racing up to see if I was all right because she could see perfectly well that I wasn't. Instead, she went looking for help in the guise of a uniformed park employee who dropped the broom he was wielding and led me to the First Aid Station. It seems to me that it would have made sense to have a branch office a lot closer to the damned Tea Cups.

So I went to the infirmary. Mel stayed long enough to be sure I was in good hands, then she bustled off to "let everyone know what's happening." I stayed where I was, spending a good part of day three of our Three Day Ticket Pass flat on my back on an ER-style cot with a very officious nurse taking my pulse and asking me questions.

"Ever been seasick?" she wanted to know.

"Several times," I told her. I could have added every time I get near a boat, but I didn't.

"Do you have any Antivert with you?" she asked.

"I beg your pardon?"

"Antivert. Meclizine. If you're prone to seasickness, you should probably carry some with you. Without it, I can't imagine what you were thinking? Why did you get on that ride?"

"My granddaughter wanted me to."

She gave me a bemused look and shook her head. "That's what they all say. You'd think grown men would have better sense."

She was right about that. I should have had better sense, but of course I didn't say so.

"We don't hand out medication here," she said. "Why don't you just lie there for a while with your eyes closed. That may help."

When she finally left me alone, I must have fallen asleep. I woke up when my phone rang.

"Beau," Ross Alan Connors said. "Where are you?"

Connors has been the Washington State Attorney General for quite some time now, and he was the one who had plucked me from my post-retirement doldrums from leaving Seattle P.D. and installed me in his then relatively new Special Homicide Investigation Team. The previous fall's election cycle had seen him fend off hotly contested attacks in both primary and general elections. With campaigning out of the way for now, he seemed to be focusing on the job, enough so that he was calling me on Sunday afternoon when I was supposedly on vacation.

"California," I told him. "Disneyland actually."

I didn't mention the infirmary part. That was none of his business.

"Harry tells me you're due back tomorrow."

Harry was my boss, Harry Ignatius Ball, known to friend and foe alike as Harry I. Ball. People who hear his name and think that gives them a license to write him off as some kind of joke are making a big mistake. He's like a crocodile lurking in the water with just his eyes showing. The teeth are there, just under the surface, ready and waiting to nail the unwary.

"Yes," I told him. "Our plane leaves here bright and early. We should be at our desks by one."

When Mel had broached the Disneyland idea, she had wanted us to pull off this major family-style event while, at the same time, having as little impact as possible—one and a half days' worth—on our accumulated vacation time. We had flown down on Thursday after work and were due back Monday at noon.

On my own, I've never been big on vacations of any kind. Unused vacation days have slipped through my fingers time and again without my really noticing or caring, but Mel Soames is another kind of person altogether. She has her heart set on our taking a road trip this summer. She wants to cross over into BC, head east over the Canadian Rockies and then come back to Seattle by way of Yellowstone and Glacier. This sounds like way too much scenery for me, but she's the woman in my life and I want to keep her happy, so a-driving we will go.

"Mel can go to the office," Ross said, "but not you. I want you in Ellensburg at the earliest possible moment."

If you leave the Seattle area driving east on I-90, Ellensburg is the second stopping-off place after you cross the Cascades. First there's Cle Elum and next Ellensburg. Neither of them strikes me as much of a garden spot.

"Why would I want to go to Ellensburg?" I asked.

"To be there when the Kittitas ME does an autopsy. Friday afternoon some heavy-equipment operator was out snow-plowing a national forest road over by Lake Kachess where he ended up digging up more than he bargained for. This is number six."

I didn't have to ask number six what—I already knew. For the past two months S.H.I.T. had been working on the murders of several young Hispanic women whose charred remains had been found at various dump sites scattered all over western Washington. So far none of them had been identified. As far as we could tell, none of our victims had been reported missing. We'd pretty well decided that our dead girls were probably involved in prostitution, but until we managed to identify one of them and could start making connections, it was going to be damnably difficult to figure out who had killed them.

These days it's routine for the dental records of missing persons to be entered into a national missing persons database. That wasn't possible with our current set of victims. None of them had teeth. None of them! And the teeth in question hadn't been lost to poor dental hygiene, either. They had been forcibly removed. As in yanked out by the roots!

"Same MO?" I asked.

"Pretty much except for the fact that this one seems to have her teeth," Ross said. "So either we have a different doer or the guy ran out of time. This victim was wrapped in a tarp and set on fire just like the others. The body was found late Friday afternoon. It took until Saturday morning for the Kittitas County Sheriff's Department to retrieve the remains. Unfortunately, their ME has been out of town at a conference, so that has slowed down the process. They put the remains on ice until she returns and expect the autopsy to happen sometime tomorrow afternoon. That's where you come in. I want you there when it happens in case there's some detail that we know about that the locals might miss."

"Our plane's due in at ten-twenty," I told him.

"That'll be cutting it close then," Ross said. "God only knows how long it'll take for you to get your luggage once you get there."

Thanks to a legacy from Anne Corley, Mel and I had flown down to California on a private jet. All we'd have to do was step off the plane and wait for the luggage to be loaded into our waiting car before we drove it off the tarmac, but rubbing my boss's nose in that seemed like a bad idea.

"I'll make it," I said. "I'll drop Mel off at the condo to pick up the other car and then I'll head out."

"All right," Ross said. "Be there as soon as you can."

"Do you have a number for the Kittitas ME's office?" I asked.

"Sure. Can you take it down?"

I had no intention of telling him that I was flat on my back in the first aid station and I wasn't about to ask the nurse to lend me a pen or pencil.

"Can you text it to me?" I asked.

This was something coming from someone who had come to twenty-first-century technology kicking and screaming all the way. I'm surprised

I wasn't struck by lightning on the spot, but that's what comes of having Generation X progeny. I had learned about text messaging the hard way—because my kids, Kelly and Scott, had insisted on it.

"Sure," Ross said. "I'll have Katie send it over to you."

Katie Dunn was Ross's Gen X secretary. Knowing Ross is even more of a wireless troglodyte than I am made me feel better—more with it, as we used to say back in the day.

I had just stuffed the phone back into my pocket when the nurse led Kelly into the room.

"How are you?" she asked, concern written on her face. "Mel told us what happened and that you needed to take it easy for a while. Are you feeling any better?"

I swung my feet off the side of the bed and sat up slowly.

"Take it easy," the nurse advised.

But the nap had done the trick. I was definitely feeling better. "I'm fine," I said. "One hundred percent."

"Mel went with Jeremy. He's taking the kids back to the hotel," Kelly explained. "She'll help get them fed and make sure the babysitter arrangements hold up. If you're still feeling up to having that dinner, that is."

That was what Mel said, of course. And that's what she was doing. But the reasons she was doing those things were a whole lot murkier—to Kelly at least if not to me.

Kelly and I haven't always been on the best of

terms. In fact we've usually not been on the best of terms. She had run away from home prior to high school graduation and managed to get herself knocked up. Her shotgun wedding had ended up being unavoidably delayed so Kayla had arrived on the scene before her parents had ever tied the knot. I have always thought most of this Kelly-based uproar is deliberate.

Mel takes the position that it's more complex than that—both conscious and not. She thinks Kelly's ongoing rebellion has been a way for her to get back at her parents—at both Karen and me. Although I didn't know about it at the time, Kelly was mad as hell at her mother for coming down with cancer and dying while Kelly was still in her teens, and she was mad as hell at me for having been drunk most of the time while she was growing up. And now she's apparently mad at me for not being drunk. When it comes to kids, sometimes you just can't win.

So Mel had designed this whole Disneyland adventure, complete with inviting my son and daughter-in-law, Scott and Cherisse, along for the ride, for no other reason than to see if she could help smooth out some of the emotional wrinkles between Kelly and me. So far so good. As far as I could tell everyone seemed to be having a good time. There had been no cross words, at least none I had heard. And I suspected that was also why Mel had sent Kelly to drag me out of the infirmary.

"I should have gone on the Tea Cups with her," Kelly said as we walked toward the monorail.

"Jeremy won't set foot on one of those on a bet, but rides like that don't bother me. They never have. And Kayla loves them so much. She rode the Tea Cups three more times after you left. She didn't want to ride on anything else."

I stopped cold. Kelly turned back to look at me. "Are you all right?" she asked.

It took me a minute to figure out what to say. I now knew something about Kelly and her mother and her daughter, and it was something she didn't know about me. As I said already, I was mostly AWOL when Kelly and Scott were little—drinking and/or working. Karen was the one who took them to soccer and T-ball and movies. She was also the one who "did the Puyallup" with them each fall. When it's time for the Western Washington State Fair each September, that's what they used to call it—"Doing the Puyallup." It was Karen instead of me who walked them through the displays of farm animals and baked goods; who taught them to love eating cotton candy and elephant ears; and who took them for rides on the midway.

"You're just like your mother," I said, over the lump that rose suddenly in my throat and made it difficult to speak. "And Kayla's just like you."

"What's that supposed to mean?" Kelly asked. She sounded angry and defensive. It was so like her to take offense and to assume that whatever I said was somehow an underhanded criticism.

"Did your mother ever tell you about the first time I took her to the Puyallup?"

"No," Kelly said. "She never did. Why?"

"She wanted to ride the Tilt-a-Whirl, and I knew if I did that, I'd be sick. Rides like that always make me sick. So I bought the tickets. Your mother and I stood in line, but when it came time to get on, I couldn't do it. She ended up having to go on the ride with the people who were standing in line behind us. Here I was, supposedly this hotshot young guy with the beautiful girl on his arm, and all I could do was stand there like an idiot and wait for the ride to end and for her to get off. It was one of the most humiliating moments of my life. We never talked about it again afterwards, but she never asked me to get on one of those rides again, either."

Kelly was staring up into my face. She looked so much like her mother right then—was so much like her mother—that it was downright spooky. It turns out DNA is pretty amazing stuff.

"So why did you do it?" she asked.

Now I was lost. Yes, I had been telling Kelly the story, but her question caught me off guard. I didn't know what "it" she was asking about.

"Do what?" I asked.

"If you already knew it would make you sick, why on earth did you get on the Mad Hatter's Tea Party with Kayla?"

"I thought maybe I'd grown out of it?" I asked lamely.

Kelly shook her head as if to say I hadn't yet stumbled on the right answer. "And?" she prompted.

"Because my granddaughter wanted me to?" I added.

The storm clouds that had washed across Kelly's face vanished. She reached up, grabbed me around the neck, and kissed my cheek.

"Oh, Daddy," she said with a laugh. "You're such a dope, but I love you."

See what I mean about Mel Soames? The woman is a genius.